DEATH
AND
TAXES

DEATH AND TAXES

A Jill Smith Mystery by

SUSAN DUNLAP

Delacorte Press

Published by
Delacorte Press
Bantam Doubleday Dell Publishing Group, Inc.
666 Fifth Avenue
New York, New York 10103

Library of Congress Cataloging in Publication Data

Dunlap, Susan.
     Death and taxes: a Jill Smith mystery / Susan Dunlap.
        p.   cm.
     ISBN 0-385-30443-9
     I. Title.
PS3554.U46972D4   1992
813'.54—dc20   91-33109
                                                           CIP

Manufactured in the United States of America

Published simultaneously in Canada

April 1992

10   9   8   7   6   5   4   3   2   1
                    BVG

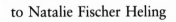

to Natalie Fischer Heling

Thanks to Rita Wilson, Larry Minney,
"Pretentious Artist" Richard List, and
Inspector Robert Maloney of the Berkeley Police Department.

CHAPTER

1

"People who don't send in their taxes sleep in jail, Howard, not in the prize bedroom of a brown-shingled house." I might as well have called it a brown-shingled other woman. But I didn't. A homicide detective hates to sound petty, particularly here in Berkeley, California, where the politically correct tone is laid-back snide.

I was sitting cross-legged on the bed in the prize room tensely pulling strands of brown hair loose from the clasp at the nape of my neck. It didn't ease my tension any to watch Howard pacing in long-legged strides between his work table and his newly painted wall. Spatters of white paint marked his jeans and the forest-green turtleneck I'd given him. The room had smelled of paint for a week now, but it was better than the downstairs where he'd just sanded the dining-room floor. It seemed the stench of sawdust and singed wood never cleared there.

Seduced by the hint that the owner of the decrepit five-bedroom house he leased and loved might consider a purchase option, Howard had devoted the last three months to refurbishing the aging siren. His latest gift had been an expensive *Azalea magnifica* he'd planted next to the front door like a Mother's Day corsage.

I knew what this house meant to him and why it was so important. But I was coming to hate it.

This morning Howard had commandeered an oak door he'd been refinishing and turned it into a table that took up half the free space in his bedroom, *our* bedroom. Howard appropriating part of his oak-trimmed inamorata was like Romeo using Juliet's balcony for ballast. Now the door-cum-table sagged under piles of tax booklets, schedule As and Ds, form 4562s, yellow pads, pencils, pens, erasers, hillocks of receipts, and mountains of eraser dust. On top was the 1040 that proclaimed that Howard owed the IRS a bundle. That bundle, alas, Howard had already spent on paint, varnish, and the azalea.

And the table was so close to the king-size bed that one communal tumble could create a tornado of tax forms. The prospect of organizing caresses to suit a 1040 is hardly an aphrodisiac.

"Deductions," Howard muttered now, running a hand through his curly red hair. "I must have been to twenty charity dinners this year. I've got to have more to deduct." He extricated the 1040 instruction booklet from the mire on the erstwhile door, leaned back in his director's chair, propped ankle on the opposite knee, and read sarcastically: " 'Gifts to Charity.' What 'you MAY deduct' is one paragraph, followed by three paragraphs of limitations. What 'you MAY NOT deduct' is a whole fucking column and a half."

"Who said it's better to give than receive?"

"More *blessed*. Not *better*, Jill," Howard corrected.

If he'd caught my disingenuous tone, he wasn't commenting. But we'd commented on less and less over the months since I'd moved in here. The only thing we both had wholly endorsed lately was the tacit decision to avoid conflict. I didn't know how we'd landed at this impasse. My first marriage had ended in screams. Then Howard had been my buddy—funny, sexy, anxious to protect me, and ready to accept that a homicide detective doesn't need protection. I was the one who pushed people, baited them till they talked. I was always taking chances. But here I was paralyzed.

"Besides," Howard said, "if the IRS believed in blessings, they'd tax them too." He turned back to the instructions. "You may not deduct 'travel expenses (including meals and lodging) unless there was no significant element of personal pleasure, recreation, or vacation in the travel.' I drove to San Francisco to speak to the Nob Hill Club. Does the IRS mean if I got caught in rush hour and sat on the bridge for an hour and was teed-off the whole time, then it's okay to deduct the mileage? But if I missed the traffic and the sun was shining, there's no deduction?"

I had no more idea than he. What I did know was that I needed to get out of here. Particularly since my own tax return had required nothing more than a 1040 and W-2. Lack of possessions has its privileges. In contrast to Howard with his five-bedroom albatross, I had lived on a porch for two years and house-sat for months. Moving here had taken only one trip in Howard's Land-Rover. I liked the freedom of traveling light, of needing no more than a sleeping bag, a deck chair in the living room, and a single 1040.

Howard stood up, stretching to his full six feet six inches, and began pacing around the bedroom, which now boasted an undercoat of white that barely veiled the dark green beneath. "And when I went to a charitable dinner that I didn't speak at and paid a hundred dollars"—Howard cringed slightly, and I could guess that he was balancing that chicken dinner against the flock of azaleas he could have had nesting in the front yard —"does the IRS say, 'Thank you, Detective Howard, for being so generous'? No. No thousand points of light for them. What they say is "Well, Seth, you ate the bird, didn't you? You're going to have to subtract that dinner from that C-note.' "

"So you deduct ninety-five instead of a hundred dollars. It's not like they served pheasant under glass."

"Aha! Logical thinking! IRS hates that. They don't care what the dinner was worth; they want to know what the restaurant would have charged for the meal." He put down the booklet. "Jill, we're talking neckbone marinara." Howard's blue eyes narrowed, his lantern jaw jutted forward, his curly red hair virtually vibrated with outrage. Felons who had seen that look were now in San Quentin.

"I take it the instruction book is no help?"

"It says 'Get Pub five-twenty-six for details.' "

"So why not get it?" I said, more snappishly than I'd intended.

But he was too deep in the world of revenue to notice something so mundane as pique. "Where do you think you get Pub five-twenty-six? The IRS office, right? The IRS office, which is closed on weekends!" Howard slammed his fist on the table.

Scraps of paper bounced.

I hadn't realized the IRS was closed. The two hours I'd spent on my return was on a Wednesday, or maybe Thursday. (It was so long ago, I couldn't remember, but I restrained myself from mentioning that. I didn't want to *appear* petty.) In a show of support, I said, "Why don't you call Pereira?" Patrol Officer Connie Pereira was the department's financial maven.

"On patrol," Howard growled. "By the time she gets off, I'll be staking out People's Park." At work, Pereira's commitment to financial maneuvers was equaled only by Howard's love of stings.

The sting Howard would be orchestrating tonight had been weeks in the planning. At midnight, Howard would reel in one of Berkeley's biggest drug dealers. Normally, just hours before countdown he would be pacing around, worrying about every detail, compulsively discussing every option, weighing his assumptions against my opinions, coming up with six variations on the theme. The Howard I loved. I realized with a start that I had been counting on this sting to resurrect him from this coffin of a house.

"Forty dollars! That's what the Nob Hill Club charges for their meal! It couldn't have cost them more than three. They must have found the chicken in a taxidermist's trash!" Howard broke pace and stalked toward the phone. "No way is IRS going to screw me. I'm going to get every ingredient in every charitable meal I ate, and deduct the real price. Let the bastards challenge that!"

I didn't think much of Howard's chances, but at least thumbing his nose at the nation's most powerful bureaucracy was better than obsessing about the advantages of azalea over alstroemeria, or hornbeam over hackberry trees. It was a bureaucratic sting. "Look, Howard, I'll go by the station and get Pereira thinking about your talks, dinners, and deductions. I'm going out anyway."

"Ah, free time."

Before Howard could go on, I walked downstairs, careful not to run my hand along the stripped and splintery bannister, across the newly stained floor, and out past the hornbeam or hackberry (whichever) and the *Azalea magnifica,* destined to produce large white flowers with a splash of pink, Howard had told me more than once. So far, it and its numerous cousins had produced only green leaves and resentment. I headed to the Mediterraneum Caffè on Telegraph for a *caffè latte* and a slice of Chocolate Decadence. I had cashed my refund check yesterday. I planned to spend it all on coffee and chocolate—and if things didn't improve at Howard's, on the first, last, and cleaning deposits on an apartment.

I had to admit that Howard's oak-paneled, balconied, brown-shingled place had lots of potential. A speculator could have renovated and made a bundle. But parting with it, regardless of the profit, would never cross Howard's mind. For him the house brought back—with the immediacy of smell—a big old house his aunt rented for the family one summer in some California Valley town.

Howard had spent his childhood on the move. His father had been off somewhere on ever-longer jobs. His mother (I met her once—a fey woman with strands of red hair running through her gray like single-lane roads in the desert) was there and not there. She moved around on the spur of the moment to cities and towns in California. Howard would come home from school to find his clothes in cardboard boxes. He was lucky to be tall, good-looking, and most of all athletic. A boy athlete can fit in anywhere. And he grew up playing football on small-school teams or pickup basketball in the cities. He learned to garner confidence quickly. But the teams and the friends could be snatched away by the cardboard boxes. The only place he'd ever felt at home was his aunt's summer house.

And now this one.

I knew how much it meant to him. I wished I could share his love for it. Or even feel neutral about it. But every time I walked inside, it felt as if all the air had been sucked out if it. I wanted to open all the windows and knew they were nailed shut. Of course, they weren't—that's just how it felt. I wished I could figure out why it unnerved me. It wasn't just its other-womanness. It was something more basic than that. Something I couldn't draw into consciousness.

It was after ten thirty when I finished a second *latte* and headed for my car on Regent Street a block above Telegraph by People's Park. The rain had stopped, but the night was still windy for April. It had been one of those warm dry winters that are becoming all too common here in drought country. And then in March, when every county in the Bay Area had instituted water rationing, it poured and turned cold. Now the wind sliced between the cotton fibers of my jacket.

I was turning onto Regent when I spotted the double-parked

patrol car near the far end of the block. Its pulser lights flashed red on the white wooden and stucco buildings, and turned the macadam brown. The squeals from its radio pierced the wind.

Behind me in People's Park men's voices provided an ominous counterpoint.

People's Park, the symbol of the flower-child era years ago, had changed. No longer was it the site of free flowers, vegetables, and love. It'd been taken over by the homeless, the dealers, the addicts. And in that mix the just plain homeless walked warily and slept with both eyes open. Near People's Park there were too many drugs and too many nervous dealers with weapons that we on the force only dreamed of. Add to that, paranoid users, fed-up neighbors, students, and street people, and the old-time crazies—and it was a recipe for violence. All too often a crowd's anger coalesced and turned on the one outsider, the cop.

Already I could see figures ambling out of People's Park. Whoever had left the patrol car there tonight might be real grateful for an assist. I picked up my pace. The patrol car was still half a block away but I could make out a blond officer bending over a man.

The street was dark there, shaded by one of the paperbark trees, the wind thwarted by the squat apartment buildings on the west side of the street. Still I got a whiff of decay from the paperbarks—they all had that foul smell.

It wasn't till I was nearly to her that I realized the officer was Connie Pereira. "You call for backup?" I asked.

"Full moon," she said, explaining why they had been detained. "I'm waiting for an ambulance too."

I looked down at the form on the ground—a thin, dark-haired man lying facedown, arms at his sides as if he'd fainted. He hadn't even lifted his hands to break his fall. Pereira was on the far side of him, feeling for a pulse. The red pulser atop her patrol car turned her tan uniform an odd shade of army green;

her blond hair danced in the light and disappeared in the darker darkness that followed. But for the victim it did nothing. He seemed to consume its light with his own darkness. His hair was brown and curly, a Jewish Afro unmoved by the wind. Turned to the right, his nose just touching the macadam. Dark jeans covered thin but muscular legs. And despite his position, the flesh of his buttocks hadn't relaxed; the muscles looked firm, as if he'd been standing. A black windbreaker hugged surprisingly narrow ribs; excess fabric lay at the sides—definitely not a natural way for it to have fallen. Closer now, I could make out the moisture on his hair—sweat. And that windbreaker—stuck to his shirt with sweat? He still wasn't moving.

I looked more closely at his face. The eye I could see was open. It was so deep a brown, I couldn't tell how much the iris was dilated. But the man's expression was not that of someone who has eased into collapse. His face was locked in fear.

Behind me I could smell the aroma of dirt-matted sweat—street people trying to see if the fallen was one of their own. They stood silently, but on the sidewalk a man was muttering to himself. Had we been in another neighborhood, house doors would be opening, neighbors wandering out. But here a body on the street was not an uncommon sight. In the shabby student apartments, group houses, and three-story flats, radios blared, but the curtains didn't move.

"What do you think?" I asked Pereira.

"He's not moving. But he's still warm. Hot, really."

"On a night like this," I commented, pulling my jacket tighter around me. "ID?"

"Empty. No wallet, no cash."

"How long has he been lying here?"

Pereira shrugged. "No witnesses. To the accident or the disappearance of his wallet. Big surprise, huh?"

I moved farther into the street where I could form a blockade against any driver who might see only the patrol car and not the victim.

On the sidewalk the crowd was growing, separated into dark clumps of street people, brighter clumps of students taking a break, and a third gathering of miscellaneous folk who milled together and apart like charged particles in a changing magnetic field. All three groups were oozing toward the spaces between the parked cars. In a minute they'd be pressing in on the victim and blocking the ambulance. "Keep back," I yelled, letting my gaze move slowly from group to group. "Stay on the sidewalk." The victim might have been rolled. Any one of them could have done it—a student on a dare, one of the users—for cash or at the whim of voices the rest of us couldn't hear.

My gaze held them only momentarily. Damn. Where was the backup? Where was the ambulance? I glanced over at Pereira. She was hunkered down by the victim's head, looking from him to the crowd, protecting his head. In the pulser light I couldn't see the wry competence that was her trademark but a wary look as she eyed the growing groups on the sidewalk. She wasn't trying CPR; the victim was breathing on his own.

I caught the movement from the eyes of the crowd first. Then I registered the footsteps. To my right, a guy was trying an end-around behind my car. "Moving," I said to Pereira.

Then, careful not to race, not to up the anxiety level, I ambled over and stopped in front of him. He was under six feet, but he still had three or four inches on me and probably sixty pounds. He was wearing a brown wool cape and a green felt hat with a wide floppy brim with one of those party noisemakers in the band where a feather might have been. He didn't have a handlebar mustache. Maybe he hadn't thought of it. Maybe the goatee was enough.

"Stay on the sidewalk," I said, not raising my voice. I've seen cops create incidents because they come on too strong. Mine may not be the popular method, but I try it soft first.

He strode more determinedly. "I have to see him."

"Do you know him?"

"I must see him!" His voice was louder.

"Your name?"

"Now, madame!" No one on the sidewalk needed to cock an ear to catch that.

We're trained to grab an arm and twist it behind. But that doesn't work with crazies in capes. "We've got an injured man here. He needs his space," I said, loud enough for all to hear. The crowd murmured uncertainly, finding it hard to choose between defying a cop and denying a fellow Californian his space. I hoped the ambulance would get here before they decided.

"Madame, I have to see that man." He projected to the second balcony. His right hand held the edge of the cloak. He looked like a seventeenth-century Dutch flasher. Or an actor portraying one. And clearly I was the foil in his performance. The guy himself was harmless—probably—but he could trigger the crowd. It wouldn't take much to knock them off the fence. And once they came down, they wouldn't be rooting for me.

We were by my car now. He moved slowly, each step long, with a choreographed swagger. I did the only possible thing. I upstaged him. I stepped back into the street, forcing him to turn his back to the crowd. Then, using the width of his cape as a shield, I coordinated with his movement, and as he sauntered forward, I grabbed the edges of the cape and shoved him against my car. His shoulders hit the metal, his head jerked, but the floppy hat softened the effect for the audience. "This isn't a stage here," I growled. "We've got a man seriously injured. We've got our hands full dealing with him. You want to perform, try Berkeley Rep!"

Even I was surprised at my anger. I hate these grandstanders. Little boys who rule by tantrum.

"Release me, madame!" His voice was louder.

The crowd moved to its left, pressing behind the old Datsun. I could smell the dirt and sweat, the beer, and the heady anticipation. Behind me came music from newly opened windows. Footsteps slapped the sidewalks. We needed backup—now. But neither Pereira nor I could get free to call in.

I could toss this guy in the cage in Pereira's car; that was the regulation move. But with this crowd it would be disaster, particularly in the full moon. I decided on a gamble. Lowering my voice, I said, "Give me a good reason, and I'll walk you by."

His eyes shifted. He was weighing his options—going for the maximum exposure? Finally he said, sotto voce, "Maybe I know him."

I ground my teeth. I could hear my mother's voice saying "If you'd said that when I asked . . ." Part of the reason I became a cop was to spite my mother. I never dreamed how often I'd end up sounding just like her. I eased my grip. "No theatrics!" To this guy I might as well have said "No breathing."

Dammit—on any other night, three patrol cars would have rolled up by now. "What's your decision?" I said.

"Okay." Still sotto voce, but in twentieth-century English.

"You're going to walk calmly, right?"

He grunted.

"Yes or no?" A grunt is nothing in this type of situation. A yes is commitment, for what that's worth.

"Yes."

"Okay. We'll walk by him slowly, not stopping. If I let you stop, everyone on the block's going to want a look. We'll have people tramping on his hair, you understand?"

"Yes," he muttered. He was shaking, restraining himself. Seeing the victim was more compelling than a great performance. It made me curious. And worried.

But I'd committed myself. If I reneged here, word of it would be all over Telegraph Avenue by morning, and every patrol officer would lose credibility. I started toward Pereira, still holding on to the man's cape. Pereira was standing now, hands on hips. The pulser light turned her blond hair orange. It glistened on her keys, radio, the butt of her gun as they hung from her belt. In the distance I could hear a siren. Minutes away. Whatever happened here would go down in thirty seconds. I could feel the crowd moving with us.

We passed the patrol car. He was moving faster now. I was holding him back by the cape.

He came abreast of the victim, still lying in the street, still not moving. He yanked free and squatted down, the brim of his felt hat an inch from the victim's. Before I could grab for him, he started to laugh. A deep natural laugh that quickly gained resonance. He stood up and threw his head back, flung open his cape, and guffawed for the last row.

He was facing the audience. I was just about to spin him around, the hell with the consequences, when he let his laugh subside. He turned to half-face me and said, "You are an officer of justice, right?"

I didn't respond.

"Well, madame, here you have justice."

"What kind of justice?" someone in the crowd called back.

Turning to them, he pronounced, "This man, who lies in the street like a defunct possum, waiting to be spat upon, trod on, run over—do you know who he is?"

"Who? Who?" they yelled.

"He is a revenue agent! With the IRS!"

CHAPTER

2

Anywhere else in Berkeley—hell, anywhere else in the continental United States, Hawaii, Puerto Rico, and Guam—the becaped thespian's announcement would have drawn guffaws and cheers. But here, right off Telegraph by People's Park, he'd misjudged his audience. Had he declared the injured man a Cal professor or a police officer, he would have garnered applause. But an IRS agent lying in the street—that got no rise from this crowd of students and street people. Half of them hadn't filed more than a 1040EZ, and the other half never would.

He had made his announcement and flung open his cape to near silence. Only Connie Pereira, who'd had her hassles with the IRS, cracked a smile, and one glance at the victim wiped that off quick.

Removing that cape exhibited a T-shirt with a huge foamy white *OO* on top, a small sketchy city skyline beneath, and the words *MOON OVER BERKELEY,* in this case apparently a double moon. "Mason Moon," he announced in a tone that hoped for a glint of recognition. But I was too caught up in the shock that I hadn't gotten his name before. It's the first thing we do. Always. It said something, something bad, about my state of mind that I hadn't. I asked for his address.

While I was writing that down, a fire engine pulled up, and two firemen jumped out. I could see the worry on their faces.

Firemen know first aid, but they aren't medics; they're not trained to carry the whole load of the injured. We should have heard the siren from our ambulance by now. There are only two rigs in Berkeley. We roll the fire trucks because we've got them at every station and they're likely to make it to a scene well before either of the ambulances. But one ambulance was only a mile and a half away. It should have been here by now. The fact that it hadn't meant it was out picking up some other full-moon casualty. Our IRS man would have to wait for the other rig, or failing that, one from Albany to the north. The pull of the moon wasn't as strong there.

Another patrol car rolled up. Pereira motioned the driver to crowd-control while she stayed with the firemen. One of them knelt by the victim's head trying to get a pulse at the carotid artery. Giving up, he put his hand by the victim's nose, hoping to get some sign of life. The victim had been breathing adequately before. He was fading. If the ambulance didn't make it soon . . .

But there was nothing I could do for him. A cop can't wallow in pity, sorrow, fear. If you can't shift gears, you don't make it in this kind of job. I turned away and focused on the problem at hand—Moon. Shepherding him to the far side of the street, I asked for identification.

"Mason Moon," he repeated.

"Driver's license?"

"Take my word." His volume was increasing.

Plenty of our citizens change their names, some at the behest of their gurus, some to align themselves with nature, some to separate themselves from their debts. Looking pointedly at his T-shirt, I said, "Maybe you drag out this name every full moon."

Moon looked from me to the T-shirt and back again. His expression changed from incredulity to affront. He fondled one of the foamy O's. "Madame, perhaps you lack artistic sense."

Seeing the hand there clarified what his skill in textile art had not. I'd grown up in Jersey near the Garden State Parkway toll booths where mooning was born. Even then it had been considered a tacky outgrowth of youth and beer. *Moon over Berkeley*. I restrained comment.

Moon reached into his pocket and produced a card. Underneath the T-shirt picture was *Mason Moon, Artist of Opportunity*. The name was vaguely familiar, but neither that nor the card proved it was real. As for the T-shirt, the most it proved was that Moon was not a craftsman. "I still need the driver's license."

In the distance the siren rose shriller, louder. I felt a shiver of fear deep inside. The crowd felt it too. They quieted, a somber hush, and turned from Moon and me toward the victim in the street. Odd that ambulances are never seen as vehicles of hope, rushing the injured to the miracles of healing as opposed to providing a stop on the way to the morgue.

Maybe the siren affected Moon too. Whatever the reason, he pulled out his license and handed it to me. I glanced at it— Mason Moon was the name listed—and said, "So, Mason, who is the treasury agent in the street?"

"I don't have a name. I've just seen him around." He pocketed the license without fanfare. We both knew his show was over. The onlookers had shifted their allegiance to the firemen and the body in the street. Moon didn't look at them, but he cocked his head, listening, getting the feel of them, poised for the chance of a comeback.

"So how do you know he's IRS?" I said, pulling his attention back.

"He's auditing a friend of mine. She's bitched enough. When she saw the guy sitting in the Med, drinking a cappuccino like a decent citizen, it was all she could do to keep from punching him out."

I allowed for hyperbole. "What's her name?"

"I don't—"

"I'm not asking for the fun of it. This guy's barely breathing. When the medics get here, they're going to start pushing drugs into him. We need medical information. Is he allergic? Does he have some condition Advanced Life Support needs to know about? Your hesitation could kill him."

"Okay, okay. My friend's name is Lyn Takai."

"Address?"

"I don't know."

"Think! His pockets are empty; we've got no ID. The man could die, Moon!"

He shook his head. His party whistle unrolled and snapped back. "Did you look at his bike? Maybe he's got one of those carrier bags."

This was the first I'd heard of a bicycle. "Where is it?"

"Under that streetlight." He motioned across the street by a house up on blocks, one of the post-earthquake casualties.

"So you saw him ride up?"

"No. Look, I know from Lyn the guy rides a bike. When I recognized him, I looked around for it. Lyn said the guy was so paranoid, he chained both wheels to her railing every time he came. She does a great imitation of him, checking this, checking that, bending over, eyeing the lock from the bottom."

I could imagine the man the firemen were still working on being suspicious; that fit with the awful picture of fear imprinted on his face. But there was a step missing in Moon's recitation. The telephone pole at which Moon pointed was too far from the victim for Moon to have noticed. "Who was it who saw him get off the bicycle?"

He hesitated, then shrugged and glanced around. I wasn't surprised when he said, "A guy I've seen on the Avenue, not one of the regulars. He's not here now. He probably split when you showed."

"Because?"

"A sensible sense of self-preservation."

"What would we know him from?"

"Perhaps you don't."

The siren silenced the crowd once more, longer this time. It was near enough so we could hear brakes shrieking and tires squealing. I looked over at the victim. The firemen were checking the carotid for a pulse again, a routine they'd do every couple of minutes. I heard one of them say, "Cyanotic."

"Moon, we're going to find that witness. Make it easier for us."

Moon took a step toward me. Even he seemed affected by the controlled desperation of the scene. "Lyn Takai lives on Derby, a couple blocks below the Avenue. Behind a violet stucco with a white picket fence. But this guy who saw him stumble into the street—I really don't know. I've just seen him around. I think he boosts bikes."

Moon's identity I had. Pereira could get a patrol officer to baby sit him on the Avenue till he spotted the booster. "Okay, so he was eyeing the bike when he spotted the flashing lights and split. What did he say about the victim?" If Moon's story was true, the victim must have looked bad enough that the booster didn't expect a fight over the bike.

"He said the guy came down Dwight, real slow, made a wide loop at the corner, coasted to a stop, and got off."

"Not fell off?"

"No. He fiddled with his locks. Then he started across the street and fell on his face."

"And your guy left him there and headed for the bike?" I said, disgusted.

Moon shrugged. "He took a look around."

"How do you know?"

"Because he was so pissed off. Kept saying if he hadn't

screwed around taking precautions like his old lady kept telling him, he'd be riding instead of walking."

I headed for the bike. Moon followed.

The bicycle was an old white racer with long narrow baskets on either side of the back wheel. It was probably a twenty-eight incher, which seemed about right for the man on the street. The only thing unusual about it was the two-pad seat, reminiscent of Mason Moon's T-shirt. I'd heard those seats were more comfortable, and from my brief foray into bike riding as an adult, it was a fair guess anything would beat the knives that pass for regulation seats. Still, an old bicycle with seats added for comfort would not have been the means of transportation I would have imagined for a treasury agent.

Bending, I looked closer. The plastic was torn where the two seats met in the back. It looked like a recent tear that someone may have tried to fix with what seemed like a mixture of chewing gum and plaster of paris. We would impound the bike. An errant tear like that and the tan-and-white specks of "fix-it" would be the meat of Raksen's day in the lab.

A small carrying bag fit in the angle of the crossbar and one of the descending ones, but there was nothing inside. "Are you sure it's his?"

Moon was already hunkering down. "Look at the chains."

He had a point, *if* his story about the victim was true. Plastic-covered chains were looped through the spokes of both wheels. A lock caught the ends of one, but its tongue hung open. On the second one the ends of the chain hung loose. It looked like the work of a finicky man who was losing control, actions done from habit but beyond his waning physical ability. It suggested he'd gotten off his bicycle, been in good enough shape to try to lock it, then walked into the street and fallen.

Moon verbalized my suspicions. "What do you think—drink or drugs? God, Lyn's going to love it."

Another patrol officer pulled up just as the ambulance

rounded the far corner. I motioned the officer over to protect the scene around the bike.

With the pulsers from the fire truck, ambulance, and patrol cars, and the radio squeals coming from all directions, the street was like a movie scene. The medics jumped from the ambulance and raced to the victim. Their energy seemed to pick up the flagging spirits all around. I headed toward them.

Moon straightened his shoulders and followed. "Think about it," he said, "IRS agent on drugs. It'll make the best courtroom drama of the decade. Everybody he ever screwed will be demanding blood."

One of the medics held the victim's arm, spreading a vein lengthwise, waiting to see if it would fill back up so he could use it for the catheter. The vein must have faded. The medic stuck the catheter in the carotid artery. His partner conferred with the firemen, then yanked the gurney from the truck.

Another patrol car pulled up. Murakawa got out.

The medics rolled the gurney to the ambulance and slid it in. I started toward them, Moon on my heels. I motioned Murakawa to take him. The drivers shut the doors and ran to the cab. The ambulance rolled with lights and sirens.

I was sure of the answer before I asked Pereira, "What's the prognosis?"

"Better than if he wasn't breathing. That's what they said." Her blond hair hung limp over the collar of her tan uniform jacket. Under the streetlights she looked washed out, exhausted. "I still don't have an ID," she added, a tacit appeal that I track it down. It was a request not from a district officer to a detective but from friend to friend.

"I'll take care of that." I didn't want to go home anyway.

Out of the corner of my eye I spotted Mason Moon moving toward us, Murakawa five yards behind. Quickly I said to Pereira. "In case the victim doesn't make it, keep the scene secured until you can get Raksen out from the lab. Right now, if the cyclist dies, we've got nothing."

Moon stopped beside me, rubbing his hands in glee. "Time for the audit in the sky! Lyn's going to love it."

CHAPTER

3

Three patrol officers were already checking out the crowd, taking preliminary statements, getting names and addresses, and IDs where either of the former seemed ephemeral. Pereira called in a request for backup to canvass the neighbors. Neither of us had noticed an open shade, but maybe there'd been someone putting out the garbage or the cat when the bicycle coasted to a stop. Pereira would gather the reports from the scene. If the victim died, she'd turn them and the case over to me. (In Homicide-Felony Assault Detail we handle all questionable deaths.) If he lived, we'd have what they called in bureaucracies a challenge: justifying all this manpower for a guy who stumbled off his bicycle. I'd hope when the next budget hearing came up that this didn't.

I left Mason Moon in the squad car with Murakawa, who'd take Moon's statement. And irritated as he was at Moon wriggling past him, he'd be delighted at the prospect of squeezing out an ID for the thwarted bike thief.

With luck, I'd have the victim's name in half an hour. With at least that much luck, the victim would survive that long. By now, Advanced Life Support would be pushing drugs into his system, hoping to find the right combination before the drugs started to contradict. They'd chase this thing till the last minute. And when the victim hit the emergency room, they'd start the clock there. Six minutes with no response, and it'd be all over.

Even if I couldn't get an ID in time for the doctors, it was still vital. Somewhere in Berkeley a wife or lover, father or daughter, could be waiting for that bicycle. Getting bad news in the middle of the night was never pleasant, but getting it after hours or days of waiting and dreading was torture.

The address Mason Moon had given me for Lyn Takai turned out to be a rear cottage south of campus. Although it was a high-density area tenanted by students and young families, at midnight the streets were empty, and few house lights were lit. I made my way between the violet stucco cottage and a two-story wood house. The path was narrow enough that I could almost have touched both dwellings. The only light came from a fixture in the backyard.

The yard behind the stucco cottage was typical of Berkeley land usage. Real-estate values have risen so sharply here that lots sell for what houses used to, and leaving a backyard for recreation is wretched excess. The rear cottage was tiny, but so was the yard. The stucco shoebox hugged the property line. Its front door couldn't have been more than six feet from the main house. And those six cemented-in feet were decorated not with potted plants and deck chairs but appliances. Under the cottage's picture window where a planter box might have stood were an old refrigerator, an apartment stove, and a scratched metal table. Beyond, on their sides, were two porcelain bathroom sinks, one decorated with a blue-tulip motif, one merely sporting a crack, but both meant for corners of a pint-size bathroom. With all this out in the yard, what was left to be inside? "Less is more," as our former governor said.

There was no bell. I knocked and waited. I wouldn't mention the victim was likely to die. The dead are barely cool before even the staunchest enemy stops speaking ill of them. And speaking ill is the bread and butter of my business.

I was about to knock again when stronger lights came on and the door opened. The woman in front of me was short, with light-brown pixie hair and a mouth that was surprisingly wide for her delicate oval face. She wasn't wearing lipstick, only eyeliner and shadow, but even with that effort she hadn't managed to correct the imbalance. She looked to be about my age, midthirties, but already there were creases beside her mouth—none by her eyes, just the mouth—as if her irritation had all settled there. She was wearing a black V-neck leotard and shorts, and despite her slight build, the muscles in her legs and shoulders were clear. And I noted with surprise, even on this cold, windy night there were no goose bumps on her bare legs.

"Yes?" It was more a demand than a question.

No one wants to see a cop at the door at midnight. Tough-guy mouths like hers are usually clenched to hide quivering jaws. "Detective Smith, Berkeley Police," I said, holding out my badge. In cases like this I don't say "Homicide." There's rarely a need to frighten people more than they already are. But when there is, it's nice to have kept "Homicide" in reserve.

She held the shield under the light. She could have saved the effort. The shield was no proof; anyone with the right resources could have made a good copy. But she scrutinized it, her brown eyes unscrunched, her lips neither pressed together nor pursed. "Do you have a driver's license?" she asked in a quiet voice, a softness that comes from assurance, like the perfunctory bark of a St. Bernard.

I showed her the license. Caution like hers is a trait we encourage in women living alone. But I wondered how much the tension of being ever watchful, ever vaguely afraid, had contributed to those defensive lines around Lyn Takai's mouth.

As she looked from my license to me, her finger moved across it from *Brn* (hair) to *Grn* (eyes) to 5-7 (I had the feeling she knew I'd stretched the truth there, but maybe that's just the paranoia of the shortest officer in Detective Detail), to *120* (actually that was more than the truth too; the Howard house diet, in which food disappeared regularly from the fridge, had slimmed me more than I'd intended).

Handing back the license, she said curtly, "I'm in the middle of my practice."

I glanced into the room behind her, hoping to see what it was she was so adamant about practicing in the middle of the night.

The first thing I noticed was myself, then Lyn Takai's straight muscular back. Reflected in mirrors on the far wall. And that was about all there was in the twelve-by-twenty room. It was bare but for a pile of two- by five-foot rubber mats, wooden handrails on the walls, and ropes hung next to the mirrors. The setup suggested a dance studio, a dance studio with ropes. Exotic dance? Erotic dance? S-and-M dance?

One rubber mat lay alone in the middle of the floor, three thick books piled on the end. Slow dance with reading material?

Takai bent her right leg, braced her foot against the left thigh, put her palms together, and balanced on one leg like a stork. "I teach yoga. I was doing a forward-bend series." She indicated the rubber mat. "I was teaching a private class this evening. It's easy to pick up students' energy and be too wired to sleep. Sitting on the floor bending forward relaxes the body and calms the mind. I'm limber enough that I can reach beyond my feet. That's what I've got the books for."

I nodded. Lots of people in Berkeley did yoga. I was not one of them.

But Takai must have taken my nod as encouragement, for she continued, "Forward bends not only calm the mind; they massage the digestive organs, tone the urinary system, the abdominal muscles, and strengthen the entire back. If you practice them daily, you—" She stopped abruptly. I was sure she'd slipped into a spiel from one of her classes. "My first class is at nine thirty. So if you can be brief . . ."

A woman used to being in control. I said, "I need to identify a man in an accident. A friend of yours, Mason Moon, said the victim was an IRS agent who'd been dealing with you."

She sucked her lips in. It looked as if she didn't have lips at all, at least not in the middle of her mouth. For another person it might not have been much of a response, but for a woman who had shown nothing but controlled impatience, this was the kind of reversion it would take a lot of forward bends to rectify. "What kind of accident?" she asked in a completely different tone of voice.

"Bicycle."

She waited. I didn't elaborate but said, "His name?"

"Drem," she snapped. She shut her eyes momentarily (a little forward bend of the lids?) and said only slightly more calmly, "Philip Drem. *D-r-e-m*."

"Does he live in Berkeley?" If he didn't, Pereira could call his jurisdiction and have them deal with the family.

"I don't know. We didn't deal in small talk. Now if you're finished . . ." She glanced toward the door. It was virtually beside her since she hadn't encouraged me in farther than was necessary to shut it.

I hate to leave when people want me to go. I took a step away. "Was Philip Drem difficult to work with?"

"He was here to audit me!" she said in an exasperated tone that conveyed not only her opinion of the event but of me for being dense enough to question her.

Defensiveness like that is a flashing red light. "Was he overzealous? You complained enough about Drem to Mason Moon."

Takai let her eyes close again. When she opened them, they looked different. "It's hard not to grumble when someone demands money. But Mason tends to dramatize everything. Any-

way, that's over and done with. Drem's out of my consciousness. Before you brought him up, I hadn't even thought about
him in ages."

Whether by visualized forward bend or whatever, she had
managed to tone down her response. I wasn't sure where the
truth was between Moon's flashing red version and her pallid
gray one. If I'd had another ten minutes, I could have found
out. But if Drem survived, it wouldn't matter; if he died, I'd be
back. Now I wanted to get the ID to Pereira. Philip Drem's six
minutes would be long gone. But maybe he'd done better than I
imagined; maybe the ID would help him.

Before I finished telling Takai I'd probably need to see her
again, she had closed the door.

I hurried past the fridge and that odd tuliped sink around the
side of the house to my car. Since it was my own car rather
than the patrol car, there was no radio.

I flagged down a patrol car on Telegraph and called in the
ID. Then I drove back to the scene of the accident. Almost an
hour had passed since I'd left. I looked quickly to the end of the
street by People's Park, but there was no sign of Howard's
sting. He'd have reeled in his victim by now, and the action
would be down at the station.

Regent Street too looked merely middle-of-the-night now. A
pair of patrol cars was still there, parked by a hydrant and in a
crosswalk, lights out, radios off. And the slow progress of the
officers going house to house would have been noticeable only
to someone spending the night looking out a darkened window. I waited till one of the uniforms emerged from a house
near the spot where Drem's bicycle had been abandoned. It was
Leonard, a short gray-haired guy who'd been a veteran when I
started in Patrol.

Leonard had been laid-back before the term entered the
realm. There was a disarmingly shambling quality about him.
He was the kind of cop who knew everyone on his beat and

found a soupçon of decency in felons the rest of us would have classified as pornographic (no socially redeeming qualities). Because of that, he'd managed to get case-breaking hints from guys who knew they were on their way home to Q. (Or maybe they couldn't quite believe this cop whose shirtsleeves were always wrinkled, whose pencil point was always broken, could be smarter than they were.) Whatever the reason, patrol was Leonard's forte, and he knew it.

Leonard should have gone off duty at eleven o'clock. It was going on 1:00 A.M. now, but he didn't seem to mind. The wind had picked up, and it flapped at the sides of his tan jacket, the summer-weight jacket. But he seemed no colder than Lyn Takai had.

"So," I said, "you manage to massage anything out of the neighbors?"

"It was late, you know. A time people are watching the tube, or listening to the stereo, or getting ready for bed."

From another man, that might have been an excuse for coming up empty. From Leonard, it meant full pockets. "Someone saw Drem get off the bike?"

"After a fashion." Leonard hated to overstate.

"The house right by the bike, the one propped up, with the foundation damage," I said, looking over at one of the earthquake's casualties. The whole crawl space was open to the air. "Are there people living there?"

"No. Anyway, it wasn't the neighbors. It was one of the street people, guy named Sierra. Mason Moon spotted him. Murakawa passed him on to me. You heard of Sierra?"

I shook my head. It had been years since I'd had this beat.

"Well, he's not someone you'd want to take on the stand, if you know what I mean. And really, Smith, when you find out what he said . . ." Leonard shrugged, *the* motion for which his shambling body seemed to have been created. "It's no help, but he's the only one who saw anything. I'll have another go at him tomorrow. He could have been hoping for a few bucks from the snitch fund. Maybe he really didn't see anything at all. It doesn't make much difference."

"Leonard!" I said, exasperated. No wonder felons let down their guard with him. "What did Sierra see?"

Leonard leaned an arm on the patrol car. His tan shirtcuff stuck out beyond his sleeve, wrinkled. "Sierra said Drem looked shaky, like he was on something, which is an area Sierra knows about. Said Drem propped the bike against the phone pole and had to brace himself on it before he squatted down and fiddled with his locks. Said he didn't think a guy in that condition could get them out of his baskets and through the tires, but he did. Got them partway locked, and then it seemed like he didn't realize they were still open. He pushed himself up and staggered into the street."

That confirmed what we'd figured, but it broke no new ground. And if I knew Leonard, it wasn't what his pockets were full of. "And?"

"And then, Sierra said, a patrol officer came."

"Pereira?"

"Now that's the odd thing that makes me wonder if Sierra really saw anything. He says a dark-haired officer in uniform. Came up to the bike, but didn't see Drem."

"Looked at the bike and left?" I asked, amazed.

Leonard shrugged again. "Like I said, it's not worth much. Probably nothing. I'll catch him again tomorrow."

"Could have been his own private screening," I said. "Whatever Sierra saw, it was not a patrol officer eyeballing the scene and wandering off into the dark." No Berkeley patrol officer would have left the scene—I knew that, I believed it. But just in case, I was glad to have Leonard following up.

 I walked back to my car and headed for the station. I thought Howard and his crew might be there celebrating his sting. They weren't. I'd hoped Raksen, the lab tech, might have seen something telling on Drem's bike. But it was way too soon for the compulsively thorough Raksen to say anything. What I wasn't expecting was Pereira.

I walked in from the parking lot through the squad room. Seeing me, Pereira jumped up and raced toward me, her face flushed. "Philip Drem," she said. "Do you know who he is?"

"An IRS agent."

"Not just any Treasury agent, Smith. Philip Drem is the Al Capone of the auditors. When word that he's been hospitalized hits, half of Berkeley will be sighing in relief."

When a young, healthy-looking man stumbles into the street and collapses, it makes me wonder. When he's one of the most hated employees of the nation's most-loathed bureaucracy, I get suspicious. And when I hear a cockamamy tale about a patrol officer ignoring his fallen body, eyeing his bicycle, and wandering off into the night . . .

I had the feeling that this case was going to blow any minute. But before the eruption came, there was not a thing I could do to contain the disaster.

I pulled my car into Howard's driveway, wishing Pereira'd had some conclusive word on Drem's condition. Drem was still alive, barely. I kept picturing him lying in the road with that terrified look. The face I saw wasn't the "Al Capone of the auditors." It belonged to someone who'd nonchalantly climbed on his bike, turned downhill, and ridden straight into the angel of death.

But there was nothing I could do now. My skin felt clammy from exhaustion, and it quivered from stress that wouldn't dissipate before I was called to the next crime scene. It certainly wouldn't ease up enough so I could sleep tonight. I'd spend the night thrashing around. I'd probably kick over Howard's tax door-table, knock his tax forms all over the bedroom, and break my foot in the bargain.

And to make matters worse, I was starved. I'd bought a quart of Chocolate Chocolate Shower ice cream yesterday. What were the chances of any of it still being in the freezer? Yesterday (Thursday) had been the beginning of spring break for Howard's tenants (two students, one prof, and one TA, all of whom would have dropped out before taking a class that met on Friday). They'd all packed and departed for beaches, friends' houses, or places where they could do even less than they managed here. I would have bet my car that my Chocolate Chocolate Shower had left inside of one of them.

But at least they were gone. And the brown-shingled other woman was empty of the increasingly "tolerant" tenants Howard was forced to accept in order to pay the rent. The only ones who were willing to join his indolent assemblage of lessees, their ever-changing live-in or -out lovers, tabbies, beagles, and, on one occasion, boa constrictor (who was reputed to have disappeared into the pipes) were more of the same. Howard's house was one of the few places where I could be living in sin and still feel like a mother superior.

I came around the front of the house. The wind ruffled the leaves of the hornbeam or hackberry. My skin was still quivering and cold. It wasn't just from the wind or the Drem case. I stopped and glanced up at Howard's bedroom windows. The panes were dark. The chill in my chest faded. It didn't take a shrink to interpret that. But I was too tired to ponder the house and the reason I didn't just resent it but was physically uncomfortable every time I had to go inside. It was decrepit, of course, but I'd lived in worse places. Shabbiness had a certain appeal to me. And for Howard, every scraped or nicked doorjamb was part of an elegant entryway waiting for rebirth, an entryway to one of the future rooms of his dreams. He couldn't understand why I didn't see that. I wasn't sure either, but I didn't. For me, those oak doors only swung closed. And locked.

If I'd had this reaction to anything else, I would have worked it through by talking to Howard. God, I missed the old Howard: leaning back in his chair, his long legs extended, feet the size of skateboards tapping against the coffee table, and that wry grin on his face as he elucidated the male point of view. Or lantern chin extended, blue eyes scrunched as we considered the problem and played through and discarded the options. The old Howard would have asked if my reaction would be the same to any house that captured Howard. Or was there something unnerving about this particular house? But the old Howard was little more than a memory, and even the new Howard wasn't in sight. He was probably out celebrating with Castillo and the other guys on his sting.

Pushing aside my irrational discomfort, I opened the door and stepped into the dark foyer. The cavernous living room seemed dark and empty, but I could make out the pale glow in the fireplace.

I sighed. Damn—one of the tenants hadn't left. I'd come in on romantic scenes here before. The Never-on-Friday set had lots of time for liaisons of the heart, which frequently ended up liaisons on the sofa. Passion, I've found, is not so attractive to the observer as to the participants, and I was too tired to deal with one of those awkward conversations where only one third of the conversants is clothed. I moved as silently as possible, giving the sofa a wide berth.

I was almost at the corner of the dining room when the figure on the sofa rose to sitting. Alone. It was Howard.

"What are you doing here in the dark?" I said. "I figured you'd be off celebrating Hentry's collar."

"No collar," Howard snapped.

"Oh, no. How could it . . . Damn!" I sat down next to him and turned on the light. "Did Hentry spot the trap?"

"By the time Hentry got there, there was no trap." Howard spoke through gritted teeth, directing his comments to his knees. The fire was down to embers. The flue, one of the many marginally working items here, must have been about a third open. The whole room smelled of smoke, the dark-green walls almost invisible, and it was cold. Howard, in a cotton shirt, didn't seem to notice. But I was shaking. I pushed back into the sofa cushions and drew my feet up under me.

Howard's sting had been half a block from Drem's accident. Could the crowd left over from Drem have derailed Howard's plan? Surely Pereira and the backups had gotten them dispersed well before midnight. Surely . . . "What happened?"

He sucked in air through his clenched teeth. "Okay. You know the setup. Castillo's already in People's Park with the regulars there. He's got his sleeping bag and a backpack full of gear. All the guys in the park—the street people, the homeless guys, the winos, the addicts, the runaways—they all think Castillo's a regular too. He's spent a month of his life sleeping in shelters, or in the park, or in alleys. He's eaten in soup kitchens. He's worn the same stinking clothes for a week at a time. I mean, I could barely stand to talk to him. You can imagine what his wife thought."

I didn't have to imagine. Eve Castillo had been to a party with us. She decreed Castillo celibate until he'd been steam-cleaned.

"So, everything is set. I've cleared and recleared with the campus cops."

I nodded. The university owned the land People's Park occupied; their police patrolled it.

"I've planned this baby down to the minute. Damon Hentry's convinced Castillo's the go-between. Hentry's supposed to be there on the stroke of midnight. Hentry's the kind of dude midnight in the full moon would appeal to. I'll tell you, Jill, I could get a research grant for the amount of background I did on Damon Hentry."

"You're an artiste," I said, giving his hand a squeeze. He'd talked about the sting between azalea runs and consultations with roofers. I'd caught glimpses of the old Howard. "Castillo's spent the day acting crazy. The park guys are giving him a wide berth, like they do with crazies. At eleven thirty he's sitting in the wet grass by the garbage cans, waiting. I'm in an unmarked across the street. Everything's perfect. I can just about feel Damon Hentry's wrists as I click the cuffs on him. I can smell his shock. I've never had a setup go so smoothly." His eyes softened. A wistful smile creased his cheeks. I could see the sting through his lenses, feel the heady rush of triumph.

The smile vanished. "And then, Jill, this goddamned jogger comes tooling along. Eleven thirty at night, for godsakes! Out jogging as if she doesn't have a home to go to." Howard turned and glared at me. "Everyone knows how the park is. Even the homeless are nervous there. *They* complain about the dealers."

Suddenly the smoke seemed thicker. I breathed in through my mouth. "And there was quite a crowd around there tonight?" Surely we'd gotten the crowd from Drem's accident dispersed before . . .

"Buncha guys, buncha drugs, and one goddamned woman jogging in skintight Day-Glo Lycra like she's a gift from another planet."

"No matter what you're wearing," I said, feeling my shoulders tighten and hearing the edge to my voice, "People's Park's not a wise spot to run by. You don't think she was Hentry's lure, testing the waters?"

"No. And she didn't run *by*. *Through*. She came from the far corner, and when I spotted her, she was in the middle of the park with five guys on her tail."

"Oh shit!"

"You can believe, Jill, that I did not want to go plowing into the park, advertising Police Presence. I know Damon Hentry too well. He had someone watching the park since sundown. As soon as his man spotted me opening the car door, the deal would be off, and the slime would be a whole lot more slippery the next time we tried to set something up. So I'm sitting tight, pulling for the damned woman to make it through. And she almost does. She's fifteen yards from the fucking sidewalk when one of the guys grabs her shoulder and knocks her down." He stopped, took a breath, and stared straight at me with a look so hostile, I barely recognized him. "So I get out and run across the street. Castillo's slipped back under the trees with the rest of the homeless. No need in both of us blowing our cover. By the time I get there, the woman's standing up, surrounded by these guys."

"Who? Transients?"

"Three guys I didn't recognize and a couple of crackheads. I've busted these two before. I know what they're capable of. To them rape would be just the beginning. So I come up and plant myself between her and one of the crackheads. I ask what's going on. Calm, authoritative, Mr. By-the-book. The crackhead tells me it's none of my fucking business. And then the chorus starts."

Howard didn't need to describe events in greater detail. I'd seen enough crowds feeding on each other, buoying up leaders, egging them on to do stupid macho things. By eleven thirty, it was a safe guess that the crackheads would be high or crazy, or both, the winos way up or way down.

"So everybody's mouthing off. I'm trying to keep order and get things calmed down before guys are coming out of the shrubbery and up off the Avenue. Before we're the top of the bill. But the crackheads get the pack of them wired. Guys who would have been slinking off are shoving and yelling 'Who the hell do you think you are, telling us what to do? This is our turf.' They're closing in around me. And her."

"And no way to call backup." He'd have been counting on Castillo to get to a phone.

"And then *she* starts in on them, yelling at them to keep their fucking hands off her. Riling them up. That's the last thing I need. The crackheads're already straining at the leash. The whole situation's ready to blow. I'm yelling at the bunch of them to knock it off, but things are so far out of control that I'm just adding to the noise." He waited till I nodded. "So I did the only thing possible."

"Which was?"

"I removed the provocation."

Textbook crowd management. Defuse the crowd first.

"I told her to get in the car. She balked. I said to her, 'Lady, you see these guys? Do I have to spell things out?'" Howard shook his head. "It was like she grew up on another planet. She planted her Day-Glo legs and said she goddamn well wasn't going anywhere. She has just as much right to be in this park as anyone else. By this time, I can see shadows moving toward us. I say, 'Lady, get in the patrol car now!' She digs in her heels. I don't have time to argue. I grab her arm and yank her across the grass. The pack follows. I get the door open. She braces against the side of the car. I shove her in. I've still got the mob to deal with. It's a full minute or so before another car pulls up. Took Castillo that long to get to a phone."

"So the whole sting's blown, and Castillo's cover too?" I said woodenly.

"Oh, yeah. Castillo's shot to hell. He might as well be the dealer's poster boy. But that's not the end of it, Jill. As soon as patrol gets there, I get back in the car. And what do I get—thanks for saving her ass? Not hardly. Fucking bitch is still screaming at me. Why have I arrested *her*? Why not the men? By then, they weren't the problem. *She* was." He turned and glared at me. "What kind of idiot woman gets out in the middle of the night in feel-me-up clothes, leaves her house where she's safe, to run through—"

"She should be able to run when she pleases," I said, my voice cracking with anger.

Howard stared, "Jees, Jill, you of all people—"

"If a guy parks his Maserati on the street overnight, we don't throw him in the cage because it gets stolen."

"And when he gets tired of worrying about being ripped off, he can get a Ford. You tell that to a woman who gets raped and ends up with AIDS. She can't trade in her body."

"So what—she should stay inside every night and be safe? Be a prisoner!" I was yelling.

"Common sense—"

"Common sense is the status quo. Common sense says the world stays as it is—"

"Well, you can't—"

I jumped up and glared down at Howard. "Common sense says men go where they please and women huddle inside and hope none of those men decide to break into their *supposedly* safe houses."

He let a beat pass before saying, "I can't go wherever I please."

"When was the last time you couldn't walk across campus alone at night because women might be aroused? When did you change out of your cutoffs because your legs looked too good? When did you not stop in a bar by yourself?"

"I don't go to the Oakland housing projects."

"Hardly the same thing."

"No, but I understand—"

I stood up and glared down at him. "No, you don't, Howard. You're six foot six, and a cop. All the streets lead outward for you. You don't know what a roadblock is. Or a prison."

"Jill, I can't believe you—"

"Believe it!" I stalked to the door, opened it, stepped out, and slammed it. The cold air iced the sweat on my face. I breathed in hungrily till my lungs couldn't take any more air. It had been as if I'd been breathing through a thick towel before.

I slid into my VW and backed out of the driveway, feeling the rough fake leather of the steering-wheel cover, inhaling the

thin smell of gasoline from the spill on the side of the car. I'd
loved that smell as long as I could remember. And when I
shifted into first, I could see the road winding endlessly ahead
of me. I turned the radio to blare and stepped on the gas.

I didn't want to be tied down by the house, or by Howard.

It was probably less than half an hour later when I realized I
had no idea where I was going. It was 2:00 A.M. I was cold and
tired, and I felt that queasy mixture of anger and sorrow that I
always do when I lose my temper, as if I'd burst free for a few
minutes, only to find myself in a bigger cage. The cage of the
police department where I was the only woman in detective
detail, where the rules were made to suit men and I was judged
on how well I adapted. Or maybe it was the larger cage of
society and its view of women.

Howard had hit a nerve with the jogger. I felt as I had when I
was fourteen years old when my older brother, Mike, drove
across country, camping. I'd thought that trip the ultimate ad-
venture. I'd started to plan my own trip to follow my gradua-
tion when my mother said, "You can't do that. You're a girl."

But how much of this was my reaction to Howard and the
time he spent on the damned house? I sat, shivering, considering that. I hadn't been just angry when I was yelling at him; I'd
been panicky, caged in that house just like the jogger in the
patrol car. Just as I had when I'd been left at my grandmother's
for months while my parents moved. I jolted. I hadn't made
that connection before. Odd, the things about your life that
would be so obvious to anyone else. I'd never liked my grandmother, a brittle woman in a house so cluttered, every step was
potential disaster. I'd hated being abandoned there when my
parents and Mike went off to settle in our new house in New-
ark, Delaware; Frederick, Maryland; Plainfield, New Jersey.
But her tiny house near the sawmill bore no resemblance to
Howard's. Why would it . . .

But I was too tired to try to find the answer. The only thing I could think of now was bed—the one place I wasn't about to go. Instead I dragged a blanket out of the trunk, folded down the backseat, and curled up on the scratchy convex surface.

I could have driven the car back into Howard's driveway and been safe. But I was damned if I'd do that. I tucked my purse with my revolver under my head, pulled a blanket over me, and fell asleep, thinking how glad I was to have a car to be in.

About five-thirty I woke up with the remnants of a dream of an infant in an overflowing tub. It didn't take an analyst to decipher that one. And now after a bit of dream clarification I knew I wasn't about to throw the baby Howard out with the dirty bathwater of what he had never had to experience enough to understand.

It wasn't till I pulled up in front of the house that I saw the form my own sting would take. The ideal sting would have started with raising Howard's house onto wheels and carting it off, but in an imperfect world, idealization isn't always possible. Slightly less satisfying would be the *Azalea magnifica* sting.

Gracious woman that I am, I didn't dig up his *Azalea magnifica*, not entirely. Just halfway. The roots were still in the ground. But it would take neither a gardener nor a detective to jump to the conclusion the *magnifica* had been imperiled.

I washed and dried the shovel, put it back in the garage, and headed to the house for my swimming gear.

5

I keep my swimbag packed so I don't find myself toweling dry later with no underwear or makeup to put on. I don't eat before swimming—too much to drag around the pool. So all I have to do is slide into my sweats and VW. The bug almost drives itself.

I left the house before Howard woke up, closing the door silently, passing the *Azalea* a bit less *magnifica*, tilting inebriately half out of its hole.

The pool is always crowded at 6:30 A.M. In the fast lanes, if you swim too slow, someone taps your foot and sprints around you. It's humiliating to be the tappee, and for the tapper infuriating to have to break pace. Swim instructors tell you to take the first laps slowly. Doing that would be like pulling onto the freeway in first gear. The difference is that on the freeway it might get you killed, but at least you wouldn't have to face the people you've held up day after day, afterward—when you're naked in the shower. I've got my diver's watch (good to 150 feet below, about 135 more than I'm likely to go). I set the stopwatch, and I go all out till my mile is done.

I was standing at the end of lane 3 adjusting my goggles when Howard walked out on the deck. Lane 4, the other fast lane, was twice as crowded, but he didn't even waver toward mine. Nor did he give any indication of having noticed the azalea. I pushed off, kicking full out for the next 5,280 feet.

I was out of the pool and in the redecorated women's shower before it occurred to me to wonder if Philip Drem had made it through the night.

Saturdays, Inspector Doyle takes off. Today I was up; I subbed for him. It was 7:35 when I got to the station, which meant no time to do anything but snag a donut from the dispatcher's box and check the In-Custody tray. Only two prisoners still in from last night. I stashed the donut in my office, gave one of the in-custodys to Al "Eggs" Eggenburger, and hunted up the rap sheet for the other, one Erin Williams.

Williams had a couple of priors in Contra Costa County to the north. True to form, the rap sheet listed the arrests but not the outcome. I'd have to call Martinez, the county seat in Contra Costa County, for that. In the meantime there were the patrol officers' reports to scout up. I found them in the patrol sergeant's box, got the file to the court liaison officer at 7:43, and slid into my chair for Morning Meeting just as Chief Larkin settled in his. Jackson, my fellow in Homicide Detail, passed me a mug of Peet's coffee, liquid adrenaline.

"Bless you," I mouthed.

Chief Larkin had already started the meeting by the time I spotted Pereira. Beat officers don't come to Detectives' Morning Meeting unless they have something germane to report. Griseki, from Vice and Substance Abuse, summarized a cocaine bust on Grizzly Peak Boulevard, but the chief didn't call on Howard to report his disaster. I took that as a good sign.

Heling, one of the patrol officers, recounted the latest altercation of the People's Park free box. "Berkeley's answer to the Bavarian Christmas Pageants," she said. "Just as reliable, but more frequent. Citizens leave clothes in the box, street people come to get them, the university starts hauling off the box, a mob forms, Campus Patrol hauls off the demonstrators in the

park, we pick up the ones on city land. In a day or two the
university relents, and the box returns. At least there were no
injuries this time. But tonight's Saturday night, *and* virtually
the full moon. It could mean another round."

I was listening to Heling but watching Pereira, illogically
hoping she had taken the squeal on a bank robbery or collared
the guy who'd been boosting Mercedes sedans all over the East
Bay—anything but bad news on the body I'd last seen being
shoved into the ambulance. But when she spoke, it was about
Philip Drem. Drem had died in the emergency room. That panicked expression of his flashed somewhere in my consciousness.
Not bewildered, as a man would be if he were suddenly taken
ill, but terrified, as if his worst fears had come true.

"Drem was the most hated of the hated, the bulldog of the
IRS auditors, to quote Rick Lamott, the hotshot of tax accountants," Pereira said. "But as far as PIN and CORPUS go, he's
clean." PIN is the Police Information Network, with data on
warrants statewide. CORPUS lists arrests in the county. Drem's
showing up on neither was no surprise. Most law-abiding citizens wouldn't.

"But on Records Management, Philip Drem was a star."

I waited for Connie to go on. The Records Management
system is where we keep note of everyone who has had any
dealings with the department. You complain about your neighbor's dog barking, you make it into Records Management.

"Two citizen's arrests of responsibles who smoked in nonsmoking sections."

"Oooohhh," Griseki chided. "Wha'd he do, find the last two
smokers in town?"

"That's not all. He accused a Chinese restaurant of using
MSG. They advertised that they didn't. We told him that was a
civil matter. But it didn't stop him. The next week, he complained that the bakers of a chocolate fudge cake had sneaked
in espresso beans."

Griseki shook his head. "How will Berkeley survive without this guy? We'll never take another easy breath or bite."

"Yeah, but we'll file our ten-forties a lot happier," Eggs put in. There was an unusual edge to his voice.

"Anything else, Pereira?" Chief Larkin reined in the Saturday looseness.

"No dependents. His doctor said we should all be in such good health."

"And it's your case, Smith?" the chief asked.

I nodded.

Then the meeting was over. They're short on Saturdays. I glanced over at Howard, hoping we could avoid being in our office at the same time. At the best of times the former closet is cramped, but when Howard and I are arguing—or worse, avoiding argument—it's as if the air were cement. Now Howard was on the far side of the meeting room talking to his inspector and Chief Larkin. He'd be occupied long enough for me to get down to the office and eat my donut.

"Five minutes?" I called to Pereira. I needed the details on Drem. And if Howard was in our office when she arrived, she'd provide a diversion.

"Give me twenty and I may have a surprise for you, Smith."

"What kind of a surprise?"

"A good one."

For that I could wait another fifteen minutes. There's never a danger of idle hands in DD. We've always got paperwork. I headed down the tan corridor to my office. At the stairs, Eggs, my fellow Homicide officer, caught up with me. Eggs was unfortunately nicknamed. Eggenburger had been shortened to Eggs for as long as I'd known him, but it had been only in the last couple of years that he'd lost his hair. Right now, his expression suited a grumpy hard-boiled. With bifocals.

"Bad time with your in-custody?" I asked.

"Nah." He braced an arm against the wall. "Good thing

Drem is yours, Smith. If he were mine, I'd be tempted to congratulate the perp." He pushed off and turned toward his office.

I grabbed an arm. "Wait a minute here. Let's have a little background on that one."

"For cause of death you don't have to consider heart attack. With Philip Drem, there'd be nothing to attack." Eggs was grinning.

"Eggs! Stop gloating over the dead and explain!"

"Can't now. I've got the DA's liaison due in . . . Hell, he can wait. Come on."

I followed him to his office, *the* Homicide office. When I'd been promoted to detective, he and Jackson had already been settled in there, in the corner office with the ledge that the Homicide squirrel visited daily for tribute. The room was three times the size of the dark hole Howard and I shared. Such were the perks of longevity, Eggs had insisted. Jackson's desk was forever strewn with reports, pictures of his wife and kids, the morning newspaper, thermos and coffee cup, and scraps of paper with notes that went back years. On Eggs's desk every square inch of blotter would be visible. When Eggs went to the men's room, his desk looked better than Jackson's when he'd taken his kids to Texas for two weeks.

"Shh!" Eggs opened the door slowly and pointed to the window. Porter, the squirrel, was on the ledge. Eggs walked over, settled in his chair, and placed his glasses on the desk. Then he extricated a pouch, pondered the contents, and selected a hazelnut for Porter.

Porter showed no such deliberation. He grabbed and carried. When the culinary consultation was completed, I said, "So, Eggs, what's the story on Philip Drem?"

He reached for a Mazda brochure in his IN box and handed it to me. "What do you think of this one, the RX-Seven?" he asked with a mixture of pride and reservation.

I glanced down at the sleek convertible and back up at Eggs. What was *with* those car-model letters—RX-7, XL, DX? Did the Y chromosome lust after these *X*'s? Dismissing the speculation, I said, "Going to spruce up your image, eh?"

"I'm going to take the RX-Seven for a test drive after lunch. Want to come?" He bounced a still-shelled walnut in his hand. It was the most excited I'd ever seen reserved, analytical Eggs, the tan-sedan man. I was kind of sorry to miss this drive.

"Can't. I'm nowhere with this Drem case. I can't cut out now. Take me for a ride after you've bought the RX."

Eggs smiled. "Okay. You'll be the first."

"I'm honored. Now, tell me about Philip Drem."

Eggs leaned back, pulled open his drawer, and glanced at his handcuffs inside. He was wearing his standard wash-and-wear pale-blue shirt, his standard dark-blue tie hanging over his shoulders like loose suspenders. I could more easily imagine him on Drem's bicycle than in a twenty-five-thousand-dollar sports car. He said, "You remember when I got divorced five years ago."

I nodded. It had been a year or two before my divorce, long enough before that I wasn't drawn to the topic. The reason I recalled the event at all was that I'd been so amazed Eggs had ever been married. He seemed like one of those men who padded through life and at some point realized they'd overlooked marriage.

He pulled open the handcuffs and clicked them shut. "Justine and I had been married since college, seventeen years. I was surprised when she wanted the divorce. Nothing had happened. She said that was the reason. We hadn't grown apart, we'd faded apart." He shrugged. "It was true. I didn't mind much when she left. Mostly the problem was new inconveniences—keeping food in the house, doing the laundry. I found I liked having the place to myself. I liked to sit and listen to symphonies and watch the fish in the tanks." The clicking stopped. He looked up, suddenly embarrassed. He'd said more about his divorce now than in the previous five years.

I nodded, appreciating the freedom of that empty apartment. If my sting with Howard didn't work . . .

"My point is, Smith, that we had an amicable divorce. Justine hadn't worked in years. She needed time to train for a decent job. I didn't want her working in a dime store, or waiting tables, or whatever a B.A. in English qualifies you for seventeen years later. So I agreed to pay alimony while she went to school." He'd begun working the cuffs again, pull-click, pull-click. "Most of her expenses were coming right away. She had to move, pay first and last, buy furniture, pay tuition, get her car fixed so she wouldn't be stranded in a parking lot after a night class. She needed money right away." He snapped the cuffs faster. "I did the decent thing. I arranged to give her the whole year's allotment. I had to take a loan to do it, but I figured so what? So I gave her the check. But the day I put it in her hand, the day she deposited it, was one day before the divorce was final. I didn't think about that." He pulled the cuff arms hard and didn't click them back. "But the next year, when Philip Drem was circling over the pickings looking for the unsuspecting divorced who might make mistakes he could latch on to, he found me and that alimony payment. Guess what, Smith?"

"What?"

"Alimony's not deductible if it's not ordered by the court." He smacked the cuffs back together. "And it's not ordered by the court until you're legally divorced. And since I'd been decent enough to pay it early, no go. No deduction."

"But surely he could understand your intent—"

"He didn't give a shit about intent. Either it fit the rules or not."

"But—"

"And before you ask, Smith, he told me every time I asked

that agents don't interpret the rules—agents only enforce them."

"Like newspaper machines? Only take your coins and give you a paper."

Eggs smacked the cuffs into the drawer. "Or take the money and give zip. There's nothing you can do about it."

"But IRS agents have to have some discretion. Otherwise, the government would use computers instead of people," I insisted.

"Sure. Agents can decide whether you are lying or not. But Drem had already made that decision. Dealing with him made me sympathize with the guys we get with rap sheets long enough to cover their beds. Drem was willing to give me the same benefit of the doubt." He slammed his drawer shut. "Between the loan costs, the extra taxes, the interest on those taxes, and the penalties, it took me three years to get back to the point of having extra money. By then, car prices had shot up." He stood up. Slowly a smile took hold and sat awkwardly on his long sallow face, as if the muscles were pulling in unaccustomed ways. "But now justice has prevailed. I'm going to be test-driving an RX-Seven, and Drem is dead!"

I hadn't been shocked by Mason Moon's comments on Drem or Lyn Takai's, but Eggs's dance on Drem's grave brought home just how despised my victim was.

I followed Eggs out of his office and walked downstairs to mine. The one small window badly needed cleaning. Porter wouldn't deign to visit our window, even if we had a ledge, which we didn't.

The sun was out, but not much light had made it through the small grimy window, just enough to show the spots on the green paint where we'd mopped at sprayed coffee. Our metal desks faced opposite walls with three feet of space between. Over my desk was a bulletin board with a collage of notices. The city'd run out of corkboard by the time Howard moved in, so he'd been left to decorate with Scotch tape. Memos and announcements were forever pulling his tape loose, leaving beige rectangles in the green and sheets of paper on desk and floor.

There were still five of Pereira's twenty minutes left. My donut was still on my desk, so I knew she hadn't come by early. I had it half unwrapped before I thought of Raksen, the lab tech. He had Drem's bicycle. There was just time to call him. With each thing I heard about Agent Drem, an innocent fall off a bicycle seemed less and less likely. I rewrapped the donut, got pencil and paper ready, and called the lab. Raksen was off duty. Few others would I have risked calling at home on their morning off, but for Raksen talk of scratches and toxins was as exciting as a stolen caress. Besides, if he'd planned a passionate morning, he'd have turned off his phone.

On the third ring, Raksen said groggily, "Yes?"

"It's Jill Smith in Homicide. I'm sorry to get you up."

"You're calling about the bicycle?" His voice sounded middle-of-the-day.

"Right."

"Was it you who spotted the tears in the seat?"

"Right."

"Good move, Smith. Place where those two seatpads come together, fabric was torn. Metal cylinder'd been wedged between. Some kind of copper alloy."

"How long a cylinder?"

"Well . . ." Raksen was tapping his teeth. He was a short, wiry terrier of a guy whose teeth were sharp and pointy, ready to snatch a scrap of information so he could race off and chew on it. "Couldn't've stuck up much higher than the seats; deceased would've spotted it. But, no way to tell."

"No way" was a big admission for Raksen, for whom an unanswered question was a bone dangling out of reach. But Raksen didn't sound defeated. "So, Raksen, what did you find?"

"Residue of a central-nervous-system depressant. Can't say which one. Could take weeks to run enough tests to find the right one."

"So what do you think was wedged in between the seats—a miniature hypodermic?"

"I don't like to guess." Raksen *hated* to guess.

"I just need a hint."

"Well . . . based on very preliminary examination"—cases had gone to court on less evidence than Raksen considered very preliminary—"my guess, just a guess, is a small needle filled with the depressant solution. Some trigger mechanism to set it off when the victim sat down."

A needle in the seat might appeal to someone who wanted to kill a pain in the ass. But it would be asking a lot to expect that pain to sit down on it and pay no attention when the needle penetrated his butt. "Do you bicycle?" I asked, though it was hard to picture Raksen enjoying such an imprecise, unscientific pastime. Terriers seldom cycle.

"No. But I did call a friend in the Berkeley Bicycle Club." I'd never known a case where Raksen didn't have a friend who was an expert or knew an expert. "Some riders start off standing, pedaling to pick up speed. But they sit as soon as they can."

"But surely Drem would have felt it when the needle went in."

"Maybe. But, Smith, street paving isn't Berkeley's forte." A couple of weeks ago Raksen had lost a case of samples to a pothole. Clearly he still hadn't finished the grieving process. "On a bicycle, a man gets a lot of sensory input, particularly in the butt. And my guess—don't repeat this till I have something solid—is the needle was embedded in a soft plaster-of-paris mixture, made to fall away after the initial pressure. But don't quote me."

"Your secret is safe with me."

As soon as I hung up, I put in a call to the ME. He'd finished the postmortem. Nothing was definite, of course. Toxicology tests take two to four weeks. But he did find a puncture wound in Drem's buttock and residue of a substance that fit Raksen's central-nervous-system depressant.

I leaned back in my chair in the uncomfortable luxury of my empty office. Someone had wedged the tiny hypodermic between the seats of Drem's bicycle, which meant either his killer had lucked upon the bicycle when he happened to have the poison hypodermic in hand or he knew where that bicycle would be. Drem sounded like a man of set routines. Now, if I could just find one person in all of Berkeley who didn't hate the man, one person who had tolerated him enough to know what those routines of his were . . .

Pereira's twenty minutes had come and gone when she trotted into my office and established herself in "her" spot on Howard's desk. She shoved open the bottom drawer, plopped her feet on the edge, and favored me with a smug grin. Then she looked around for coffee and donuts to mooch. Howard's absence made it harder on Pereira. I moved my cup of Peet's out of her reach and kept my hand on my donut. It had been the only chocolate old-fashioned in the box.

"So," I said, "what's your great surprise?"

"A coup, Smith." Pereira's grin grew wider. Her blond hair nearly twitched with smug. "When I tell you Drem's name has come up at parties, it probably won't surprise you. The man's famous. Even among auditors, Drem's a bulldog. He gets his TPs—that's taxpayers to us TPs—by the throat and doesn't let go until they pay. He never initiates an audit that ends up with a No Change." Connie eyed the remaining half of my donut.

Had it been a merely a glazed instead of a chocolate old-fashioned, I'd have relinquished it. I broke off a quarter and plopped it in my mouth. "What's No Change mean?"

"Exactly what you think. When you get audited, either you

pay, or the IRS admits you don't owe more—No Change. They hate that; it wastes their time."

"So he just kept digging till he found errors?"

Connie eyes opened a smidge wider, as if to say that things weren't that simple. They never were with Pereira and finances. The stock-market pages were her Disneyland, bankers and brokers her Mickeys and Minnies. I remembered now that about twelve hours ago, before Drem's death and our argument, I'd promised Howard I'd ask her about his charity deductions and Publication 526. That could wait. I leaned back in my chair and braced my feet against the back of Howard's. If he'd been here, he'd have had his chair angled toward the door and his long legs stretched to the wall beside my desk. I pushed the thought of him out of my mind.

"Smith," Pereira said, "there are different types of audits and auditors: office auditors, field agents, collection agents—"

"Wait! What's an office auditor?"

Connie eyed the chocolate old-fashioned. I could divert her with my coffee, but I nixed that idea. Another, albeit lesser, donut I could get from the box, but machine coffee and Peet's were not the same species of liquid. I handed her the donut.

She took a bite. "There are three categories of initial audits in the IRS. The easiest is when a form comes in the mail for you to send in some information. The assumption there is that you will admit your guilt and pay up. The second is the office audit. For that, you and your accountant show up, records in hand. Then you pay up. And the third is the field audit. They save this for businesses with records too cumbersome to carry into the office, or TPs with operations they want to eyeball. Then there are agents in collections. By rights, Drem should have been one of them, packing a rod and facing down the Mob. But maybe that was too dangerous for Drem. Anyway, he was a field agent."

"So he was likely to have been out seeing someone, someone

who may have profited by his not being around to continue the audit, the afternoon he died."

Pereira nodded.

"We'll need a list of his victims, or whatever IRS calls them."

"Fat chance, Jill. You won't get that without a warrant and a big fight, and even then . . ." She grinned.

So this was the coup. "So?"

"Well, Smith, seems Drem was the apple of his group manager's eye. Always up on the Procs and TDs—"

"*What?*"

"Revenue Procedures and Treasury Decisions. Didn't shoot the breeze or bitch about the irates."

" 'Irates'?"

"The TPs who call with questions or complaints."

I took a long swallow of coffee. It was lukewarm now, but still good.

"And then I heard that the group manager was sick last year, and Drem, not the senior agent by any means, took her place at the Fresno meetings, which is as close as you get to conventions in the world of IRS. It's where they look over the TCMP figures and set the local DIFs."

I didn't even bother to ask. I'd decode those later.

Pereira plopped the last vestige of my donut into her mouth and smiled as she chewed. "So, Smith, it was an easy guess that our Phil would have a few enemies in the IRS office."

I took a final drink of my coffee and handed Pereira the remains. "And you found one?"

She finished it in a swallow. "Better than that. Found and just interviewed. And guess what he told me?"

"At this hour Saturday morning, either everything or nothing."

Connie shrugged. "My source, whose identity I swore on my mother's grave I'd never reveal—"

"I'm sure your mother will appreciate that when you tell her."

"As much a pain as she's been, she should be pleased to be some use. But anyway, my source was in the office Friday and just happened to look at Drem's log and—"

"Saw who his last appointment was?" I asked, excited.

Pereira handed back my empty cup and stood. "Right. It was Lyn Takai."

So Lyn Takai had been Philip Drem's last business appointment before he was murdered. She hadn't mentioned he'd been in her studio just hours before he was killed. In fact, what she'd said was "I hadn't even thought about him in ages." All in all, that was a big lie for an innocent citizen to present to the police. She wouldn't be as cool as she'd been last night—not explaining this.

I left the patrol car in front of the violet house with the white picket fence and took the walkway between it and its neighbor double speed. I wouldn't have been surprised to find Takai, the yogi, doing a headstand on the cement patio between her cottage and the violet house. Or braising tofu on her stove out there. Or washing off bad karma in the blue-tuliped sink, or more ascetically in the cracked sink, had either been upright and usable.

But she was doing none of those. The stove and refrigerator stood untended, the tuliped sink lay on its side, and the cracked sink was gone. A healthy set of police raps on the door convinced me Lyn Takai was gone too.

Disgusted, I drove back to the station, called in a favor from Tim, the DD clerk, and got him to move the background on Takai to the top of the pile. I didn't expect much. What could a woman who displays her appliances in her front yard be hiding? Takai seemed like someone who'd consciously opted for a life with little excess. Yoga, I gathered, was called the eight-fold path; it was a safe guess that that path rarely led to riches.

While I waited, I checked the reports Pereira had collected. She'd sent Acosta to Drem's apartment on Milvia Street. No one was home, and a canvass of the ground-floor tenants in the fourplex indicated that Drem lived alone and pursued the type of life that would make him eligible to represent accountants in any 1950s movie—no entertaining, no loud music, and most of all no women (in fact, no friends at all). Drem's flat was on the second floor next to a female hermit whom neither of the ground floor tenants had ever seen. According to them, Drem's only interests were bicycling and badgering them about car emissions. One suggested Drem could improve his image by imitating his next-door neighbor.

Acosta's report indicated he hadn't found Sierra, the street person Mason Moon had fingered as having seen the "cop" by Drem's bike. It wasn't out of the ordinary for a street person to transfer himself to another street. I was sure Acosta would find him and discover Sierra hadn't seen the patrol officer at all. But I'd feel a lot more comfortable when the question was closed.

I filed Pereira's report and tried Lyn Takai's phone number. No answer. I called Tim. He growled something about patience. Something else about half an hour. There are few tyrants like a clerk.

I walked out to the squad room looking for Pereira. She'd signed out an hour and a half ago. She'd been on Evening Watch last night—3:00 P.M. to 11:00 P.M. With Drem's death, she couldn't have gotten home before 2:00 A.M. And up for Morning Meeting. It didn't take a wizard to figure what her plans would be today—sleep, with the phone turned off.

The tax accountant she'd quoted on Drem was a Rick Lamott. I dialed his number. On the Saturday before April 15 I expected a secretary to answer, but the voice said, "Rick Lamott. What can I do forya?"

"Detective Smith, Berkeley Police. I need some background on the IRS."

"You know Connie Pereira?"

"She's the one who suggested you."

"Well, for Connie. Whataya need?"

"Tell me about TCMP, DIF, and Philip Drem."

"Pothole and paving roller. You got an hour?"

"It'll take that long?"

"You look like Connie?"

"Not a bit," I snapped.

"Okay, so I'm superficial. Slide down the surface, and you get to the bottom faster."

"You must have a pretty raw butt."

He laughed. "Yeah, and a flock of feds who'd like to make it a lot redder. Hey, it's lunchtime. I'll buy you lunch. I'll be by in ten minutes."

"Make it noon. Front desk. Ask for Detective Smith." I hung up. The guy sounded like the one who made you say never again to blind dates. But he wasn't a date; he was a source. It's wonderful not to be a teenager anymore, to be a cop with a gun. Still, I ran him through files before he came. No priors, no warrants.

I sent Heling to reinterview Drem's neighbors on the ground floor of his fourplex. They might have a clue about Drem's relatives, hobbies, or habits. If Drem ended his workday at Lyn Takai's, that still left a lot of time before he died. Maybe he'd stopped home. Maybe he'd stayed at Takai's. That would be a good explanation of why she'd lied and why she wasn't to be found at home now.

I tried Takai again. Still no answer. I was just about to dial Tim when he pushed open my door and poked a sheaf of papers at me. "Voilà!"

"Thanks, Tim. We're square."

He grinned. "Which means you are once again ripe for the picking."

I read through the report. I'd been right and wrong. Right that Lyn Takai didn't own much. Wrong in thinking of it as nothing. She rented her studio. No reportable assets, except for one. Lyn Takai owned a property on Carleton Street called the Inspiration Hotel, in partnership with Mason Moon, a Selena Hogan, and an Ethan Simonov. The quartet had an eighty percent mortgage and a ten percent second. Nothing murder-inducing about that.

It took me a moment to recall the Inspiration, a shabby, transient-type place that was in the process of being renovated.

And as for Mason Moon being one of the co-owners, I wasn't so surprised about that. Berkeley is the town to which the sixties retired. Aging hippie on the outside and successful entrepreneur underneath was hardly an unknown combination. There just wasn't a catchy name for it yet. What amazed me was that Moon would be involved in a renovation project that required sustained work.

But Tim hadn't stopped with the background on Takai. He'd also run detailed background checks on the trio and turned up a better than average number of entries. Selena Hogan had two warrants outstanding in Nevada (speeding—not uncommon for those racing up to Reno to get rid of their excess money. And having left their cash there, few rushed to pay the traffic tickets they associated with their rotten weekends). Mason Moon was the star on the Records Management System that lists citywide contacts with the department: trespassing, disturbing the peace, failure to disperse—the plop artist's roll of honor. And Simonov had been indicted in Oregon for tax evasion. Tax evasion—now that was interesting. I moved Simonov up on my list of prospects.

A yogi, a plop artist, a racing gambler, and a felon. Just what kind of property did these people own together? I was just about to head out to find out when the phone rang. Rick Lamott was in the lobby.

Rick Lamott had probably been waiting fifteen minutes when I opened the double doors to Reception on the second floor. From the main door downstairs two wide staircases lead upward, hugging both pale-beige walls. A WPA Tara. The stairs end at a balcony-hallway that forms Reception: a row of plastic chairs facing the desk clerk's window. The only thing that makes Reception tolerable to our guests is the knowledge that their next stop may be worse.

Now the chairs were occupied by a white teenager in a down jacket that smelled of long-term sweat and dirt, an elderly black woman with a cloth shopping bag between her feet, and a leather-jacketed eighth-of-a-ton-er who looked like an over-the-hill Hell's Angel. The kid and the woman were seated as far away from him as possible.

But planted in front of him, only slightly taller than the seated Angel, was a sandy-haired guy in an expensive choco-late-brown suit wagging a finger at the bearded face. "*They* call it tax evasion. But you don't have to put up with that crap. We'd label it tax avoidance. Avoiding taxes is every citizen's right under the Constitution." He turned to look at me. "Smith?"

If I hadn't seen the scene, hadn't known the background, I would have assumed from his tone that he'd had his secretary summon me here to his meeting.

Before I could answer, he turned back to the ersatz Angel. "Get yourself a good accountant. You can't afford me, but you can do a lot better than what you've got now." Then he made for me, grinning anxiously. "Come on. My car's double-parked."

"You double-parked in front of the police station?" I asked, amazed. "Did you want to save us the tow?"

"I won't have a ticket. Trust me." He was already three stairs down.

Anyone else I would have cut short, but I wasn't about to miss the scene by his car, or more likely the empty spot where his car had been. At the front door I caught up with him, racing through like an engine with the idle turned up too high. He was a little guy, not quite my height, and his face had an aerodynamic look: light-brown hair blown back, narrow face, sharp cheekbones, long nose, slash of eyes yellow as a cat's—a sports car of a man.

He hit the street not running but with one of those Manhattan walks that could trample six unwary tourists and still break the four-minute mile. He made a sharp left. I didn't have to ask where he was headed. The crowd was already there—five or six uniformed officers huddled around a red sports car. Closer up, it was clear that this car, designed to look like it was going sixty sitting still, was the automotive equivalent of Lamott. When we were within ten feet of it, he slowed and strolled proudly forward, ready to accept kudos.

What he did accept was a parking ticket. Berkeley is a city of many inefficiencies. Delivery of parking tickets is not one.

I was still laughing when he grumbled his last answer to the uniformed enthusiasts. He held open the door of the red convertible, and I swung in.

"While the cat's away, Smith?" It was Redmon, from Vice and Sex Crimes, Howard's detail.

"Research," I said and shut the door, a not wholly effective move since the top was down. But then the cat had only the afternoon off. He wasn't likely to be farther away than the nursery buying another azalea.

"Lotus Elan SE," Lamott said, starting the engine. "Zero to sixty in six point seven seconds."

"Great. The guys on Traffic will appreciate the chance for as close a look as Parking Division had." Lamott revved the engine, obliterating the quiet of the noon hour.

Ignoring the patrol car pulling into the parking lot, Lamott hung a U and headed south toward Ashby. I'd done that maneuver often enough myself, but it was class-A illegal, and I hated to think that Traffic was letting Lamott off because he was with me.

"Tell me about TCMP," I said.

"Taxpayers Compliance Measurement Program, or how the IRS uses you to screw others." He hung a left onto Martin Luther King Jr. Way, raced through the yellow light at Bancroft, and jammed on the brakes at Haste. In front of a funeral home. It seemed apt.

"How so?"

"Well, Jill, they've got to know who to audit, right? How would ol' Phil Drem, the defunct, know if you claimed too much for, say, casualty and theft losses? How does Drem know whether to believe you when you tell him you've had leather coats stolen out of your car six times this year because your job takes you into bad neighborhoods?" He hit the gas and then had to brake before the next corner.

"The lights are staggered here, set for rational drivers."

Ignoring that jibe, he said, "So what the IRS does is pick at random a small number of unfortunates and audits them. Not the normal audit, nothing that easy. No, these poor suckers, who haven't done a thing except have the wrong social security number, have to hunt up proof for every item on every line of their returns, down to birth certificates and marriage licenses."

"Why?"

"So the agency can figure what the average legitimate deduction is for each item. So when you file, Jill, and you claim thirty-five hundred dollars for lost coats, the computer will see that's twenty-four hundred dollars in excess."

"And bump me to Audit?"

The light at Ashby and Martin Luther King was green. Two lanes of cars crossed toward us. A pickup signaled for a left turn. Facing it, Lamott cut left in front of a cement mixer with inches to spare and a blare of horn from the mixer.

"How large a carpet do you see this car as?" I asked. With another driver, I would have been out of the car back at Haste, but there was something fun about cocky little Rick Lamott. I had the feeling he was used to pushing the limits but not crashing through them. It was a kick riding in the new red sports car with the top down and the windows up and the breeze catching the top of my hair. Just like high school. All options open, no doors closed, and thousands of miles of highway calling.

He braked at Adeline. "You don't go straight to Audit for one offense. The system's cumulative. Computer gives you black marks for each excess. You get enough, it kicks you out."

"And then I get audited?"

"Nope. Then classifiers for Ogden, Utah, send the batch of you to district offices. The group chief there divides the files between agents." He hit the gas, but now the traffic was too heavy for anything more than normal tailgating. "Then the agents go over the records, and they choose the cases they think will generate revenue. They're in the business to make money." Lamott glared at the line of cars, then cut left in front of an AC Transit bus onto Hillegass—my street.

Pereira had said the district IRS powers met in Fresno to set local figures. "And the figures are adjusted to reflect different spending in different areas, right?"

"Right. If they had one national figure, they'd end up pulling files, spending hours on them, and then making a No Change. They hate that; wastes their time. They don't care about yours."

We passed Howard's house. As I'd expected, the azalea was once again centered in its hole. Howard was nowhere in sight, but the curtain nearest the newly planted azalea was pulled back.

To Lamott I said, "So what are these area figures?"

Lamott laughed. "Jill, they don't make them public. That's why there are guys like me, who can outwit them." He pulled sharply around the corner and screeched to a stop. A cement barricade blocked the street. Traffic diverters—Berkeley's big on them. City fathers see them as traffic erasers rather than driver annoyers.

I expected Lamott to be one of the seriously annoyed, but he was already backing back into Hillegass before it occurred to me he hadn't paid enough attention to be bothered. "See, Jill, it's a game for them. It's a game for me. Their weapon is the audit. Scares the pants off the average TP. But not me. Let them audit. I'll go to their audits, eat up their time. I'll take them to court. You know the system, you like the game, you can beat the bastards. And, Jill, I love it." He hit the gas and raced forward.

In your face barely did justice to this guy. The IRS must have hated him. "What about Philip Drem?"

"God, I'm sorry the bastard bought it!"

I almost gasped. "That's one of the most heartfelt—"

"Don't think I liked the asshole. He was a first-class prick. The tightest, most niggling, goddamn line-by-line . . ." He shook his head. "It just won't be the same dealing with the nearly normal ones they've got left. It's like asking Joe Montana to play against the second string."

Now I did gasp. I understood the sports car; I realized Lamott was taken with himself and his image. But to see himself as Joe Montana! That was as close to sacrilege as we come in this secular corner of creation.

Thinking of Lyn Takai, I said, "What odds would you give about Drem sleeping with one of his auditees?"

Lamott slammed on the brakes at the stop sign. He was

laughing. He turned to me. "Assuming one of his victims could still stand to be in the same room with him, much less naked? Not unless he could find a necrophiliac."

My beeper went off. "Damn. I'll have to get back."

"Let it go."

"Lamott, I'm the police. We don't beep to impress people. Make a left."

"Hey, they'll find someone else."

"Not as good as me."

He looked over, caught my eye, and grinned. The route to the station didn't take us back past Howard's house, which was just as well.

"I'll call you tomorrow," Lamott said as he squealed to a stop and I jumped out.

"If you're alive," I called, already racing inside. We're not profligate about calling officers in the field. I took the steps two at a time, panting by the time I reached the dispatcher.

"Memo on your desk," he said before I could ask.

I ran back down the stairs and yanked open the office door. The memo was from Heling: "Philip Drem married to Victoria Iversen, the 'hermit' next door to him."

7

When a man's wife becomes a hermit, it doesn't speak well of him.

It had been fourteen hours since Drem's accident. I hated to think what shape she might be in now. I got her phone number, called, and let the phone ring. If there's one thing you should be able to count on with a hermit, it's that she is home.

"Yes?" The voice was faint. She'd picked up the phone on the sixth ring. How long had she been sitting there, wondering why Drem hadn't come back, worrying, embroiled in that awful combination of grief and uncertainty?

"Victoria Iversen?"

"Yes?"

"I'm Detective Smith, Berkeley Police. Has one of our officers contacted you yet?"

"No." I could hear the dread in her voice. I felt that familiar mix: a dread at having to break the news, yet a quickening of excitement to see her reaction and fit it with what I knew of the deceased. It wasn't the type of thing I'd admit to my mother. But it was during those moments of shock that survivors had given me evidence they would never have divulged later. "I need to ask you some questions. I can be at your door in ten minutes."

"What is this about?"

I'd been hoping to avoid giving her the news over the phone. "I'm afraid your husband has been in an accident."

"On his bicycle?"

"Yes."

"Is he all right?"

"I'm afraid not. I'll be right out."

She gasped, a small shrill sound. Then she put down the receiver.

I grabbed my coat, flicked on the answering machine, and headed for a patrol car.

Victoria Iversen's and Philip Drem's addresses were on Milvia Street, site of one of the city's latest ecological idiosyncrasies. Milvia used to be a normal residential street that ran parallel between Shattuck and Martin Luther King Jr. Way, two of the crosstown thoroughfares. A handy shortcut in a city where automotive convenience is anathema.

In the seventies the city installed bike lanes and barricaded intersections (thus creating routes for bicyclists and rude shocks for drivers). "Too little," environmentalists claimed. And a decade and a half and half a million dollars later were born seven blocks of the Milvia Slow Street: a series of speed humps (humps are more gentle than bumps) interspersed with cement peninsulas, each holding a sapling and extending six feet out from the curb—two to a block on each side of the street, *not* across from each other. Skirting these odd peninsulas of curb, the white line waves back and forth. It's not a street for one given to motion sickness.

Bicyclists loved it. It was the perfect street for Philip Drem. Normally I liked it. Driving in first and second gear, bouncing slowly over the speed humps, swaying back and forth, was almost surrealistic. To put it more mundanely, it forced me to calm down. But now, hurrying to a woman whose reaction I couldn't gauge, lurching around the trees and hurtling over the bumps (*humps*) at twice the posted 15 mph was infuriating.

The apartment house, built when stucco box was modern, would have been ugly anywhere, but here it seemed less out of place. This block was something of a throwback to Berkeley before real-estate inflation made every dwelling an investment. In the 1970s foxtails, foot-long brown grass, and bare dirt were not so much a sign of slovenliness as an indicator that residents had other priorities. Now, perhaps, it was a statement of drought consciousness. Or maybe that interpretation put too Berkeley a spin on it. Maybe the owners were just lazy.

Drem's building stood behind four parking slots. The two on the right held not cars but lines of planters with nothing growing in them. More water conservation? Or maybe the tenants were just lazy.

I left the patrol car in the driveway behind the bare boxes and climbed the cement-slab stairs on the right. The second-floor landing ran around the front corner, creating a few square feet of balcony over the parking spaces. A picture window looked out on the whole unappealing scene, and the window was covered in plastic. Back east, plastic was the poor man's storm window, but in California, with neither hurricane winds nor gusts of snow, I couldn't imagine what Victoria Iversen was protecting herself against.

The door was on the side by the stairs. I was surprised it wasn't already opened or that it didn't fly open as soon as I rang the bell. But nothing happened. I was about to knock when I heard a tapping on the nearest window.

An intercom crackled: "Are you the policewoman?"

The interior light was off. The window was covered with plastic. And all I could make out of the speaker was that she was a slight woman with no color in her face, hair, or clothes. "I'm Detective Smith."

"You've come about Phil?" When she said his name, her voice caught, just as any concerned wife's might. It took me a moment to realize that her reaction was not extreme; it was just the first mention of Drem that had not been spit out in anger, disgust, or glee. "I don't want to talk here. Go around to Phil's place, up the stairs on the other side of the building. His key is in a fake stone in the corner of the planter nearest the house."

"Ms. Iversen, why don't you just let me in here."

"I can't. Trust me—this is the best way."

Strange. But that went with the hermit territory. I headed down, extricated the key from the planter, and hurried up the south steps.

Drem's flat shared an interior wall with his wife's. It looked to be the mirror image of hers. The curtains were drawn. I unlocked the door, walked into the darkened room, and nearly tripped over a bicycle tire. Irritably, I flipped on the light, reminding myself that it wasn't as if Drem had invited me. He hadn't planned to die and have an unexpected guest wander into his living room.

If *living room* was the right choice of words. Men I've known have had eccentric tastes in parlor furnishings. I wasn't at all surprised to find the bicycle tire in here, the rest of a racing bike hanging from hooks on the wall, an open kit for bike repair, or even a variety of bike helmets, special shoes, and a pile of those black stretch shorts I'd seen cyclists wearing. I was quite willing to accept that Drem got dressed to ride as he rushed out the door.

And once I'd thought about it, I wasn't so surprised to find posters lined up on the walls: *No Smoking, Ban Styrofoam, Clean Up Toxic Wastes, No Dumping in the Bay*. They suited the Drem who'd made it into Records Management by complaining about MSG in a Chinese restaurant.

The floor was bare. A wooden desk was covered with papers, a table with stacks of fliers. It could have been the office for any ballot-proposition campaign. The only thing out of place was a stuffed chair that faced the inside wall. I might have guessed that Drem practiced some meditation technique of a particularly comfortable kind in that stuffed chair (though from all I'd heard of him, it could not have been a very beneficial technique).

But Drem's chair wasn't facing a bare wall. It was inches from a purple-flowered drape that covered the wall. As I moved toward it, the curtain drew back. What it revealed was another picture window and a view of Victoria Iversen's flat.

I moved up behind the chair, getting nearly the same view Drem must have had. The room on the other side of the sheet glass was indeed the mirror image of Drem's, except that it was empty and almost entirely colorless. All that was in the room was a futon sofa covered in beige flax, a television, a phone, a shallow clear plastic box inside of which I could make out a newspaper, and a straight pine chair next to the adjoining window.

Victoria Iversen was dressed in a white shirt and pants that hung loose on her tall, unhealthily thin body. Her hair was so short it was almost a crew cut, her skin was blotchy, and her blue eyes, opened wide in fear, stood out from her bony face. She had to be in her thirties, but there was a waiflike quality about her. She drew up the wooden chair and sat so her knees were right next to the window. She stared at me for a full thirty seconds before she could bring herself to say, "Phil's dead, isn't he."

"Yes."

She let out a shriek, reached for her face as if to bury it in her hands, but stopped just before her fingers touched. Her hands squeezed into fists, and she sobbed. Her whole body shook, vibrating the loose cloth around her. She looked desolate in the midst of her hanging clothes. Even her own hands couldn't get near enough to help. Her sharp, agonized shrieks seemed to sear her lips. They reverberated over the speakerphone that connected us.

That may not have been the most helpless I'd ever felt, but I

didn't want to think what the other times had been. I wanted to
. . . but there was nothing I could do. Except note the reality
of her distress and wonder what she had seen in Drem to merit
it. I sat in Drem's chair and waited, hoping that at least the
presence of another human being was some cushion against the
desolation that screamed from her and doubting it.

When she was quieter, I said, "Why don't you let me come
over there?"

She looked up at me, face already puffy and painfully red,
and began to laugh hysterically. "If I could let you in, I
wouldn't be crying. Phil wouldn't be dead."

"Why is that?" I said softly.

"Because I'm allergic."

"To?"

"The whole fucking planet."

CHAPTER

There's no rule about survivors. Some fall apart right away; some hold together in a fog of seeming normality for six, twelve, eighteen hours and then go to pieces. Some need to be protected from the piercing facts. For others, even the most gut-wrenching details are at least a bit more of their husband's or daughter's life.

With Victoria Iversen, I chose to start with what she'd given me, her consuming allergies. Now her unbleached cotton clothes, the bare floor, the plastic-shielded windows, the hermitlike existence, made sense. Another odd facet of Philip Drem's odd life. Glancing back at his racing bike hanging on the wall, I wondered how she reacted to the sight of it, such a symbol of open air and muscle tone—and freedom.

I laid my notepad on my thigh. "Tell me about your allergies."

"I haven't always had them, if that's what you're thinking. There was an explosion in the studio I was sharing with three metal sculptors. I was farthest from the door. By the time they got me out, the gases had burned out my immune system." She gave a little lift to her shoulders, the suggestion of a shrug. "It's not a very scientific description, but it gives you the picture. That was three and a half years ago." She waited for me to finish writing in my notepad. "You're probably eyeing my skin and saying 'What could a man like Phil have seen in her?' But I didn't look like discarded cotton candy before."

I pressed my teeth together to keep from reacting. Her description was perfect. She did look dry, brittle—as if an unplanned touch could crumple her.

Behind her I could hear an appliance going. An air filter, perhaps. Whatever, it was too common a sound for her to notice.

She said, "Phil and I spent our honeymoon hiking the Appalachian Trail. We were going to travel. None of this middle-class, pension-oriented life for us. I did stained glass. One of my windows is in the library in Montclair, New Jersey. I had shows in New York, and in Cincinnati when we lived there. If I'd stayed in New York, I could have done more adventurous pieces, bigger ones in more important places." She made a move with her mouth as if to laugh, but the pull on her rash-roughened cheeks looked too painful. "Sometimes you have to choose. Phil wanted to travel, and I wanted him and the world more than a hefty reputation at thirty. There was always time. Or so I thought.

"So we went to Cincinnati and New Orleans and Santa Fe, spent a winter in Mexico, and then we came here. We were going to do a big work binge to save up and then head for Asia. Six months here and four there, you can't do more than little windows and repair stained-glass lampshades, whatever the trade brings, but it was okay. After all, Phil was doing accounting, and he hated that."

"He hated accounting?" I asked, amazed. The impression I'd gotten was that he savored every minus sign he made.

"It was just a way to get by. It came easy to him—he graduated in three years. He could always get a job. And he never had to think about it after work."

"A colleague at the IRS described him as committed."

"Phil?" Again she almost smiled. "Hardly. He hated the government."

"Then why—"

"Why did he stay for four years? Because I couldn't do without the medical insurance. That's one of the ugly kickers about being sick. If you're not as lucky as I am, having a husband with a group medical plan, you can spend hundreds of dollars a month to get minimal coverage at some HMO, *if* they'll take you at all. If they won't, you devote most of your time to sitting in the waiting room at the county health department picking up every virus around. And I couldn't do that. I'm allergic to the glue in the carpets, the chemicals in the air-filtration system, to perfumes, hair sprays, the smell of stale smoke that covers a smoker even when he's not smoking. My immune system is shot. Out there I'd be dead. But still I can't take the chance of no insurance."

"Don't you ever leave here?" I had to struggle to keep my voice from cracking. My skin felt clammier than it did at Howard's house.

"The last time I went out was two years ago. My last doctor's appointment. Into the office and out, just long enough for him to tell me he couldn't say what had caused my allergies and couldn't suggest anything but more steroids, and those only made things worse. They depress the immune system, for chrissake."

"Why didn't you try another doctor?"

"Because I'd already been to half the doctors in the Bay Area. First I went through the ones on Phil's medical plan, got second, third, fourth opinions. They didn't know what to do; they blamed me, said I was hysterical." She brought her hand near her cheek, near but not touching. "Does this look hysterical? Okay, so I probably sound like I'm crazy. . . ."

She was wound frighteningly tight now. Tight and controlled as opposed to the panic that I had to force down. I needed to run out into the fresh air, to Rick Lamott's convertible and speed with the top down, the wind blowing free . . . I swallowed hard and forced myself to lean back in Drem's padded chair. A depression was worn deep in the seat. Drem must have sat here a lot.

Victoria Iversen sat remarkably still—no handwringing, no clutching or twitching. I wondered if she had trained herself not to scratch or rub, the mental equivalent of the mittens my mother had put on my four-year-old hands at night when I had chicken pox. Was Victoria Iversen's whole life a mitten now?

More calmly, she said, "After that, it was the counterculture doctors. Herbs, needles, potions, mind control. I did it all, till I began to think that the original doctors were right—I was crazy. And physically I was only getting worse. It's gotten to the point that I react to everything but porcelain. Everything that comes into the flat is a potential danger. I don't go anywhere. I don't have a job. But there are days I'm exhausted by the time Phil gets home from work because I breathed in the smell of the newsprint while I was putting the paper in the plastic box. Then I've had to spend the day watching every breath I take, keeping aware of how the early-warning spots on my skin feel, trying to decide if I'm going to be sick, and if I am, should I take a cold bath or do relaxation exercises or just give the hell up. I get so tired of it all, I could scream." She wasn't clutching the arms of her chair. Instead, her hands were poised above them, fingers bent and stiff. Her control was so tight that when she did let go, the explosion could be total.

I hesitated but finally asked, "How did Phil handle your situation?"

"Not as well as I."

"Why not?" I snapped. After all, he was the healthy one. He got to go out every morning, even if it was to the IRS office.

She didn't react to my tone. Her control held. "There was a point when I realized that the only thing that would help me would be to live on an island in the middle of the ocean. Or maybe in the wilds of Alaska where there's no technology and it's too cold for pollens. Then I figured that if I was going to isolate myself, I might as well do it in Berkeley where I can talk to friends on the phone and listen to KPFA and watch people like you go flying over the road bumps." She almost laughed again. "Once you realize things are hopeless, you spend a lot less energy fighting them."

"And Phil?"

"Phil couldn't believe this was it, that we'd never be closer than sitting on either side of this window."

"How long—"

"Since even if he showered twice and left his clothes in the bathroom, there was still too much of the outside on him? Two years."

I wanted to ask why he didn't leave. What I did say was "How did he handle it?"

"Most marriages break up. The healthy partner realizes he doesn't have to live this way. He stays for a while, maybe from love, or loyalty, or because of the insurance. But eventually he can't take the confinement. He gets out. I would if I could."

I expected her eyes to well with tears, to reflect the panic I felt, but again she showed no reaction but that tightly controlled tension. She leaned back against the slatted back of her chair. That position looked no more comfortable than the other. It was not a chair built for comfort.

"So what did Phil do for sex—you're wondering that, aren't you? They all do. Most don't ask. But you're with the police, so you will ask." The corners of her dry lips twitched as if beginning to smile, but she controlled herself before her skin pulled. "I encouraged Phil to do whatever he chose, sleep with whomever. He said he didn't want anyone else." Her expression remained unchanged, but she didn't have the same control of her voice, and there was a different tone to it—softer, as if hugging the memory to her, and yet defiant.

"Did you believe that?"

Again she almost smiled. "I chose to. What good would it do me otherwise?"

I wished I could have seen Victoria Iversen before she'd gotten sick. She would have been a lot easier to judge. Now there were too many variables guiding her reactions—sickness, hopelessness, grief, and doubtless ones I didn't know about. If she wanted to hide something, she'd be a master at it. "Did Phil come right home every night?"

"No," she said. "That I did insist on, that he have at least the freedom he did before. Then he went up to the Med for coffee on Fridays and to Black Oak Books for readings. And he had his bicycle races. If you look in his desk—I'm sure you'll do that—you'll find his time records. That's what he did, timings, where you ride against your last time. He's done twenty-five miles in fifty-four point twelve minutes. The world record for seniors—that's eighteen to thirty-four—is just under fifty. He's real good. He should be. He's out there every morning before he leaves for work, doing calisthenics, stretches, aerobic rides. He had to fight the Service so they'd let him ride to his calls, but he won."

"Is the riding at work part of his training?" I said, slipping into the present tense she was using.

"Not really. You can't train on a bike with a basket. Phil says he'd be humiliated if any of the racers saw him on his city bike with its bourgeois baskets."

Drem with a sense of humor?

"The reason he rides," she went on, "is so he doesn't create more pollution."

That sounded more like our Drem. I glanced back at the various *no*'s on the wall. "Is that the reason for his posters here too?"

"Right. Phil was never political before, but my accident changed that. He's totally committed to cleaning up what he can." Now she looked at me, and her face seemed to fall. "Or he was."

For an instant I thought she was going to cry. I had to look away, swallowing again. If she broke down in her glass prison where I couldn't even reach out a hand . . . I swallowed harder, jammed my teeth together, and looked back, hoping my anguish didn't show.

But Victoria Iversen wasn't looking at me. Her eyes were closed. Picturing Drem? "Phil was like I am when I have to worry about the smell of the newsprint—watching, always ready to take action. It's just that he did it out in the world. He was responsible for three restaurants going totally nonsmoking. He got petitions signed by so many customers, the owners couldn't say no."

I leaned back, focusing totally on Philip Drem, trying to fit this view of Philip Drem into what I'd already heard. Was the Drem the world knew a fraud? Could the bulldog of the IRS, who shook his victims till their every secret seeped out, truly have hated the IRS? But I'd known people like that, guys who hated law enforcement. Rather than quit, they'd taken out their anger and frustration on the perps, or the victims. They'd been the cops everyone hated and feared. I could believe Drem was like them. But there was another possibility. Alone here day after day, his wife could have created a fantasy of the fairy-tale prince: eternally loving (indeed with no other friends), totally accepting no matter how disfigured she became, serving her automatically, and sexually neutral. Prepubescent prince, or the nicest of dogs.

In a while I would ask Victoria Iversen how she would manage. I'd make a couple of calls. Now I had to give her the answer to the question she hadn't asked, that I could barely make myself answer. "Ms. Iversen—"

"Tori—that's what people call me."

"Tori." I took a breath. "Phil didn't just fall off his bicycle and die. He was killed."

"I know he was killed."

"No, murdered. Someone planned it and killed him. Can you think of anyone who would want him dead?"

She shook her head.

"Think about it. Tell me any theories, no matter how tenuous."

Slowly she said, "I can't imagine time without Phil. It's like knowing dawn will never come again. He gave up his life for me. Not one in a thousand men would do that. How could anyone want to kill him?" Her voice was low, her tone flat. Desolate.

I found myself biting hard on my lip to keep it from quivering and loosing tears of sorrow and panic. Whether her picture of Drem was fact or fiction, her pain was all too real. I bit down harder. Sweat ran down my back.

When I was sure I could keep my voice steady, I said, "Tori, people kill for all kinds of evil, misguided, confused, misinformed reasons. They kill good people as well as bad."

She didn't say anything. I had the feeling that on her side of the glass she was holding tears in tighter than I.

"Has Phil ever mentioned the name Mason Moon, or Lyn Takai?" I wasn't expecting a response to Moon, but I didn't want to offer only Takai.

Her eyes widened momentarily. "No. He didn't talk about his work."

"You do recognize one of those names, don't you?"

"No," she insisted. "Well, not in the sense of knowing them personally. But I listen to the radio all day. I feel I know half the people in Berkeley. I've heard Mason Moon interviewed on *Probabilities*. He's a plop artist, one of those guys who hires a crane to dump his fourteen-foot metal monster on the marina grass and dares the mayor to be bourgeois enough to haul it off." She nodded, as if assuring herself her story was going okay. But her shaky voice gave her away.

"Moon is a metal sculptor? Is he the sculptor you shared a studio with?" Concentrating on Moon, I could feel myself slipping back into the protective camouflage of the police detective. More calmly I said, "Tori, someone murdered Phil. You've got to help me find him."

"I will, but it wasn't Mason," she insisted. "Mason was there when the gases exploded, but he wasn't responsible. It burned out his nose. He can't smell anymore at all. He was a victim too. Phil understood that."

Maybe Tori's Phil understood, but did Agent Drem, IRS? And if Agent Drem pondered the books of a partnership in which Mason Moon was involved, might he not have wondered if the same lack of care went into those as the gases at the art studio? I asked Tori about Moon, but she insisted she hadn't seen or talked to him since she got home from the hospital after the accident. Putting a question mark beside Moon's name in my notebook, I said, "And Lyn Takai? What do you know about her?"

"Nothing. That's the truth."

Her expression gave no clue whether it was fact or not. I moved back to the lead she'd given me. "Tori, tell me about Phil's plans for Friday."

"His schedule?" she said, clearly relieved. "Fridays, after work, he went to the movie at Pacific Film Archives. He had dinner somewhere before. Phil really liked foreign films. We watch a lot of movies here on Phil's VCR, but it's too far away for me to read the subtitles. Besides, I'm not so interested in foreign countries anymore. When you know you'll never be able to go to those places, they lose something. So Phil goes to the museum alone."

"And you didn't mind?"

"I told him to go out two or three nights a week. He wasn't sick; he didn't need to be confined here. But he insisted one was all he wanted. He knew how much I looked forward to his getting home."

I took a breath. She was already so close to the edge. . . . But I had to ask. "When did you expect him back Friday night?"

"By ten thirty. The movie's usually over by nine."

But Drem had fallen off his bicycle after ten. The spot where he died was only about four blocks from the museum. And closer than that to the property on Carleton owned by Mason Moon and company. What had Drem been doing for over an hour? "Could he have had plans afterward? Or decided to stay for the second movie?"

"Once or twice he went to the Med for coffee and didn't get home till eleven. But he would have called if he knew he'd be late." She stared at me a moment. "Someone got to him there, didn't they?"

"I don't know. Can you think of anyone?"

"No, no one," she said just a bit too slowly.

Tori watched through the series of windows as I checked Drem's flat. The desk drawers in the living room and the kitchen and bathroom cabinets revealed nothing more about the man. I pushed open the bedroom door and stood staring at Drem's bed—a single bed pushed up against the connecting window next to Tori's on the other side. I turned my back to the window so Tori wouldn't see me force back tears as I thought of him rolling over in half sleep, seeing her face next to his, reaching out . . . and touching only the cold glass.

I thought of Howard, wanted to clutch him to me, feel his body against mine, and hang on to the moment. This sting of mine, would it close the gulf between us or would it build a wall of glass?

But I couldn't let myself get caught in personal issues now. I pulled open the top dresser drawer and checked the contents like a rookie with her instructor watching. It took me half an hour to finish the dresser and the closet. And as I left I forced myself to look once more at that solitary bed.

I walked outside and stood breathing in as much fresh free air as my lungs would hold. I could smell the crab apples, the flowering plum blossoms, and the unmowed grass in the yard below, and the dust, the exhaust fumes, and the tar fumes from a roofing job down the street. I breathed it all in greedily, making it all a part of myself, melding myself to it all.

Then I hurried back to the station and called Rick Lamott. Tori Iversen might believe Drem wouldn't harass her old studiomate. Maybe she was right. Or maybe every time Philip Drem rolled over in bed and reached for the wife he could no longer touch, every time his hand hit the cold glass that walled her in, he thought of Mason Moon.

CHAPTER

9

"Lamott," the accountant barked into the phone.

"It's Smith, from the Berkeley Police. I—"

"Jill! Great to hear from you. Listen, how about dinner? There's this great little place in Stinson Beach."

I laughed. "You're the angel of death, aren't you." The road to Stinson Beach was narrow, windy, and cantilevered high over the Pacific. For Rick Lamott it would be a launching pad. "The way you drive, we'd be halfway to Japan before we hit water. Besides—"

"Augusta's, then? You're going to need an insider's eye on the IRS, and there's no one who keeps tabs on them better than me. You could ask half the doctors in Berkeley—if they were home. They're not. They're off in Maui living it up on the money I saved them on their tax shelters. The IRS hates tax shelters almost as much as they hate unreported income."

"Since you offered your expertise," I said, ignoring the dinner part, "would it have been possible for Drem to extend his audit to a TP's partnership books to harass one of the other partners?"

Lamott hooted. "Possible? With those bastards, anything's kosher. Rule number one: You can't sue the government without its okay. Rule number two: You can't sue a government employee for doing his job. Rule number three: IRS can audit anyone it damn well pleases. They see a write-up about some guy in the newspaper, they can pull his file. They get letters from ex-wives, ex-employees, ex-friends, they send out an audit notice. They've even got a special form, Form two-eleven, to make a contract with informers—"

"The trio of *ex*'s?"

"Maybe, but see, Jill, anyone can send a squeal letter—their term, not mine—and IRS is allowed to pay the squealer ten percent of any extra they collect. But the squealer better get it in writing first. Otherwise, no ten percent. They pay no more than they feel like. No honor among thieves."

"Rick"—I leaned back in my chair, staring absently at the strands of dark brown hair I was winding around my fingers— "could Drem decide to audit you just because he didn't like you?"

"He could jab a pen at the phone book. They call cases that aren't assigned through normal channels individual pickups. But would he have audited me? I doubt it."

"Why not?" If Drem was a bulldog, Lamott was a crow. I could picture him swooping down teasingly, inches from the floppy jowls, or landing lightly on the furry rump and digging in a claw just before he took off. Drem must have loathed him.

"See, the bottom line is money. And Drem would have known that he'd be making about thirteen cents an hour dealing with me. IRS is only going to pay him for that once in a while."

"And there's nothing to make you think Philip Drem wouldn't use that once-in-a-while for vengeance?"

Lamott just laughed. But I was willing to bet Mason Moon wouldn't be amused.

I swung by Peet's for a *doppio cappuccino* to fight off a wave of exhaustion. A night in the car isn't free. Working when you can barely stay awake is something you learn early in the department. Cops who go home for a nap don't make it. I took a last swallow and crumpled the cup. I could still think, but emotions floated in and out, each more muted than the last. I was thankful to have Tori Iversen buried beneath the smoke of exhaustion.

Ten minutes later, I found Mason Moon in his "studio," a garage with a workbench. There was no esoteric equipment to suggest metal sculpture. Moon was carving a slab of wood the size of a coffin, creating what looked like a dead body. Without his brown wool cape and floppy-brimmed green felt hat with the party noisemaker in the band, he looked almost normal. Or as near normal as a plump man with flowing brown hair and orange goatee (new gray mixed with old red) could. Moon hadn't normalized enough to forgo his Moon-over-Berkeley T-shirt, though.

I said, "So you shared the artists' studio with Philip Drem's wife. Drem took his wife's injury very seriously."

"We all did!" Moon put down his tool. "Some jackass leaves his gas spigot going and nearly blows us all to Mars. I can't smell at all now. And I lost a year's work. Some of the best metal work I did. Gone. Forever. I'll tell you, after that, I was so freaked that I'll never go near metal or gas again. It's wood for me now. Whatever you can say in metal, you can say in wood." He stood up and stepped back, as if to take in his entire work.

I allowed my attention to be drawn down to it. "Is this plop art?"

Moon flung out a hand. He needed his cape and chapeau to achieve the full effect. "Yes and no," he said. "Plop art is not just the piece. It's the concept, the statement. It's communication. Sometimes it's political, sometimes whimsy. I play off the energy that's going on," he said in classic Berkeleyese. "It's not just my thing, but it forces people to participate."

"For instance, this . . ." I looked down at the dried-out piece of wood.

"Well, on one level it's a bench. But of course it's also a corpse. And then anyone can make the leap to realizing it's a bench for people society treats no better than a corpse."

"And you plop it down . . . ?"

"In the spot that symbolizes that degradation." He looked me full in the face. "Of course, I can't tell *you* where that will be. Police are not always supportive of the arts."

I said nothing, allowing him to keep his secret. Later I could speculate on which section of People's Park he'd choose.

"See," he said, warming to his subject, "I practice what Lyn Takai and the yogis call *ahimsa*, nonviolence, in my art. Part of my statement is that I don't harm the space I use. When I make delivery, I don't endanger other people, or me."

"You mean you don't deliver at night?"

Moon laughed. "Right, but not just because of *ahimsa*. You haul a huge sculpture into the middle of the campus at two A.M., and you freak the campus cops. Do the same thing at two in the afternoon, and everyone thinks you work for the art department. Cops clear the way, students offer to help." He turned around, reached for his fedora, and plopped it on his head. "Besides, it's more fun to do in daylight. And there's a chance of making the evening news."

I couldn't help smiling. There was something disarming about his straightforwardness. But I doubted it would have endeared him to Philip Drem. "Moon, were you responsible for the gas explosion?"

"No!" No theatrics. This looked like real shock.

"You were close enough to damage your sinuses."

"I had nothing to do with the gas."

"Did Drem believe that?"

He picked up his wood-carving tool and held it in both hands. "Who knows what that crazy bastard thought? I liked Tori. But after the accident I kept away."

"And then Drem audited your partner Lyn Takai. If Drem

had moved on from Lyn's audit to the partnership, there would have been no way for you to escape him."

"It's been three years. He probably calmed down," Moon said with a remarkable lack of conviction. "Besides, there's nothing in the partnership's hotel books, even if he did decide to summons them. Take a look at the building. Do you think there's an extra cent in it for even the IRS to squeeze out? Someday when we turn it into a bed and breakfast, maybe. But not now."

I walked out past the Inspiration Hotel next to Moon's studio and sat in my car staring at it: a clapboard affair from the 1940s that might have been apartments or flats but was now passing as a hotel. But there were really two hotels. The dilapidated building I saw and the bed and breakfast that existed in the minds of its owners. Which was the real Inspiration? And which Philip Drem was the true Drem—the bulldog or the faithful, loving pet?

But unlike the hotel, Drem wasn't an either-or question. Drem was a habitué of the Film Archives. Over the months there a faithful pet would have made friends at the Swallow Café next door. A bulldog wouldn't have set jowl over the doorway. I had just time to make it to the Swallow.

CHAPTER

10

The Swallow is like a diner that's moved up in the world. Specials run to ratatouille and pizza rustica, fruit spritzers and *caffè latte*s, blondies (caramel brownies) and slices of chocolate decadence. Instead of booths, there are small tables, and out the window is the graded grassy yard of the University Art Museum. Had it still been light, I could have sat on a bench and contemplated the three-foot metal ball with the hole in the middle. I'd named it Cannonball Karma.

I asked the guy at the counter if he had worked Friday. He hadn't. Nor did he know who had. So I switched to the reserve plan and sat in the café, drinking my *latte* and eating a salad—I consume a vegetable every now and then to remind myself why I don't more often—and eyed the other patrons, trying to get a line on who might be theater regulars, people who could have known Philip Drem, film aficionado, aka family pet.

I checked bejeaned legs for bicyclists' leg clips or ridges left from them. When I spotted "ruffled" cuffs on the beige cords of a guy reading the *East Bay Express*, I smiled, picked up my *latte*, and walked over. "Do you know Phil Drem?"

"I don't think so."

"Cyclist. Medium height. Wiry brown hair. He's here most Fridays."

"No, I wouldn't. My *shiatsu* group meets on Fridays."

No fast fix here. I chose a spot along the window rail and sat nursing the *latte*, letting my mind drift in that dusky halflight of wired sleepiness. In that grayness you make connections that the glare of alertness would burn through. I found myself watching for potential witnesses and thinking about my grandmother's house, that small, crowded gray frame house in a neighborhood of small, shabbier houses. It looked nothing like Howard's house. I couldn't really summon up a picture of it, no more than its aura. But I felt all the muscles of my back clenching.

I sipped the *latte* and glanced at the pantlegs of three newcomers, but there were no clamp marks. The reason I couldn't "see" the house was that it was always behind me in all those early memories. Ahead of me our white Chevy sedan was pulling out of the driveway. My brother Mike was in the backseat waving, my parents in front, driving off to the new house in the new town my father had talked about for months, where everything would be new and exciting and fun, where life would be Technicolor. I clung to the car with my eyes till the white blur was long gone.

A guy with a bike helmet walked in. I called to him. He'd been here Friday, but he didn't remember Drem.

By seven, I'd finished a piece of chocolate cake and a second *latte*. The dinner flock was thinning. Now people were rushing in for espressos before the film started. But they were in groups —chattering, excited, or intense—closed units that would have neither drawn nor admitted Drem. It was just as well. Two *latte*s have their effect. I had just time to make to it the ladies' room before the opening credits.

When I opened the ladies'-room door, I spotted her. Maria Zalles her name turned out to be, but it could have been Tori Iversen. There are people in Berkeley who believe that every person lives many lives simultaneously, that each time you choose between two paths, life strolls on from both of them, a family tree of the potential self.

Maria Zalles looked like the Tori Iversen who had decided not to go to the studio the day the gas jet blew. She was healthy, even a bit plump, with shiny blond hair brushing her shoulders, blue eyes shaded with enough eye shadow and mascara to make Tori sick for a month, and clothes bright enough to be a kindergartner's dream. I stared, stunned. The reality of what Tori had lost struck me anew. No way could Philip Drem have resisted Maria Zalles.

She was washing her hands when I asked if she knew him.

"Philm? Sure." Even her voice was like Tori's, or what Tori's might have been if she'd had this woman's energy and enthusiasm. My skin was quivering from caffeine, and sorrow, and the futility of it all. "I call him Philm," she explained, "because he's here so much."

Cute. Tori wouldn't have dealt in cute. "Did you see him last night?"

"Oh yeah. Actually, I almost didn't. It was a Greek movie, and I'm not crazy about them, but my roommate was having her boyfriend over to watch basketball, and I can't handle that, you know. I mean you see the last two minutes, you've seen it all, right? And subtle—no way. So I came on here."

One of the stall doors swung open, and a woman hurried out. It reminded me why I'd come in here and how serious my need was after those *latte*s. Professional that I am, I focused on Maria Zalles. "But Phil likes Greek movies?"

"Phil will watch anything set outside the continental United States. I've told him he might as well stay home with *National Geographic* for all the discrimination he has about art." She pulled a towel loose and began drying her pudgy hands.

I could picture Drem looking at those hands, contrasting them to the thin, cracked hands Tori had been pressing against the chair arms. Tori said she had encouraged Phil to see other women and he had refused. I wondered. "How did Phil take being called bourgeois?"

"He laughed." She tossed the towel in the wastebasket.

I eyed the empty stalls, but there was no way I could take the chance of Maria Zalles leaving, catching me with my pants down, literally. I stood very still. "Maria, I have bad news about Phil. He's dead."

"You're joking, aren't you?" Her face had gone as pale as Tori's.

"I'm afraid not. He died last night. I'm with the police, and—"

She let out a scream "No!"

"I'm sorry," I said, glancing at the door, expecting to see it fly open and every film buff in the lobby race in and demand to know what I'd done to this woman.

"How could he—" She burst into dry sobs, jamming her fists into her eyes and wailing so her whole body shook. The picture flashed in my mind of Tori Iversen, letting out that one shriek and never allowing her hand to touch her face.

It was five minutes before Maria Zalles was calm enough for me to lead her back to the café. I got her a cappuccino; for myself I couldn't even bear to have a cup of liquid in front of me.

She wrapped her hands around the cup, oblivious of the hot ceramic. Her face was flushed, and despite rinsing and dabbing with towels, smears of turquoise and black ringed her eyes. "He was here Friday. We sat in our seats, in the back row, and watched the whole movie. He was right here," she said accusingly.

"And then what happened? When you left the movie?"

"Nothing," she choked out. She sniffed back sobs and began pulling the napkin apart. There were people at the next table six inches away, but their only reaction was a momentary pause in conversation. The California commitment to giving people their space has its good points.

I put a hand on her arm and said softly, "Nothing?"

"No. He just went home." She wadded up the remainder of the napkin and rubbed it across her eyes. The blue and black makeup streaked like a raccoon mask, but if she suspected the effect, she couldn't be bothered to check it. The absolute inverse of Tori. Philip Drem *had* to have been seduced by her.

I waited till she was quieter. "He didn't go home."

"Well, I don't know what he did. *I* went home." There was an edge to her voice I hadn't noticed before.

"And that was unusual—for you two to leave like that?"

"We always had coffee or something. We always talked about the movie afterward. I mean, that's the reason you go to movies with someone, so you can talk about it, right?"

One of the reasons. "But you were more to him than just a friend. I can see that."

She hesitated as if she understood I was manipulating her, then, as if she couldn't be bothered worrying about that either, said, "I don't know what I was to Phil. I used to think that we were at the beginning of something, you know? I mean he was so seductive."

"How so?" The Philip Drem I'd heard about couldn't have attracted an escapee from a convent. And Maria Zalles was the kind of trusting, cuddly girl—more girl than woman, though I would have guessed her to be about twenty-five—who'd have men lined up to protect her. I couldn't picture Tori Iversen ever being that innocent.

Maria brushed the rubble of paper shards to the floor and wrapped her hands around the cup again. It would have fit her image better if the cup had held cocoa instead of strong coffee. Gazing into it as if it held her memories, she said, "He was so intense. And he really listened. He was interested in everything. He found out I'd done some scuba diving, and he wanted to know all about it, not only the mechanics but how I felt under-water, was I scared, and stuff like that. Sometimes he just stared at me as if that would help him take in what I was saying. Other times he sat with his eyes half closed as if that let him focus all his attention on listening. And then occasionally, when we were in a place with a mirror, I'd think he was look-ing away, and I'd find him staring in the mirror, watching me, watching us both."

I felt a tug of sorrow for Maria Zalles, so entranced by the illusion of being cherished. And for Philip Drem. It was easy to imagine Philip Drem looking in the mirror at the couple he and Tori might have been. What had it been like for him when he went home to the real Tori? "Maria, how long had you been seeing him like this?"

"A little over a month."

"That's a long time for things not to go anywhere."

"Well, I was just getting over a relationship, and I didn't want to get involved with anyone, and so I probably put up some barriers."

Compared to the walls Drem was used to, Maria Zalles's barriers must have been like doorsills. And yet there was some-thing about Maria Zalles that didn't fit. She thought the rela-tionship was going somewhere; she was confused about Drem's reluctance; she was holding off. I kept trying explanations, like Halloween costumes, looking for the right one. Had she just moved to town and was trying to adjust? Was this air of inno-cence no more than a veil she'd chosen to wear for Drem, or for me? Or had the shock of Drem's death juggled her reactions so none seemed quite real? Like most survivors, she was going through the "Fun House" stage of death recognition, riding along the tracks of the present dealing with my questions when suddenly out of the blackness up popped a skeleton: "Phil is dead!" Was it just that? I couldn't tell.

I hesitated a moment, deciding which path to take. Only one

of my choices was going to have a life. I decided to go with my hunch. "But you thought Phil was about to make a move."

"Thought? Hoped? I don't know. It had been a big deal when he suggested we have coffee on the Avenue last week. When we walked there, he put his hand on my shoulder. I felt like I did when I was twelve years old with my first boyfriend." The skeleton took her by surprise. Tears gushed again. She ignored them.

For Drem, the draw of this illusory Tori would have been overwhelming. When he reached out for her his hand had touched not cold window glass but her soft body. Drem had alleviated his misery by deceiving Maria. I was using her too. That didn't make me feel any better, about me, or him. "Maria, you are such a warm, outgoing person, I can't imagine you just waiting passively to see what he'd do."

She wiped her eyes and looked up. "It doesn't sound like me, does it? I've moved in with guys and back out in less time than that. But there was something about Phil, or maybe the aura of the films and just meeting Friday nights. Until real recently, it was a game. Like a movie, a foreign movie. I wondered if he was married, but I didn't ask. I don't know what he did for a living. It was like watching a movie where you just take what you're given and make your conclusions on that."

Wonderful! The one witness with the chance to know Drem, and she makes no effort. Or had she made that effort but was too stunned to draw up the subtleties of her conclusions? Or unwilling to tell them to a stranger and a police officer? "But, Maria, last night you left right after the movie. How come? Is that what Phil wanted?"

"Yeah." She wiped her finger around the inside edge of her cup, gathering the ring of pasty coffee. Then she sucked it from her finger. "He said he had to see a guy."

"About?"

"I don't know." She stared down at the cup, nervous, thinking now. "Phil didn't say. I did ask. It was the first time I'd broken my rules. I guess I expected an answer that would make it up to me for forfeiting the game."

"And you didn't get it?"

"I got nothing. He said he couldn't talk about it, that it was something to do with work."

I could feel my shoulders tensing with excitement. "Did you buy that?"

"Hardly."

The path forked again. The top tine said she went home; the bottom, she hung around. I chose the bottom. "What did he do?"

"I don't—"

I put a hand on her arm, and smiled. "Maria."

"Okay, so I left and got halfway home. Then I thought, Shit, who does this guy think he is? Maybe he had a wife and she was picking him up. So I came back. He must have been waiting inside here because he walked out just as I came back. It was nine thirty. His bicycle was still out there then."

"So it would have been out of his sight all that time?"

"Unless he came out and looked at it, yes. But when he did come out, he didn't pay any attention to it. He just paced up and down in front of the gate. And at ten he got on his bike and pedaled like mad up the street."

"*Up* the street? East?" To go home, he would have coasted *down*, west. "Which way did he go on College?"

"Right."

Right—south—away from home. "Did he sit on the bicycle seat?"

"When he turned, yes. It's a downslope on that street."

So Philip Drem had waited for someone who didn't show up. Then he rode off in a huff, in the opposite direction from his flat. But where was he going?

"What about his briefcase?" He hadn't been home or back

to the office since he'd stuck that briefcase in his basket and pedaled away from Lyn Takai's.

Maria picked up the ceramic cup and drained the coffee. Her hands were shaking.

"Did he have the briefcase when he got here?"

"Yeah. He always had the damned briefcase. I teased him about it. I mean, here we are fantasizing a carefree month in Samoa"—she clunked the cup down—"or Lisbon, or Paris, and he's clutching his briefcase like he can't be away from his work for an hour. It's like his anchor to his job, his life here, whatever. Like it kept him from being washed away with me."

"When he left on his bicycle, did he still have the briefcase?"

"If he went to the men's room, he took it. To be separated from it, he'd have to have been . . . dead." Her breath caught. Behind us the clattering of china and silver seemed suddenly louder. Her voice was shaky as she said, "He stuck it in his basket, unlocked his chain, and rode off. Didn't you find it?"

"No. Who would have wanted it?"

"No one. When I asked him about it, he said there was nothing that would interest anyone, least of all me."

That might have been what he said, but his actions certainly told a different tale. I said, "I'll need a written statement from you. You can come in to the station tomorrow."

She nodded. "The movie's over. Tell me about Phil. He was married, wasn't he?"

I nodded. We don't tell witnesses more than they need to know. This time I was glad. I could have said that I didn't think marriage per se explained Philip Drem's behavior, but I didn't think she needed that black-and-white version. For tonight at least, she was better left with her soft-colored memories.

CHAPTER

I took down Maria Zalles's address and phone number and arranged for her to come to the station at 10:00 A.M. the next day. When I left her, she was still sitting in the Swallow, her cappuccino cup empty but for the coffee stains.

I started on the route Drem had taken from here. He'd left the Swallow at ten, ridden the half block up Durant (a one-way street), turned right on College Avenue (two-way), cut down either Channing or Haste, and turned left again till he got to Dwight and elected to loop down half a block of Dwight against its one-way eastbound traffic. (In the secondhand report we had, the witness spotted him on that part of Dwight.) Then Drem turned onto Regent Street to die.

The only reason he would have taken that route was to get to Regent. And my guess was he would have chosen Regent as a route to cut across Telegraph (also a one-way, the wrong way) only if he was headed to Carleton and the property owned by Moon, Takai, et al.

Since I had to obey the one-way signs, it took me a bit longer to get there. It was dark now. Deciduous trees already had full complements of leaves, branches hanging low over the streetlights. Sidewalks were empty, street traffic light for a Saturday night. Of course, this was the last weekend before April 15. Berkeleyans, never ones to pay the government more or earlier than absolutely essential were home sweating over their 1040s. Howard, I suspected, was sitting home with one eye on his charitable deductions and the other on his azaleas. An uncomfortable picture, any way you looked at it.

I hung a U and pulled up across from the group's property, the fifty-year-old cheap hotel that could have as easily been cheap apartments. *Inspiration Hotel*, the sign said. Presumably the inspiration had yet to be fulfilled. The outside lighting was minimal. I doubted that had been an aesthetic decision, but the result must have pleased the neighbors (and any housebreakers with meager enough standards to bother with this place).

Lyn Takai and her partners had had the Inspiration only a year, and whatever improvements they might have made were clearly not on the facade. What had possessed a pair as indigent as Takai and Moon to invest in a long-term project like this? I walked up the cracked cement path to the door and pushed it open.

The lobby was shaped like the box of a size 15 AAA shoe and decorated about as imaginatively: a pine counter, two elderly flowered sofas, and the staircase that led up from the front door. No carpet, coffee tables, or lamps. The only light was from the overhead fixture. Not that there were any newspapers or magazines to read by it. This lobby was not a place where people would choose to wait.

"Can I help you?" The man behind the desk had an elfin look—curly dark hair caught in a ponytail that disappeared into the collar of his tan shirt, skin a little wrinkly, dark eyes with the twinkle of experiences not taken too seriously. A tan beaked cap sat on the counter, a captain's cap. Or was that admiral's?

"Detective Smith, Berkeley Police."

"Ah, the one who talked to Lyn." The most innocent of people are usually unnerved by the unexpected arrival of a police detective, particularly one they know to be in Homicide, but this man was not impressed. He was leaning forward over the counter as if he were ready to peruse a trinket I'd brought in. I guessed him to be Ethan Simonov, but I asked anyway. He was.

Simonov had been indicted for tax evasion in Oregon. Had this not been a weekend, I would have gotten the details of that case. I'd heard Simonov's name around town. It was on Howard's well-worn "in case of emergency" list of plumbers, electricians, foundation workers, roofers, and so on. The notation beside Simonov's name had been: "finder."

I said, "Tell me about the tax-evasion indictment."

He leaned toward me as if I had laid a pouch of contraband on the counter and was ready to trade. "You don't mess around, lady."

"A tax indictment is serious business. You get caught evading, IRS makes you pay. They don't send you to jail unless there's a pile of money involved—"

"Or they want to make an example of you," he said matter-of-factly.

"So what did they get you for?"

"Stupidity. Or more to the point, sloppy business practices." He stood up and tapped a finger on the counter as if waiting to see what I had to barter. When I didn't bite, he went on. "It was the kind of stupidity that comes from living in Berkeley too long, then moving away and forgetting where you are. If I'd been the swap king of Berkeley, they'd never have done more than dun me for a few bucks."

"The 'swap king'?"

"Yeah, that's what the papers called me." Simonov gave a little snort, but he failed to hide a little proud smile. "It was up in southern Oregon. I ran the biggest swap club in the state. A trombone player needed his roof reshingled, he called me. I got him in touch with a roofer who wanted a band for his high school reunion. They swapped jobs."

"And paid you a fee?"

"Yeah, though sometimes it was work instead of money."

"Didn't you pay taxes on it?"

"I did. I wasn't that stupid," he said, clearly put out. "It was my clients who didn't. Not my fault, is it? I tell the people I deal with now, they better pay."

"You reported every fee, including the work-instead-of-money?"

Simonov shrugged. "IRS would never have gone after me for that alone. They got me because I was too dumb to check out my clients and find that a bunch were growers and were paying their share in marijuana. Then one of the growers *didn't* pay up. There's nothing worse than a reneger, particularly a stupid one. The other client got pissed and called the sheriff. Sheriff couldn't find the crops, so he went after him for tax evasion. And I got caught in the cross fire. And once they had my books, they dug through them till they found the rest of the growers." He shook his head in disgust. "They dunned me for everything I had. I got out with my shoes and Jockey shorts but not much else. Never would have happened in Berkeley."

Simonov was right. Marijuana is a very low priority here. The citizens passed a nonbinding referendum to remind us. "But you're still doing swaps here?"

Simonov grinned. "For the law-abiding only. I guess I like knowing everyone, being in the middle of things, being the swap king. Maybe I'll get one of the guys to make me a crown of hammers and ladles and bronzed taxi receipts."

I had the feeling that he'd picked up my pouch and tested the biggest diamond, or toughest question, and was satisfied with the deal he'd made. I walked around to join him behind the counter. "Looks like you've got the crown around your waist," I said, indicating his tool belt.

"Be prepared. I learned as a boy. A concierge never knows when he'll have to fix a lock or unplug a toilet."

I leaned back against the counter. Simonov, I recalled, had netted a bit of fame a couple of years ago when he brought together an unemployed environmentalist campaign manager and a city-council candidate who became a champion of Berkeley's Bay shoreline. The two had parlayed their trade into an effective campaign, and Simonov had endeared himself to locals by virtually refusing to share the newspaper publicity.

I asked, "Were you manning the desk here Friday night?"

"When Drem bought it?"

I let a beat pass. "From, say, seven to eleven."

"I just fill in."

"Who was here?"

"At the desk? Scookie Hogan—she's one of us owners. But you know that, don't you."

"Don't worry about what I know, Mr. Simonov. Did you fill in then?"

He wasn't taken aback by that either. "Maybe I should worry more about you."

"Or just answer honestly."

He shrugged. "Or that. But it's so much less interesting." Noting my irritation, he said, "Okay. I was here. From four to eleven—seven long hours if you haven't brought anything to read."

I could imagine. The room with its one window way at the front was cell-like. And Simonov was the last man who looked likely to be comfortable in emptiness. He'd probably been one of those kids who'd spent hours on the jungle gyms or organized gangs of little boys to hike through imaginary deserts over chimera mountains to battle great blue dragons or eels from outer space. How had he survived being imprisoned? I wondered if the trades he arranged now—a kitchen painted in return for six hours of massage, four sessions of emergency therapy swapped for a weekend at a Lake Tahoe cabin—satisfied his need for fantasy.

"Is there any reason Philip Drem would have been headed here Friday night?"

"God forbid! The IRS is bad, but they don't send their agents like Drem out on Friday nights!"

"Could he have been coming on his own, maybe not on business?"

"Socially? Hardly." Simonov laughed.

I still felt the odds were Drem had been headed here, but whatever the reason, it was going to take some digging. "So what's your arrangement here? How many rooms?"

"Twelve," he said after a moment's hesitation. I couldn't imagine he had trouble remembering that. "Ten rooms, the honeymoon suite, and the room with a view of the boiler. Truth in advertising." He grinned and looked as if with the slightest encouragement he'd leap the counter and start pointing out the earthquake cracks in the lobby. That bratty quality would make him a nuisance as an interview, but it was also an outlook I'd always found appealing. The old Howard had it. Brattiness was what made the sting artist.

"And your guests?"

"Our guests are your guests, Detective, at least for the moment. As you can see"—he gestured to the empty lobby with a sureness I'd seen Howard use when he was diverting attention —"we're still renovating. We're doing the work ourselves— more love than money. And this way we don't have to worry about renegers." He spit out the word. Clearly the swap king aimed at his renegers the same loathing the rest of the world felt for Drem. "We've started the foundation work. Now we're dealing with the termite and water damage. Renting a room with a torn-up wall isn't every traveler's dream. Till things are in better shape, we take in whoever's willing to pay twenty-five a night." He paused and stretched farther across the counter. "Now you're asking yourself how I know we've got guys who've spent time in your nice pink jail, right? When they bitch about the cost here, that's what they throw up to us—'the fucking city provides a single room with bath and breakfast for free!' "

"The one night we provided guests with keys, it cost them fifty bucks."

He threw back his head and laughed. He was one of those little guys who seemed to burst into everything in a big way. "That was the night it opened, right? When you had the special offer for nonfelons?"

"Right." It had been a public-relations move that had paid off. Our new pink jail had been a hit with most of the citizens. And for many of our regulars, those clean, quiet, safe cells were better than they got in their SROs.

As if reading my mind, he said, "We're doing our best here. Tonight every room is full, so I guess that says something."

Overconfident sting artists can be sloppy. They forget what script they've been using. I said, "Don't you keep an emergency room for Social Services?" Occasionally the department had had to find a place for a witness or a family out of funds overnight. A hotel like this—bare bones but safe—was the economical type to use.

"Oh that.—The one next to the boiler right behind me—It's empty. I don't even think of it when I'm talking about bookings."

Mediocre save. He was skirting something, but I couldn't figure out what. I glanced at the yellowed plaster. There was a draft that reminded me of the cold night outside. In here it carried with it fetors of mildew. "Anything unusual happen here Friday night?"

He stroked his chin, pulling his fingers together as if over an invisible goatee. "Nothing happened at all. The big event was Scookie arriving with dinner at eight."

"She made you dinner when she should have been here at the desk?" I asked, amazed.

"It was a half swap. She didn't renege. She still owes me a dinner. If I'd thought to bring the book I was reading, I would have come out ahead. Scookie's a great cook."

Scookie Hogan I had met a number of times. She had run a stand near campus that sold "scookies"—a scone-and-cookie mix—to which I had been virtually addicted. She too had had her flash of fame—a story in the *East Bay Express*, an interview on KPFA—but she had shown none of Simonov's nonchalance about publicity. She'd pasted the *Express* article on the front of her booth.

"Do you think Scookie will ever cook again professionally?"

"Nah. She'd never take the chance. It's like she had one shot to make and it's gone. Sad. But you can see why I'm not grieving over Drem." He gave his imaginary goatee another pull. "Heard Drem went from a prod in the ass. I like that. Whoever did it has flair."

It was like listening to an art critic. "*Flair* is a word I'd associate with Mason Moon."

He pulled at his chin again. At the rate he was going, in a few years he'd have a goatee of skin. "Too subdued. How would Mason have killed the weasel of the paper trail? Let's see. For Mason it would have to have been something big, splashy. If Mason had killed him, everyone in Berkeley would still be talking about it. They'd have forgotten Drem and just be applauding Mason's lethal concept. Maybe he'd have rigged up a vacuum cleaner in one of the sewer grates on the Avenue and waited for the right moment." He shook his head. "No. Waiting isn't Mason's strong suit. I don't know. I'll have to think about it."

I could have given him the decision for round one; clearly he'd won. I knew there was something going on here, but he'd played the scene well enough that I couldn't get a handle on what. Witnesses hide things for a number of reasons. Illegality is only one. I handed him my card. "If you come up with anything useful."

I didn't say I'd be back. We both understood that.

CHAPTER

12

I sat in the patrol car shivering, though it wasn't much colder out here than it had been in the Inspiration lobby. The wind had picked up, clearing any residue of cloud. The moon loomed low over Berkeley, exerting its pull on the waters of the Bay and the aberrations of the crazies. Plane-tree branches brushed the streetlights and the corner lights on the sides of the hotel. All else melted into shades of dark.

I'd been chummier with Ethan Simonov than the manual would encourage. There was something about that make-me attitude that always hooked me. As a police officer, I'd learned not to come at it head-on, the way tough guys did. My strength was not bulling through but slicing in at an angle, like a small, slippery running back who splits tackles and is ten yards downfield before the defensive linemen realize he has the ball.

I reached for the ignition key, then changed my mind. I should be honest with myself—it wasn't just that the oblique run was efficient; it was that I hated bullying. I'd been in Berkeley, the seat of the underdog, too long. I had power, of course, though not the power held by departments in cities without police-review commissions and nothing near that of the Goliath IRS. But Berkeley is a city of Davids, and like virtually everyone who chooses to live here, I appreciate the well-aimed stone.

Unless it hits my own eye. And I knew if things got tough, Ethan Simonov would aim his there. And when I faced him down, he'd look for every judgment mistake I'd made. He'd be his own review commission, auditing my every hour at work, and if those failed to provide ammunition, he'd be checking out the rest of my waking and sleeping hours. Sometimes I felt as if the whole city were review commissioners. Or Philip Drems.

And yet, oddly enough, I wouldn't have changed it. There was something about the pervasive skepticism of the city that comforted me. I suspected it was the municipal expression of my own outlook. Growing up, I'd lived in eight towns in five East Coast states and never felt a part of any of them. They were just way stations before the next, better town, the one with the clean slate and sunburst of opportunities, the town that turned out to be another rest stop. Berkeley was the only place I'd ever felt at home.

And Howard was the only man I'd really felt at home with. Or I had before I'd moved into his house. Before the jogger, before my sting. But I couldn't let myself think about Howard, not now. Instead, I sat listening to the wind snap the leaves against each other, feeling the fog-cold air ice my feet.

I sat staring across at the muted light coming from the Inspiration Hotel. And the blank darkness around it.

But the dark wasn't monolithic. I squinted. A man was crossing the hotel lawn. Male Caucasian, five-ten, 155 pounds, shoulder-length brown hair, black jacket, jeans, carrying two stuffed plastic bags. He glanced back at the hotel door, then rounded the corner of the building and headed down the gap between it and its neighbor. Textbook suspicious. I got out, pressed the door shut, and moved as quietly as I could across the street.

To the Inspiration's right was Mason Moon's garage studio. I started down the narrow alleyway between. It was more like a tunnel with the roof rotted away. The garage wall had that old-wood-and-moss smell. From the ground came the stench of decaying leaves and urine. The only light was from the shaded windows of the hotel. I could barely make out the clumps of melting cardboard and mounds of debris in time to step over them. I could have brought a flashlight, but I didn't want to announce myself.

From the yard came staccato taps, cutting through the rustle of the wind. At the end of the passage I paused and glanced into the shallow backyard and down along the side of the building. The guy in the black jacket was twenty feet away, standing about two feet from the wall, arms hugged to his chest, round plastic bags hanging from his hands. Wind flapped the plastic and picked at his hair. He took no notice. For a moment I wondered if he was one of the Avenue crazies who'd been turned out of the state institutions in the Reagan-era economy moves. For years they'd wandered the Avenue in their own universes. When their universes collided with ours, we picked them up, but mostly we left them their space. Left them staring into space, like this guy.

But he was not one of them. He adjusted his bags, leaned forward, and rapped on the window. Now the window shade lifted, and I could see clearly his quivering hands and the thin cotton jacket blown against his ribs. The window opened. He grumbled something and stepped inside.

Inside the room right behind the front desk that Ethan Simonov had told me was empty, waiting for a Social Service emergency to fill it. The guy with the bags I didn't care about; Simonov I did. I ran back around the building, in the front door, to the desk. Ethan Simonov looked up from his book.

"Simonov, you've got two tenants in that 'empty' room of yours."

"You're kidding!"

He was lying. I ran past him into the hall.

"Hey, whadayou think you're doing?"

I knocked on the door under the stairs. Next to it I could feel the heat from the boiler. That might make this room undesirable to some, but to the shivering guy I'd followed, it must seem like heaven. Simonov had just come up behind me when I called, "Police! Open the door. And don't try the window. We've got men out there."

The door didn't open. But two down the hall did.

"You've got cops all around my hotel?" Simonov demanded. "You can't do that!"

I pounded on the door. "Come on, open up!"

"Hey, whadayou want with them?" A guy the size of a linebacker leaned out of the far door. At the other end of the hall, doors opened. Damn. Here I was Goliathing in front of a crowd anxious to see my eye knocked out. For guys who had nothing better to do with their Saturday nights than stay in their rooms at the Inspiration, my arrival was better than renting a movie. But there was no way for me to back off now.

I pounded on the door. "Police!"

The linebacker stepped into hall. At the other end, a door banged. Simonov put a hand on my shoulder. I shook it off and banged the door. "Open it *now*!"

I could hear the knob before I saw it turn. The door opened a crack. No one was visible. The linebacker was behind Simonov. The stench of dried sweat filled the hall. There were others behind him. I didn't look at them. Careful not to touch the door, not to force entry, I said, "Open it all the way."

Simonov stepped in front of me, his tool belt jangling. "Hey, you can't—"

"Don't interfere with a police officer!"

He took a step back.

I moved forward toward the doorway. The door was open all the way now. The room and its two inhabitants were visible. The guy I'd followed was still in his black jacket, his arms wrapped around his thin ribs. I'd seen him on the Avenue. He wasn't a street person in the sense of being homeless night after night. He was one of the marginal ones. His host—young, blond, in torn jeans and a sweatshirt—was steps above that, too clean and well fed to be a street person.

"Okay, what's the story?" I said. "The landlord"—I eyed Simonov—"told me this room was empty. You break in here?"

The street guy shrank back toward the closed window. Cops rousting him wasn't a new situation for him. He was cringing automatically. The blond wasn't cowed. He moved on Simonov. "What the hell is this, Si? We had a deal, and—"

"What kind of deal?" I demanded.

"Look, it's—"

"Wait," I stopped Simonov. "Let him tell me."

Behind him, feet shuffled. The show was winding down; the other tenants knew the rest of the script. That meant that this situation was one they'd all seen before.

"Glad to tell it." The blond crossed his thick arms over his chest. "He say I was freeloading? No way, lady. I spent the whole fucking day digging in the crawl space so the hotshot exterminators can get to the dry rot tomorrow. No sense in paying the exterminators to dig, that's what you said, right, Si? Bad enough you paid me ten bucks an hour and threw in a room for the night. Maybe I was figuring you ran a real hotel with rooms that had two beds instead of one bed and every scrap of wood whoever you snookered into doing your carpentry left around. You got a nerve asking me to sleep in this place. And now you're calling the cops on me! Listen—"

I held up a hand. Turning to Simonov, I said, "Is this right?"

He glanced nervously down the hall at the linebacker, who stood straddling his doorsill, watching from a safe distance but waiting, I guessed, to see if there were any unexpected twists. "Yeah. So?"

"So it's not what you told me."

"I don't need to clear my business with you." A murmur of approval came from the hall.

"In this case you do." I looked past the blond at the stacks of two-by-fours. They took up nearly half the floor space. Playing to the hallway, I raised my voice. "Simonov, Social Service pays you to hold a room for their clients. You take their money. You're not holding a room. You're keeping a woodshed."

The murmur of approval was louder.

"It'd take ten minutes to clear it out if I had to," Simonov insisted.

"That's ten minutes too long." I looked at the blond, ready to tell him he was off the hook. He was leaning back on his heels enjoying the show. But the guy in the tan jacket stood next to the window, still shivering from cold or fear. I felt bad about him. To Simonov I said, "I asked you a simple question earlier, and you chose to lie. Now I want the truth."

His elfin face adjusted, and I had the sense that I could see it pulling back warily and then shifting to attack. He eyed the shivering man, and then, as if reading my guilt, said, "It's too windy to stay outside. These guys need a place to sleep. We've got twelve hundred homeless in Berkeley and nowhere near enough beds for them. The city should be grateful I'm willing to let them stay here free. It's not like I'm charging them money. Even if I were, the city ought to be glad."

From down the hall a guy yelled, "Right on, man!" The momentum had shifted again. Simonov understood this crowd every bit as well as I did.

The blond stepped forward. "Hey, I'm not freeloading here. I worked my damn ass off under this place today. I deserve a lot better than sleeping with the scraps. I ache from my neck to my knees. And for that I get a cot that's so small, I can't turn over."

Simonov had had enough. He jabbed a thumb at the blond's

companion. To the blond he said, "If it's so small, how come you brought him in, huh?"

"He needed a place. Hey, man, you said it yourself. There's a hurricane out there."

The murmur from the hall was uncertain. I could feel the tension mounting, heading toward anger as it does in a game where you can't decide which team you're rooting for. In a minute they'd clump all of us together and give their frustration its head. To Simonov I said, "Let's discuss this at the desk."

He gave a quick nod. "Okay, Ron. I'll deal with this."

But Ron was no fool. He looked over Simonov's head into the hall. "The hell you will. You don't come here bullshitting me like this and then just walk off."

Simonov didn't move. He let a beat pass and said softly, "You want to work for me again, Ron?" Without waiting for a reply, he said, "We'll talk later." He turned and walked back into the lobby, took up his post at the desk, and glared at me. "You cops have nothing better to do than stir up trouble? I thought you were supposed to be hunting down a murderer."

Ignoring that, I took out my notepad and laid it on the counter, open. "So why the song and dance with me? What are you hiding?"

He shrugged. This time the movement had none of its earlier bravado. Now he looked like a dog staring up at the rolled newspaper. But hangdog was unnatural for him, and I could already see the beginnings of resurgence. "I figured Social Service might create a stink if they knew I kept stuff in the room."

"Stuff and people in the room."

"I could clear it easy. If I needed to, I'd take Ron back to my place for the night. Ron and his friend if I had to."

I waited. Odds were, I wasn't getting the full story—police detectives rarely do on the first try—but I suspected that Ethan Simonov was one of those suspicious sorts who never tells it all, regardless of how innocent it might be. When Simonov didn't offer more, I took a shot, "The other guy's been here before. He didn't pay any twenty-five dollars a night. What's your arrangement with him?"

"He's been here once, maybe twice," he said, as if that dismissed it.

"And paid?"

"I don't know. I'm not usually here at night."

"Simonov, I'm running real low on patience. You rented him that room for a cut rate, right?"

"Okay, yeah."

"So you make a habit or renting out that room, the one reserved for Social Service."

He held his hand out palm up, as if he were holding the last ball of common sense. "If we didn't let these guys stay here, they'd be out on the street, and Social Service would have to put them here!"

"So why didn't you just tell me that? I don't object to people sleeping inside instead of in doorways."

"Because you're going to report it, and Social Service is going to feel called upon to make a fuss and maybe want their money back, and frankly we're running too close to the edge here to pay back anything. Look, all four of us owners had to squeeze to make the down payment here. We were real marginal as far as getting a loan." His voice was calmer now. "Every one of us contributes something to the place—"

"What?"

"Lyn's a carpenter. She's done a lot of work. I've got a lot of connections, and I coordinate getting skilled guys to do the renovation. Like I said, Scookie is the night receptionist. And Mason does the books."

"Mason Moon is your bookkeeper?" I asked, amazed. Only in Berkeley would a hotel have a plop artist do its books.

"Yeah, he used to be a bookkeeper." Sensing the shift of

focus, Simonov paused and grinned at me. "Mason said that bookkeeping was too uncreative."

I let a moment pass, recalling my original reason for coming here. Stretching speculation into fact, I said, "Philip Drem was headed here when he died. What was he coming for? This time I want the truth."

Simonov paled. There was no questioning the authenticity of that reaction. The man was shocked. His hand was still extended, and now he stared down at it as if peering into that illusory ball of common sense for the answer. "I don't know," he said. "I almost don't want to know."

"Was he auditing the hotel?"

"No. Mason would have told us if he was. Mason doesn't take well to tragedy, and for him to have to spend hours and hours hunched over the books playing out a scene to Philip Drem's directions would have been worse than solitary confinement. You can believe we'd have heard about it. All of Berkeley would know. The publicity possibilities . . ."

Ignoring that, I said, "Philip Drem was at the Swallow to meet someone who failed to show up. He waited an hour, and then he headed here. It looks to me like he expected that person who didn't show up to be here. And the person on the desk that night was you."

"If I'd said I'd be there, I'd've been there. I don't renege. I make a deal, I stick to it."

"Maybe you changed your mind."

"I make a deal, I don't change my mind. A deal's a deal."

Obviously I'd hit a sore point with the swap king. And as obviously, he realized that he'd strayed down his own path. He smiled, the trader's smile. "But you're not asking about my ethics. You're after who Drem was looking for. Could have been anyone here. There were guests in all our rooms too. Maybe he was meeting one of them."

"What might they have told Drem?"

"Nothing. There's nothing to tell."

"Then why was he coming?" I pressed.

"Curiosity. Perversity. The hope that there's some small thing he could pick up and use against someone. Who knows with someone like that?"

I closed my notepad. I hadn't written in it. I'd have to make notes when I got to the car. I leaned an elbow on the counter and waited till I caught Simonov's eye. "Ethan, there's still something you're not telling me. I'm hunting for Drem's murderer, not for building-code violations. The more you do to help me find him, the fewer times I have to come back here."

He looked as if he might say something, then changed his mind and smiled. "I don't mind your coming back. I rather like it."

I let a beat pass. "So much the better." Before he could answer, I walked out to the car.

I finished a couple of pages of notes, started the engine. Heading to the Inspiration was an odd choice for Philip Drem. I'd suspected it, but I hadn't been sure until Ethan Simonov failed to disagree. Simonov, I was sure, knew a lot more than he was admitting. And I was also sure that knowledge was somehow connected to the hotel.

I was almost home when I remembered that it was Scookie Hogan that Simonov had been subbing for last night. If Philip Drem had been headed to the Inspiration, he might have expected to find not Simonov but her.

What had Simonov said about her when I asked if she'd ever cook again? "Not after what happened to her." Dammit, what *had* happened? Did it have something to do with the hotel and Philip Drem? I didn't know that, but I did know where she'd be in the morning. I'd seen her there often enough.

I started toward home, thinking of Tori Iversen and Maria Zalles, and Mason Moon, and Ethan Simonov. Trying to find a common thread.

Many nights I'd talked out cases, Howard and I eating pizza, chewing on possible leads. They had been good times. The memory made the chill of our distance today seem all the colder.

It also made me hungry. Late as it was, I veered north into El Cerrito and picked up a Thai pizza, family size. Howard could be counted on to put away half of it, no matter what he'd had for dinner or how recently. And with the tenants away, if a couple of slices were left, they wouldn't disappear from the fridge like lambs at the Brotherhood of Wolves banquet.

As I neared Howard's house I found myself remembering Howard glaring at me in the half-dark living room last night. And Tori Iversen behind her glass walls. And that prized azalea of Howard's I'd dug up. Had Howard ever felt so torn with any of his stings? If it failed, there'd be nothing left for us. I knew that. And still, I felt a rush of excitement.

I pulled into the driveway. Howard was probably on the phone to whatever restaurant he'd been to for the Nob Hill dinner, demanding to know how many mushrooms had been in their Stroganoff and subtracting their cost from his charitable deductions. Or, since I knew how he got once he'd started nibbling into some injustice like this charitable-deduction business, he might be talking to the wholesaler who delivered the overpriced mushrooms or the farmer who grew them. Or God, I thought, smiling. Maybe he'd have forgotten about the azalea. I'd be relieved, and yet . . . No, the issue of freedom the jogger brought up was too basic. I was handling it in an almost flip way, I knew.

But Howard and I had a tacit understanding. No heavy talks, deep thrashing of souls, at home. We spent too much time dragged into other people's misery. We needed lightness at home. It was an unpopular philosophy in the land of "relationships," one I'd given up trying to defend. But it had worked—until now. Until we banged into this issue that was too baffling to him, too integral to me. Was I asking too much of him?

And if he couldn't understand it? I felt suddenly stiff and icy. It was this issue—my brother's camping trip and my mother's comment, "You can't do that; you're a girl"—that jolted me to the realization that I wasn't *home* there. Not just not in

Tenafly, New Jersey, the town of that moment, but not home in my home, in my family. Briefly I'd thought I'd found home with Nat, my ex-husband. I'd been wrong, real wrong. As far as belonging went, Berkeley was the only place, and Howard was as close as a person had come. If I'd planned to put everything on the line, it wouldn't have been the line that lead to the azalea. But it was too late to back out of the sting now.

And the pizza was getting cold.

When I opened the door, Howard wasn't on the phone haggling about mushrooms. He was seated on one end of the sofa, beer in hand, and Connie Pereira was at the other. They were both facing forward, silent. On the coffee table were piles of papers, and the telltale blue-and-white forms of the IRS. Howard looked as if he were envisioning every serving of mushroom, mashed potato, and cup of creamed corn for the last year dumped on the table. Pereira looked as if with the slightest encouragement she'd toss those dinners in his face. Neither of them perked up at the sight of me, or the pizza box—a definitely ominous omission.

"Well, I think that's all we can do tonight, Howard." Pereira jumped up.

"Impossible," Howard muttered. I couldn't tell if he meant the tax forms or her.

Pereira grabbed her jacket. "See you in the morning," she said as she headed past me and the pizza. Pereira passing up food was like Attila the Hun skirting the Roman Empire.

I could have asked what had happened here, but whatever it was, I didn't want to get drawn into it. I followed her to the door. "When you get in tomorrow, I need you to run a background on Maria Zalles."

"Who's Zalles?" Howard growled. It was more demand than question.

"Philip Drem's wife's look-alike. Dorian Gray, except the other way around." He was in the foulest humor I could remember. And, I noted, Pereira might have already left for all the attention he paid her.

"I'll do it first thing," she said to me. The smell of curry filled the room. Pereira, apparently untempted, reached for the door.

"What's new on Drem?" Howard asked.

"He was headed to the Inspiration Hotel when he died."

That stopped Pereira. She was torn between escape and curiosity. She had the same look she did when eyeing my coffee and donut. Finally she grabbed: "Had Drem started in on the hotel's books, then?"

"Not according to Ethan Simonov."

She laughed with a scorn worthy of Howard and pried up the top of the pizza box. "Not yet, you mean. Smith, Drem was like an anteater after termites. He wouldn't have left a basement till he'd stuck his snout into every hole and sucked it dry." She pulled out a slice of pizza.

"Maybe he wouldn't have questioned anything in the hotel books," Howard said.

"Pigs may fly"—she poised the steaming slice an inch from her mouth—"but they'd make unlikely birds."

I walked over to the sofa and put the pizza on the floor. There was no room on the coffee table. Howard grabbed a piece. Already I could see one source of communal irritation here: hunger. I couldn't imagine what had kept these two from food so long. I took a slice of pizza and settled on the couch.

"Still," Howard insisted, "maybe Drem wouldn't have been able to come up with anything, no matter how many holes he sniffed out." He was looking at Pereira.

She hesitated, then stalked back into the living room and plopped down on the floor next to the pizza. "Look, IRS regulations are open to such wide interpretation that even their own advice is wrong a third of the time. IRS does not stand behind the advice their own employees give out on the phone. You do what they tell you, and they're wrong—tough for you. If their own people make mistakes, you can believe the taxpayer will." She chomped down on her pizza, staring at Howard. Then she helped herself to his beer. I took this as a sign of truce.

Or partial truce. Pereira's statement had a hefty undertone of "see!" And clearly Howard was not about to rebut it. For Howard—ever on the lookout for new stings; intrigued by each new wrinkle of perfidy the opposition created; vitalized by the new, the different, the exciting—for Howard, wading through bureaucratic regulation was like trudging across the swamp of the shadow of death.

"I wouldn't put money on the hotel books being above question either," I said. "Their bookkeeper is Mason Moon."

A lesser person would have choked. But Connie managed to hoot *and* swallow her pizza, with only one gulp of Howard's beer.

Howard got up and headed to the fridge. "But, Connie," I said, "surely Drem wasn't coming to peruse the hotel books at ten o'clock at night. Even IRS must have some standards."

"Right. Field agents don't make unannounced calls. Only special agents do that, and they carry guns and have FBI training. They usually work in pairs with the FBI. They arrive out of the blue, and they're ready to take you to jail. Compared to them, Drem was Santa."

"Rick Lamott said it was a game for Drem."

"A game where only he had access to the rulebook. He'd call you for penalties you didn't know exist and tell you ignorance was no excuse. It's Kafkaesque, all right. But there are some rules. And everyone agreed that Philip Drem would never break an agency rule. That was part of the game for him."

Howard handed us each a beer, settled back on the sofa, and nodded.

He didn't say it, none of us did, but we all understood Drem's view. When we interrogated suspects we needed to break, truth was pliable, threats and promises redeemable only as much as we needed to protect our own credibility. (I'd promised a guy who'd beaten his crippled uncle everything from plea bargain to a Big Mac. But I would have seen him eat his uncle's cane before I ordered out for him.)

"There have to be some rules," Howard said, retrieving his beer. "No rules, no victory."

Pereira glared at the pile of papers on the table. "Remember that when you insist the Nob Hill dinner wasn't worth the forty dollars the caterer charged them." Clearly, this was an area the two of them had been over more than once.

"Jill"—Howard was not about to be deterred from his argument—"I've already called the distributor who sold the caterer the ingredients."

That he was directing this explanation to me was not a good sign. It meant he'd tried it on Pereira and failed. I asked, "What did they say?"

"They laughed. How could they remember what peas cost six months ago? Maybe there was a pea sale that week and they paid less. They thought I was crazy."

Pereira nodded. She didn't say "I told you so," not in words.

Howard glared at her. "So then, Connie, if there was a special on peas, do I get a bigger deduction? Suppose I didn't eat my peas? Do I still have to subtract them? Suppose I had sixty peas and only ate twelve."

Pereira pushed herself up and stood, hand on hip. (The other hand was still clutching pizza. Even in pique, Pereira has her priorities straight.) "Howard, stop trying to make sense. This is the biggest unchallenged bureaucracy in the country. IRS makes the rules, and there's nothing you can do about them."

"I'll take them to court."

"Fine, if you want to go against the whole battery of lawyers. And if you do win, Howard, they'll appeal. And if you win again, do you think they'll change their regulation? No. What they can do is wait till someone else files suit in Oklahoma, in

Alaska, in New Hampshire. They can go to court in as many jurisdictions as they need till they get a decision they like. Then that's the one they use." Pereira took a swallow of beer and plunked the can on the floor. "Smith, you live with this jerk? Women have been canonized for less." She grabbed her jacket and left.

I picked up another piece of pizza and looked down at the tax forms. "How much difference can it make? A few dollars? Your time and sanity are of some value."

Howard glared at the forms with the same look he'd had when first pondering Damon Hentry, the drug dealer. "I'll be up anyway. I'll get the IRS while I wait for the plant thief."

I said nothing.

"Some asshole dug up my *magnifica*. In broad daylight."

I took a bite of my pizza.

"Broad daylight," Howard repeated. "Something must have freaked him. Why else would he leave the plant only half dug-up?"

Actually, the digging had been only cosmetic because I'd been concerned about the plant, about Howard, and about me when Howard found out. And because I didn't want to have to dispose of a big azalea at 2:00 A.M.

"Howard, you're going to stay up all night?"

"He comes back again, I'm going to get him."

Howard was falling in with the sting so well that if I hadn't known I was the only one in on the plan, I'd have suspected a leak. But pulling a sting on a drug dealer is one thing. Doing it to your guy is another. It didn't feel real good. "What about your taxes?"

"I slept this afternoon."

I almost protested. I wasn't going to have to show Howard what it was like being a prisoner of society. He was doing it to himself.

I shrugged and moved on. From the stairs I tossed down "It's really infuriating when the threat of danger forces you to stay on guard."

If Howard caught the irony, he didn't react. He looked tense, tired, angry. I had second thoughts about the whole sting. Second thoughts; fifteenth thoughts.

I headed upstairs to the bed.

I don't know when he decided thieving hours ended. Howard was asleep when the alarm went off. I had to shake him awake and then agreed to reset the clock for an hour later. The whole process of his grumbling, my statements of fact, and what passed for negotiating took time, and I was still in Howard's hand-me-down T-shirt (my nightwear) when Pereira called.

"I did the background check on Maria Zalles," she said without preliminaries. "No priors, no warrants, and no building at the address listed in the files."

"A fake address?"

"I wouldn't have picked up on it, but Murakawa was in running a perp, and he knows Zalles's street. He's got a Feldenkreis class there. He was sure the numbers didn't go above twenty-one fifty. So I took a pass by and . . ." We both knew the rest. Murakawa is a great observer. It's as if he could stop time and inspect every image he sees under his mental microscope. I've asked him how he does it, but it's so natural for him that he can't explain.

"Rats," I said. "What's with this woman? She gives me this song and dance about how upset she is that her almost lover is dead. Did you try reversing the numbers?"

"Of course."

"A phony address. Why?" I glanced at my watch: 9:32. "She's supposed to be at the station in half an hour. What do you think are the chances?"

"About the same as Drem being nominated for the Nobel peace prize."

By ten I had showered and was at work. Maria Zalles hadn't shown. I spent some time trying to come up with a reason why she lied. But I knew too little about her—and too much about the extraneous dealings witnesses perjure themselves to hide. Maria Zalles may have held the key to the Drem case, or she may simply have been afraid I'd discover an ounce of pot in her underwear drawer. If the latter was true, I was out of luck. If it was the former, then Maria Zalles was one hell of an actress and a woman to consider a lot more seriously than I had so far. I left word with Patrol to check with their sources and pick up Zalles the moment they spotted her.

Then I did the practical thing. I pushed aside what I didn't have (Zalles) and went with what I did. If Drem had been going to the Inspiration, chances were, it was to see Scookie Hogan. Why would he have left Pacific Film Archive, the PFA, after the person he was waiting for didn't show and headed to the Inspiration? To find the person who'd stood him up?

Things were looking up. Scookie was a regular at the Med. I could ask her there, over a cup of cappuccino.

CHAPTER

14

Scookie Hogan was indeed in the Mediterraneum Caffè, one of the old standards of the Avenue. I don't know how long it's been there—longer than any other establishment on the Avenue, I'd guess. The Med is a coffeehouse that wouldn't be out of place in San Francisco's North Beach, near the railway station in Florence, or in Greenwich Village. It's a cold-weather Italian place—long-yellowed walls, metal chairs and marble tables, the smell of smoke and roasting espresso, strident voices smacking against one another territorially, cut by the clang of the cash register.

There was a time in the seventies when the Med was dominated by Hell's Angels. Twenty or thirty of them would park their hogs outside the door and saunter in. Non-Angels gave them and the Med a wide berth. Managers were in a quandary. They appealed to the city, and the University, and someone came through with one of those solutions that make you glad to live here. No violence, no confrontation. Someone did a little research on the Angels and found that they never allowed their motorcycles out of sight. So a couple of *No Parking* signs in front of the Med, and voilà! The Angels roared off, the old clientele ambled back in, and once again the marble tables were surrounded by men in scruffy plaid shirts and worn jeans, women in shawls and faded flowered skirts, students with backpacks and biochem texts.

Now, twenty years later, the scene was much the same, with doubtless many of the same people. Probably in some of the same clothes. Scookie Hogan fitted right in. Her gray-streaked light-brown hair fell in waves that mimicked the cushions of her cheeks and was caught loosely at the nape. Her eyes were pale blue, her skin not so much sallow as dry, drooping.

Despite the chill of a morning when the fog had yet to burn off, she was wearing a V-necked cotton shirt that she had to have bought from a table on the Avenue. I recognized the shade of teal. I'd bought one myself a few years ago. The color had run every time I washed it. By now, it was one of the few off-white things I owned. Scookie's was a couple of washes behind.

I got in line for a cappuccino, added extra chocolate, and walked between the tables to the far side where she sat with her back to the wall. At this hour on a foggy morning the Med was more than half empty. A couple of regulars read papers. One of them fiddled with his wheelchair.

Next to Scookie a young woman in jeans and sweatshirt was reading Virginia Woolf. Scookie wasn't doing anything. She seemed to be neither thinking nor putting forth the effort to stare into space.

I sat down at her table and identified myself.

She shrugged.

"You've had dealings with Philip Drem," I said.

Her pale face reddened. "Bastard! That slime wrecked my life."

"Tell me about it."

"Sure I'll tell you. Glad to." She tapped a pudgy finger on her saucer. Her face was redder. Her voice had risen. The woman at the next table glanced over the top of *To the Lighthouse.* "They should have made a movie off it—a tragedy, maybe a horror story. I'll tell you, but you won't believe me. It's like something out of . . . like the Black Death. One day people were just minding their shops in Paris and Bruges. The next day they were breaking out in buboes; the next, they were dead. No reason, no escape."

Philip Drem had caused his share of misery, but hardly the equivalent of decimating fourteenth-century Europe. "Specifically, what happened to you?"

"Don't worry, I'll get to it. I'm glad to tell you. Everyone else got sick of hearing it years ago." Her voice was gruff, but there was a whine cutting through. It made me wary. "I used to have this business—Scookies—maybe you've heard of it?" She looked at me hopefully, silently begging for reassurance.

She'd asked the right person. "Of course. You had the wagon next to the ones that sell sushi and fruit smoothies up by Sproul Plaza. You sold those wonderful scone-cookies, the ones with the soft-tart interior and the crisp sweet stuff around it. And you had great fillings—cranberries and hazelnuts and chocolate. The chocolate scookies were the best. A lot of times I had them for lunch. Not *after* lunch; they were my whole lunch. You had some real fans on the force."

"Oh, yeah." She beamed, and that smile pulled her sagging cheeks taut and turned her blotchy red skin to a color that looked almost healthy. It changed her from a has-been to a woman of the moment. "The guys on beat always stopped by. The big redhead, and the pretty blonde, and"—she looked intently at me—"I remember you. Yeah, you were a great customer."

"Then suddenly you were gone. You opened a bakery, right?"

"Yeah. I needed the space, and it was time. I was doing too much business to handle out of a wagon like that. I couldn't keep up with the demand. I worked my butt off in that wagon, and in the shop too. Got up at four every morning so I could be making dough by five and have the stand open at six thirty.

The cookie people like you ate scookies for lunch, but the scone crowd—they demanded theirs at breakfast, see? I'd get the joggers lining up at six thirty, and plenty pissed if I was late." The whine was almost gone from her voice. There was just a warm gravelly quality, not unlike a good oatmeal scone.

"Wasn't there an article in the *Express* about Scookies?"

"Two columns."

"As I recall, it called you the nun of the dough world, the bride of the oven."

She laughed proudly. "Yeah, and they weren't far from right, I'll tell you. You don't have a social life with a schedule like that. Oh, I could have gotten it down to a science—make dough, shove in oven, sell, and home by four in the afternoon. I suppose I could have had a couple hours free then. But there were always innovations to try. That's how the hazelnut scookies came about. I was trying something late one afternoon. I was always fiddling with recipes, adding vanilla, trying less sugar. But you can't do that while you're making scookies for your customers. No way. You can't disappoint your customers when they're counting on their hazelnut scookie. You understand that."

I nodded with conviction and took a swallow of cappuccino.

"So, the trial runs all had to be on my 'free' time. But I'm not complaining, no way. I loved it." She hesitated, and in that moment her whole being seemed to turn down a notch. Her voice was a note or two lower as she said, "Making scookies was the first thing I ever did that was mine, the first—the only —time I did *something*, that I was *something*. You know, my real name's not Scookie." She shrugged, embarrassed. "My real name is the same one as half the other women my age. I might as well have been named Generic. It was like my parents created me to do no more than fit it, to never do anything special like make scookies." The whine was back now, like an ill-played violin suddenly clear through the melody of the orchestra.

"Philip Drem?" I prompted.

"He's a cancer."

No longer a bubo, I noted. "A cancer?"

"Right. One day you're sitting home healthy; the next—"

"Drem?" I prodded before she could launch into a new chorus on disease.

Momentarily she stared at me, affronted. Then she gave a half-shrug. If she carried on like this all the time, she must think being cut off was the norm of conversation. "One day I was baking scookies, thinking about whether to add coffee service and put some tables out front of the shop, and the letter arrived. The agent would be calling for an appointment. An appointment—no big deal, I thought. Maybe I should have known better then, but I was too busy to worry about it. I had a new recipe—with blackberry brandy—to work on."

"And he came to the bakery?"

"Wanted to see my receipts for every bag of flour, every ounce of currants, and every cranberry I bought. I brought him the box of receipts, but that wasn't enough. He had to have them in order. He was like insulted that I kept my receipts in a box! Insulted! To him, my bakery, my whole baking life, was nothing but a means to gather receipts. It was like if I had an hour to bake a tray of walnut scookies or write down every penny I'd spent that week, there would be no question which I'd do."

The woman at the next table slammed her book shut, stuffed it in her pack, and stomped out. Scookie turned, startled. "Sorry, I'm getting carried away again. After I lost the bakery, I got so out of control, I was in Herrick Hospital on a seventy-two-hour hold. I tried to slit my wrist. I didn't do it right. I'd never done anything right except make scookies. But by the time Drem got through with my records, there was nothing left.

He made me try to get copies of invoices from suppliers and estimate what I bought from the health-food store—I tried to have everything organic—and figure out what I paid for grocery stuff I couldn't get organic or had to get in a hurry, like blueberries the year everyone went wild about blueberry scookies. He called my suppliers and badgered them till they wouldn't deal with me. He contacted my landlord, at the shop and at home. He talked to the shopkeepers on either side of me. He made my life hell. I'd be rushing around trying to get the bank to give me copies of canceled checks and discover the next morning that I'd forgotten to buy flour. I'd have to race to Safeway, lose almost an hour, have nothing ready for the morning joggers. That only has to happen a couple of times before they find someplace else to eat."

She wasn't shouting, but that whine of hers had cut through every other conversation around, and when she stopped speaking, the room was almost silent but for the whir of the espresso machine and the clatter of cups against saucers.

"Did you end up paying a lot?"

"Three hundred forty-seven dollars and twelve cents. Not what's going to save the nation from bankruptcy, is it. Probably about seven dollars an hour for his time. I mean the IRS *lost* money on the deal. But it cost me my business. By the time he finished, all my suppliers and my customers had deserted me."

"So why was he after you like that?"

"I don't know. He was like a bulldog who's got you by the scruff of the neck and starts shaking. If no one pulls him off, he'll shake you till your neck snaps." Once again she stared full at me. This wasn't the first time I'd heard Drem described as a bulldog. "With the IRS, no one pulls them off. And no matter what an agent does, you can't sue them. With them, you're gallows material unless you can prove yourself innocent."

"But why—"

"What did I do? That's what you're asking, isn't it? Everyone assumes you've done something to bring this on yourself. They can't believe—maybe they don't want to believe—it can just happen. You can lose everything that mattered and end up looking at a hypodermic in the psych ward at Herrick Hospital." Her face was flushed, her hands shaking.

Around us I could hear forced conversation. Scookie reached for her cup and could barely manage getting her fingers around the handle. The cup rattled against the saucer. When she finally did lift it, she smacked it into her lip. She was fortunate the coffee was gone.

I said, "Tell me where you were last Friday night after dinner."

"Friday," she said, putting the cup down with surprising control. "You mean when the slime was killed? Mason called me. He thought I'd be delighted. But he was wrong. I was here the whole evening. I'm here most nights. Only a block away from all the action. I could have seen Drem lying in the street. I would have liked that part. But I'm not happy he's dead. Death's too easy. Death's nothing compared to knowing you had one chance and it got snatched away from you and now it's too late." She smiled unpleasantly. "Maybe I'll try to work up a belief in hell."

"Was there anyone else here that evening who might remember you?"

Her eyes widened. "Ah, just like Drem. 'Can you document your existence here?' Well, Philip goddamned Drem got every bit of documentation I am going to do. So if you want to know, you find out. If you can't, take me to jail."

Slowly I said, "The police aren't the IRS. We do have rules—and the police-review board if you feel they've been broken. I need your help—"

Her smile grew wider but not more pleasant. "But you see, Officer, I don't want to help."

I stood up and left her my card anyway. You never know

when people will change their minds. "The enemy of my enemy is my friend," the Arab saying goes. But I didn't see how I could ever manage to seem like I hated Philip Drem enough to become the swing enemy in Scookie Hogan's eyes.

I stopped in the bathroom and took a minute longer in the stall than I needed to. Sometimes witnesses are so pleased to see me leave, they don't pay attention to where I've gone. They wander in after and start talking to a friend. But when I left the bathroom, Scookie Hogan was still at her table by the wall. A tall thin man I didn't recognize was standing next to her. She'd forgotten about me. She was looking up at him with that same eerie smile in place. I veered toward them.

"Well, congratulations on your twenty-seven points," he said to Scookie. "Azrael commends you."

It wasn't till I got back to the station and hauled out my dictionary that I realized Azrael was the Hebrew angel of death.

CHAPTER

15

"Azrael commends you," the man had said to Scookie Hogan. The angel of death praises you. Now, back in my office at the station, I wished I had paid more attention to the angel's messenger. Five feet eight, long brown hair, bald dome, army-surplus raincoat. If I came across him again, I'd recognize him, but I couldn't put out a call for him. With a description like that, Patrol could pick up half of Telegraph Avenue.

I ran the name Azrael through files. In Berkeley I wouldn't have been surprised to find priors or warrants on a flock of fallen angels. But if we had angels, Azrael wasn't among them.

On the way back from the file room I stopped by Eggs and Jackson's office. Outside, the fog had thickened, the wind had picked up, and tree branches scraped the windows. The overhead light was on, and it reflected off Eggs's pale dome. In another few years what he referred to as a receding hairline would have spread like the Sahara, banishing all life across its sandy knoll. Jackson, who would have a forest of wiry hair long after he was dead, loved to tease Eggs with the prospect of one long strand crisscrossing his scalp like jeep tracks in the desert.

Now Jackson leaned back in his chair, phone propped between shoulder and ear, as he drank coffee, took notes, and grumbled into the receiver. "Hey, man, whole nations have emerged and deceased while you dangle a theory about how long this corpse was in the water. Now you think that the currents brought it from San Francisco, Treasure Island, or out from Oakland and back in to us?" Jackson reached for a paper bag, extricated an enchilada, and picked up the phone.

Across the desk Eggs put down his Mazda brochure and fingered his bifocals.

I settled myself against the windowsill. "Jackson giving the lab a hard time again?"

"You bad-mouthing me, Smith?" Jackson put down the phone. "Enchiladas don't clog the ears, you know."

I laughed. "Jackson, you've been on that guy at the lab ever since he won the Raiders bet. Rarely has one guy paid so dearly for his hundred bucks."

"Careful, Smith." Eggs slid his chair between us. "Just because Al Davis made a fool of the city of Oakland and the old football fans when he dangled the illusion of the silver and black coming back . . . Just because the gullible really believed—"

Jackson glared. He had a reputation as a cop who took no guff, a guy you wouldn't want to meet in a dark alley. Now his round face narrowed, his dark brown eyes seemed to pierce into Eggs's maroon tie. He put down his enchilada and said to Eggs, "Bald."

Eggs and I burst into guffaws. The 1980s defection of Jackson's beloved Oakland Raiders to Los Angeles had been the receding hairline of his life. When the team had agreed to return to the Bay Area, he'd had a miracle regrowth. But when they reneged at the eleventh hour, Jackson was left without a figurative hair on his head. And with hundreds of dollars of debts to cynical friends delighted to profit from his credulity. Eggs, who'd been hearing about his pale pink dome for years, was number one. And Jackson, I noted, laughed with the same enthusiastic insincerity as Eggs on *his* touchy subject.

"You guys have been around for a while," I began.

Another time, Jackson would have tossed in a comment about baldness as a sign of age, but the new parity of jibes must have stopped him.

"Ever heard of Azrael?"

"Hebrew angel of death, you mean? You getting religion, Smith?"

"Just facts, for now, Jackson." I recounted the interchange with Scookie Hogan. "Any ideas?"

He shook his head.

"Aha!" Eggs pounced. "Another game the hirsute one misjudges."

Jackson occupied himself with his enchilada. He had a comeback for everything. The Raiders was the only subject that silenced him. It made me uneasy. But Eggs didn't seem to notice.

"Game?" I prompted, hoping to steer to neutral ground.

"The death game, Smith."

"There's a death game, and we in Homicide don't know about it?"

"*Some* of you," Eggs pronounced. "Neither of you've heard of it? Well, I'm not surprised that the well-thatched one missed it. Maintaining all that cover consumes a great percentage of the scalp's nutrients. But you, Smith . . ." He settled back to enjoy his triumph.

"Eggs," I said, "either you spit it out, or you see a round of this death game played locally."

"Amen," Jackson muttered.

"Okay, innocents, there's the national death game and the local branch. The national one was written up in the *Express*. I'm surprised you two don't keep up with the commentary on your city. But no, that's okay—ignorance of the news is always an excuse." Before I could speak, he held up a hand. "In the death game the players each make a list of sixty-nine people they expect to die within the year. The nominees have to be nationally known, or known well enough to have their obituaries in the *New York Times*. For each person who dies, the player gets points. The younger the deceased, the greater the points. So if somebody over ninety goes, it's hardly worth the cost of buying the *Times*. Over ninety equals one point. Someone between eighty and ninety is two points, and so on."

Jackson put down his enchilada. "So if I dispatch a pedagogical skindome in the lobby of the *New York Times*, I'd get five points for offing you?"

"You lose again, well-tufted one. As in law, even here you can't gain from your own misdeed. Or at least on the national level."

"It's different locally?"

Eggs laughed. "It's always different here. Even in the death game, the Berkeley players did not feel constrained by national rules. God forbid a self-respecting Berkeleyan should conform. What do they care about the death of a nationally known soprano or a Canadian hockey player? The pleasure they want is to see their enemies *here* die. So here the rules are a bit different. The age rule still holds. But there's an arcane system of ratings. For instance, for politicos, they give an extra point for dead Republicans."

"Because there aren't any?" Jackson asked.

"No. Lists can contain names of anyone in the state. Plenty of Republicans down there in Raiderland."

"Because Republicans are less likely to be assassinated?" I asked.

"Right, Smith. A number of tries, but few successes. So it's two points extra for Republicans, one for Democrats, and zero for Berkeley Citizens Action."

"What about professions?"

"Oh yeah, there's a rating systems there too. The national group has to clarify some point every couple of years. The

Berkeley Obit Band—the BOBs, they call themselves—confers each year to stay on top of complaints."

I pushed up from the windowsill and paced to the far side of their desks. "Eggs, Scookie Hogan got twenty-seven points. Could that be for Philip Drem?"

"The IRS guy? How old?"

"Thirty-two."

He made a show of counting down on his fingers. "That'd be seven for age. The IRS isn't popular, but it's not like being a fireman or a marine, either. I'd think Drem would be classified as a civil servant, which would probably be worth about five points, because the worst that's likely to happen is the county car stalls in an intersection and he gets hit. That's still only twelve."

"Damn. You sure?"

"Not sure. Not with the BOBs."

Jackson paused, enchilada halfway to mouth. "Dome, I can't believe there's not some more local spin."

"You mean like the corpse urged Oakland not to take the Raiders back and keep fifty thousand drunks off the freeways on Sundays?"

Jackson didn't respond. He didn't react at all.

"But Drem'd go with an extra five points because he was murdered, Smith," Eggs went on.

"Ta-da!"

"What? Do they get a bonus if we close the file?" Jackson demanded, surprisingly out of humor.

"Who would know whether Scookie picked him, Eggs?" I asked.

Eggs glanced at Jackson questioningly and then, apparently finding no answer to Jackson's chilliness, plunged back into his topic. "As you might imagine, the death game is a pretty secret organization. I mean Chief Larkin, or the priest at the Episcopal church isn't likely to admit he's a player. All the players have game names, so they don't even know who the others are."

"What's the point of winning if you can't lord it over your fellow players, if you don't even know who they are? Is there a cash prize?"

"Zip."

"Eggs, somebody has to know," I insisted. "Games like this have a game master who keeps the official lists."

He nodded.

"Okay. So the game master would have to be someone all the players trusted. A person with a job he or she wouldn't lose if he were found out. Someone who everyone believed was reliable and who'd be able to keep up on who died." I took a step toward the door. "Do you know any of the players?"

"Not anymore. The guy I heard this from died. Went for twenty-four points. He would have loved it."

"Eggs! How do you know that?"

"In his twenties. Eight right there. Worked as a copy editor —next thing to a bureaucrat—four points. In his own home, so he didn't even have the dangers of commuting—an extra two."

"And the other ten?"

"Well, only his ex-wife got those points. Probably nobody else picked him."

"Family members get extra points?" Jackson pulled his hand back from his food. "Hey, man, this is close to the marrow, even for Berkeley standards."

Eggs flushed. In all the years I'd been in the department, I couldn't recall ever seeing his skin any color but so white that his lips seemed rouged. Now, as he stared at Jackson, his cheeks were an odd shade of orange. Could Eggs be a part of this game? Would I be greatly surprised? Eggs fit the requirements for game master as well as anyone I could think of: solitary, fair, knowledgeable, reliable. I could picture Eggs sitting in his Morris chair in front of his fish tank discussing the rule changes with his fantail fish. The death game was just the sardonic view of things that would appeal to Eggs. Being game master would suit him. I could see him in wizard's garb. Would Eggs have made that rule—extra points for close relations? There the wand faltered. That, I had to admit, would surprise me.

Eggs was facing the window, but I could see out of the corner of his eye he was concentrating on Jackson. "Jackson, it's only a game. We see a dozen corpses done more casually than these."

"Not family."

"Look, I'm sorry I—"

"Forget it, man." Jackson picked up his enchilada, took a last bite, and threw the wrapper in the trash. "I'll be back around four." He grabbed his jacket and headed for the door.

Jackson had never left without a good-bye to me. That was two firsts for this interchange. I stared at Eggs.

It was a moment before he said, "Jackson's uncle—I forgot about him. He was a big Raiders fan, season-ticket holder, had a bunch of friends he'd meet there each Sunday, flew to all the away games. He must have used every spare penny for that. When the Raiders left, he was lost. I guess he'd drunk a lot at the games, all those tailgate parties and all. But the games were his social life, and when his team left, he fell apart. Jackson and the whole family tried to divert him, but nothing worked. He died. God, how could I forget?"

"Suicide?"

"No gun. Drove off the road, drunk, on a Sunday afternoon. Same thing. Or worse."

I put a hand on Eggs's shoulder. "Jackson knows you feel bad."

Eggs shrugged.

"Look, maybe you'll lose a few hairs over it."

He didn't look up. I was beginning to feel as awkward as he

did. Eggs and Jackson had shared this office for nearly a decade. They were as close to friends as two so different men could be, and still Eggs poked a raw spot till it bled. Inadvertently, sure, but that only made it worse. Eggs and Jackson were different races, from different states, had divergent interests, but they were both men. They shared a more common background and mythology than Howard and I ever would. How could I expect Howard to understand how life imprisoned women, imprisoned me? Was I asking the impossible?

I pulled my hand back. "About those extra ten points—if they weren't for closeness of relative, for what?"

Eggs shook his head. "Individual choice. Each player chooses the name on his list he'd most like to see die. If they cash their chips, he gets a bonus."

"Add ten to seventeen," I said in triumph, "and you get Scookie Hogan's twenty-seven points."

"So Drem finally did something good for her."

"Or she decided he would." I wished Howard were here to enjoy contemplating such a macabre sting. But I'd spent enough post-sting time with him to know the smug delight that flows from the triumphant. I recalled Scookie Hogan's glee as she accepted kudos in the Med. To a serious player that victory over Drem and *because of* Drem would almost have evened the score. "Did she kill him, or was she just lucky?" I asked, slipping into death-game mentality. "Eggs, do you remember names of players?"

"Only code names. Tarantula, and Clumsy Medic, and—wait—Ice Pick, and, oh yeah, I think the game master was called Canary's Keen."

"Canary's Keen?" I smiled. In a case that had been plagued with dead ends like Maria Zalles and blocked alleys like the IRS, Canary's Keen could be a eight-lane freeway. I thought back on the game-master requirements: smart, reliable, informed, no danger of losing his job, someone people trust. I'd been speculating about Eggs. Had he been game master, I doubted he'd have admitted it. But he wouldn't lie to make up a name just because it didn't fit him. Whatever his hobbies, he was a police detective first.

"Canary's Keen, indeed. It just may be that I know that yellow bird."

CHAPTER

16

I checked my IN box, hoping for word from Leonard that he'd unearthed Sierra, the street person, and derailed his tale about the errant cop near Drem's bicycle. But the box held only the normal departmental memos. I left a message for Pereira to get in touch with Mason Moon and check out the Inspiration Hotel books. Then I signed out a car, headed up to Telegraph, and parked across the street from Herman Ott's building.

Darting through the plodding two-lane traffic, I ran toward a doorway between a take-out pizza parlor and poster shop. Fog dampened already mushy piles of discarded napkins on the sidewalk. The aroma of tomato and garlic flowed out of the storefront, and up from the debris, and followed me inside Ott's lobby. There the elevator car, one of the old ones behind a folding metal gate, sat waiting. It had been waiting for as long I'd been on the force.

Ott's building, once a sought-after business address, had fallen into hippie-pad-dom during the seventies and more recently had been occupied by Asian-refugee families who were willing to endure life in offices-cum-apartments with the bathrooms down the hall.

I climbed the two flights of double central staircase and made my way around the square track of hall that surrounded them. It had been a couple of months since I'd had reason to poke into Herman Ott's burrow. But I could sense another change in the building. The hardworking refugees were moving on. The inviting smells of satay and curry were sparser now, thinned by an odor of turpentine and chemicals. Was the landlord renovating? If so, it would be a first for this building.

Ott had been the first tenant to illegally transform his two-room office into an apartment of sorts. One room was an immaculate office. The other housed cot, hot plate, an overstuffed chair that had been spitting out its springs and batting for years, and a pile of blankets, newspapers, and clothes that covered the floor shin-deep. Had that pile been mud, Ott could have gotten federal disaster relief. I knocked on the *D* of the Ott Detective Agency in the opaque glass window.

"Who?" Ott called.

"Jill Smith," I said, omitting "detective." I didn't want to proclaim Ott's connection to our department—not yet, anyway. Herman Ott made it a policy never to cooperate with the police, at least never without a long and exceedingly tedious argument, never without recompense, and never never if it endangered one of his clients. I had gotten information out of Ott over the years, an achievement worthy of an epitaph. More amazing was the fact that for once, there were no overdue discretionary-fund disbursements outstanding to Ott. I was not indebted to him. In fact, I had done him a favor, a big one, and for the only time in the years I'd dealt with him, Herman Ott owed me. It made him exceedingly uncomfortable. Seeing Herman Ott edgy, having to choose his words with care instead of merely growling "out!" was almost payment in itself. Almost, but not quite.

I was just about to move into stage two of our encounters and start ordering him to open up when he surprised me and did. Debt was definitely improving his manners.

But not his appearance. For a moment I thought I'd woken him. He rubbed a small plump hand across his little hazel eyes and gave his stringy blond hair a shake. There was no sartorial clue to his immediately previous activity. As if sleep came as a startling discovery every night, Ott didn't own nightclothes. He fell onto his cot in whatever he had on and yanked up the clutter of sheets, blankets, clothes, and newspapers that covered the floor.

I walked into the twelve-foot-square office. Maybe I *had* woken him. Ott's office was always in order: no stray papers, pens, or newspapers. Pages of notepads with any written message were carefully torn off. Even his paper coffee cup was usually deposited in the trash. But this morning the *Daily Californian*, an eight-pager, was lying open across the scarred wooden desk. Covering something. And the cover-up had been too hurried to conceal the lump beneath but unfortunately too proficiently done for me to tell the nature of that lump.

"Whadaya want, Smith?" Ott's thin lips formed a scowl—his natural expression.

"Courtesy's hard to maintain, huh?" I shouldn't have gloated. I couldn't help it.

Automatically Ott's mouth formed a circle, ready to demand "out!" Instead he closed his mouth.

I settled in his straight-backed pine chair and watched for his reaction. "Does the name Canary's Keen mean anything to you?"

Ott's tiny pale eyes pulled back in his sallow skin. Each time I saw the man, I had the same initial reaction. *He looks even worse than the last time I was here.* With the best haircut, the best tailor in town, Herman Ott could never have looked good. But had he also been the richest man in town, he would still have been too counterculture to spend money on his appearance. His clothes came exclusively from the Salvation Army or Good Will and would have come from the free box in People's Park across the street had he not felt guilty about taking clothes out of the hands of the destitute. Today his ensemble included a lemon turtleneck with a hole in the neck seam, a tan-and-ocher argyle sweater with a stain just below the point of the V that could have been from dark curry or pale bean sauce, a tan down vest that was unlikely to make it around the arc of his gut, and spanning that gut but hanging so loose on his spindly legs that they looked more like curtains than pants were threadbare chinos with two of those brown patches that you ironed on and then waited uncomfortably as they worked loose again. I hadn't seen those since I was in high school. I wondered if Ott got them from the Salvation Army too. I had never seen Herman Ott in any garment that quite fit—anything new, anything not some shade of yellow. I repeated my question. "Does the name Canary's Keen mean anything to you?"

Ott shook his head. His thin blond hair shivered in response. Barbering was another extravagance Ott disdained.

He didn't look as if he were dissembling. But he was a pro at hiding the truth. "Ott, you may recall you owe me."

"Smith, if it'll get you off my back, I'll come up with a meaning. Canary's Keen, eh? Distress at the opera? Death at the bank cage?"

"Smartassedness is not repayment. Repayment is the truth."

"If I give you the truth, we're even? You're on. Canary's Keen doesn't mean a thing to me."

I sighed. From behind him came the burning smell of spaceheater filaments. The heater revved up slowly, groaning as if it knew how useless its efforts were in this cold room. "Ott, there are many things about you that are reprehensible. But I did assume you were honest."

Ott settled in his gold Naugahyde desk chair. "I'm flattered that you assume I know all things. But what can I tell you, Smith?" He threw up his hands.

I was beginning to have the distressing feeling that Ott might be telling the truth. Maybe this potbellied, bandy-legged, yellow-clad bird was not Canary's Keen. If I had wasted the one indebtedness I had had from Ott in three years . . .

"The death game, Ott. Surely you've heard of that," I said, as if my knowledge spanned years instead of less than an hour.

Ott grinned, never an attractive sight. He wasn't a big man by any means, not quite as tall as I am, but he had the smallest teeth I'd ever seen in an adult. Little baby teeth that stood like white pickets in a fence. Fortunately they weren't in sight often, for Herman Ott had virtually no sense of humor. "Smith," he said, "you a death-game player?"

"You?" I parried.

"This the question?" He held out his hand to be shaken.

"Ott, I saved your reputation. Is that worth no more than a research question?"

The grin faded, and the hand withdrew. Herman Ott prided himself on fairness.

"Consider it a partial. Tell me what you know about the group and Canary's Keen."

Ott sighed. "I'd like to, Smith, but what I can tell you isn't going to shave much off my debt. The local group has probably twenty-five members. They choose twenty-five 'nominees' to bite the dust."

"The national group's requirement is that a nominee must be likely to have an obituary in the *New York Times*."

"None of that bourgeois status for the locals. Here, the rule is a nominee must be known to five of the members."

"No obit in the *Express*?"

"No obit anywhere."

"So they could choose the old guy down the street if four other people have seen him?"

"Yeah, Smith, if they don't mind looking at the guy every day and getting itchy fingers when they see him cough." Ott pulled the edge of the *Daily Cal* toward him. From underneath it a corner of paper appeared.

"So who are the players?"

"I can't give you names. You understand that. Just say its a fair cross section of Berkeley."

"Do you know who the game master is?"

Ott hesitated. "No." I couldn't decide whether he knew and had considered telling me or, more likely, didn't know and hated to admit there was some clandestine position in the city limits that had escaped him.

I hurried to capitalize on this minor mortification. "Ott, so far this tells me nothing that's not common knowledge. What other requirements do they have? Any limit on professions? Like could they choose twenty-five firemen? Or all drug dealers and deckhands?" I asked, naming three of the most dangerous ways to make a living.

"If they wanted. It's Berkeley, Smith. They don't have rules, and the ones they have are by consensus." Ott rubbed his hands together as if cleaning off his obligation.

Before he could stand up and reach for the door, I said, "Okay, Ott, let me give you a for-instance—"

"Drem."

Of course he'd know what case I was working on. No one died in Berkeley without Herman Ott finding out. If I hadn't known he slept under the wad of blankets on the cot in the next room, I would have wondered if he rented a room in the morgue. "Was Philip Drem on any of the lists?"

Ott smiled again. Two smiles in one visit. "You bet, Smith. He was a nominee on five or six, and on two a bonus baby."

On five or six lists, and got the coveted ten-point spot on two! I didn't try to disguise my amazement—not that Ott knew who the nominees were but that he passed on the information without a fight. I stood up and leaned over his desk, brushing the *Daily Cal* to the right. It didn't surprise me to find tax forms underneath. Only that it was a Schedule D.

I broke into laughter. "Ott, *you* have stocks? *You* have invested in the establishment? Why did I bother saving your reputation when there's this just waiting for someone to discover?"

"It's not establishment. It's solar panels," Ott insisted, puffing up his chest feathers. "Cheap solar panels, Smith, will save the planet—if we don't fuck it up completely before that."

I found Ott's indignation and his explanation comforting. I also found it encouraging. He might not be Canary's Keen, but a man like Ott, with complicated taxes . . . "I take it from all this that you knew Philip Drem?"

Ott nodded.

"And you're not sorry he's dead?"

"I'm going to tell you something, for free. I'm not a death-game player, and, Smith, I don't wish death on anyone."

I didn't disbelieve him. That kind of fairness was part of Ott's code. He was too much mired in the sixties ethic. I glanced around his depressing office, drops from the fog streaking down its sooty windows. I looked through the doorway to the mire of blankets, newspapers, books, clothes, and God-knows-what that covered the floor. Many of Ott's clients were Avenue regulars who'd been strung out on drugs and probably would be again when it came time to pay up, or they were forever on the short end of life, Avenue street artists who'd move on or felons who'd find him expendable as soon as he delivered. No one who wasn't guided by that naive hope of the sixties could live Herman Ott's life.

"Drem audit you?"

Ott hesitated again. He really did hate to give information to the police.

"More than once?"

Still he didn't say anything.

"More than twice?"

He yanked the *Daily Cal* back over his Schedule D. "Smith, this is not part of our deal."

I stood up. "Ott, I'm going to tell you something that may amuse you."

"It won't change the balance between us."

"A gift, Ott." Seeing his small pale eyes narrow into the folds of his face, I said, "Okay, a gift, and let's just say I'm open to any return gesture. So here, Ott. Your acquaintance, Philip Drem, a man who made it onto a number of death-game lists on the strength of his professional offensiveness, had not only a wife but a girlfriend."

Ott prided himself on not showing reactions. But here pride failed. His eyes opened wide, and his fleshy arms hung loose from his narrow shoulders. "Two women tolerated him?"

"Right. You know about his wife?"

Ott gave no reply. I took that for a yes. I didn't doubt that when Drem audited him, he had audited Drem's life. I waited, watching his inner struggle, till he said, "And the other one?"

"Here's the interesting thing, Ott. The girlfriend looks like a healthy likeness of his wife. Maybe you've seen her—Maria Zalles?"

Again Ott didn't answer. But this time I was surprised. If he'd known nothing, he would have had some reaction—anger, bewilderment, or amusement (such as that might be for the humorless Ott). But this careful lack of response was significant.

"You know Maria Zalles?"

Ott reached for the doorknob. "We're through, Smith."

I didn't move. "She seems like a nice girl. She gave me a phony address. She's going to get herself in a lot of trouble. If you know her, you'll be doing her a favor by telling her to call me."

He pulled the door open.

"Ott, for her, it's like innocents dealing with the IRS. They think the government will forgive them because they just overlooked something. They're wrong. You've been audited. You know that."

He gave just a small sigh. I wondered how many dollars that exhalation reflected. But I didn't pause. "Ott, Maria Zalles thinks dealing with the police is like fussing with the house-mother at school, like a good story will make everything okay. Or maybe it'll all be all right after spring vacation. We know that's not true. Interfering with a murder investigation is a crime. Help her, Ott."

"Out."

"She calls me by the end of the day, she's off the hook."

Maybe Herman Ott would get Maria Zalles to turn herself in. Probably not. But there was nothing I could do about it till I gave him time. What I could do was stop by the Inspiration Hotel and see what my visit last night had stirred up. I could ask Ethan Simonov about the books. I pictured Simonov leaning over the desk as he had last night, elfin eyes gleaming with readiness to battle the city council or organize an expedition or create a party game. If I'd had to nominate someone for death-game master, Simonov would be high on the list.

It was just before noon when I walked out of Ott's building. The smell of tomato sauce, oregano, and garlic wrapped around my nostrils like a nose ring and drew me into the pizza shop. The dense fog had emptied the Avenue, but those who had braved the danger of wet had done it for food. The tiny pizza joint was packed. Inside the smell of tomato sauce battled with the stench of wet wool. Students in rugby shirts, shorts, and goose-bumpy legs huddled by the stand-up shelf along the soda- and sauce-stained wall stuffing deep-dish pepperoni in their mouths and mumbling about on-line access or the Cal Bears season. Discarded sheets of wax paper were mashed into the floor, and muddy tendrils marked the lines of ingress and egress.

I ordered a slice of ham and pineapple (it's better than it

sounds) and stood along the counter half-listening to conversations, hoping to overhear something worthwhile, the other half of my mind thinking about the Inspiration Hotel. Had Philip Drem been over the hotel's tax return to verify Lyn Takai's? Was Drem headed to the hotel when he died?

I finished the Coke, wadded up the pizza paper, and ran across the street to the patrol car. In the fog the car needed to idle a bit. I always forgot that. Warming up the VW bug never made any difference. Either it stalled or it didn't; the choice was its own. I listened to the squeals coming over the radio as I drove down beside the campus past Sproul Plaza, the counterculture Hyde Park of Berkeley. My favorite of the haranguers had been the spaceman selling square inches of real estate on the moon. This year's entry was a bald man in a pink tube suit giving away condoms.

I drove the few blocks and parked across the street from the Inspiration. Thick fog suited the hotel. The whir of an electric saw came from one of the yards. Like the sound of the sawmill near my grandmother's. I stared at the vague outlines of the hotel and in front of it, the cattails poking up from the hard, stamped dirt. I remembered my grandmother's front yard—I still couldn't picture the house. I saw that prickly yard as I had then, looking out the front window. Looking at it from inside, where it was safe. Inside the closed windows and closed doors. My stays had always been in summer, the air conditioner whirring but the air still moist, thick, deadeningly hot. A soggy straitjacket of air. I could remember the door opening and the searing light cutting across the sill, the smell of fresh-cut wood from the mill taunting me. But I couldn't picture myself outside, not without her dry fingers on my shoulder. Keeping me safe, she'd said, glancing pinch-eyed at the neighbors' houses and forcing me back inside to . . .

I found myself clutching the steering wheel, foot poised on the gas pedal. I couldn't recall a clear picture of the outside of that house because I'd spent those endless months inside. But I couldn't see the inside of the house either. Why was I blocking that out? But this was hardly the time. The taxpayers don't pay for self-discovery.

I hurried across the street to the Inspiration. Once inside, I could hear hammering in the back. The sawing had stopped. The lobby was empty but for the couple behind the desk. Had I not known their raison d'être, I would have taken them as an illustration of *ill-suited*. Mason Moon's bushy brown hair still showed a hat line from his floppy felt chapeau, and his orange goatee held a smattering of wood flecks. Obviously, he'd been dragged in here from his studio.

When I'd first seen Moon, he'd been flamboyantly playing to the crowd. Now he was huddled as small as his plump five-ten frame could get, like a wad of insecurity stuck atop the hotel records.

Standing over him was the reason—Connie Pereira. Dressed in her lightweight tan uniform in this winter-cold room, Pereira was sweating. Her blond hair, which never appeared uncombed at any hour of day or night, showed tracks of fingers drawn through it in frustration. The pounding in the back of the hotel was louder, more irregular.

"How's it going?" I asked.

In unison, Pereira and Moon shook their heads.

"This is a ridic—"

But Pereira overrode him. "To call this assemblage of scribbles financial records is like mistaking *him* for Henry Moore."

With an orbital spread of the arms, Mason Moon, the plop-artist sculptor, thrust himself up and glared at Pereira. "Spare me the persecution of the hirelings of the bourgeoisie!"

I stepped between them. "I take it the records are not in order. How do you prepare your taxes, Mr. Moon?"

"With pain." He slumped into the chair. But that slump did not end in the normal droop of the head over the chest. In

Moon's case his cotton clouds weren't squeezed, nor was the silver moon creased. A careful slump.

"You've been a CPA, haven't you, Mason?" I asked. Pereira stared, as amazed as if I'd suggested he'd been a diva.

"Another life," Moon muttered.

"Believe it," Pereira said. "Not only does he have no coherent record of expenses—he's got utility bills mixed in with permit payments and rooms rented with no names of clientele. I've seen people keep piggy banks with better records than this."

I looked down at the scraps of paper strewn over the desk. Although there were a number of obvious answers there, I asked Moon, "Why did you leave accounting?"

"Being an accountant is like spending your life blowing the stuffing into pillows. Your best hope is that you avoid disaster. Life should be about more than avoidance."

Pereira opened her mouth, but I gave her the "stop" look before she could speak. I knew her well enough to foresee a lecture on creative financial planning, stocks, options, and esoteric but legal ways of keeping, expanding, or hiding money that were beyond my level of comprehension or interest.

I said to Moon, "Surely you knew the limitations of accounting before you chose it."

He shrugged, a theatrical gesture aimed at the back row of the empty lobby. "I erred. The job's boring, and the competition's a nightmare. It's like selling toilet paper. One brand's pretty much like another. The only things you can sell are price differences or extras. So you spend half your time trying to convince housewives that their friends will think better of them if they have violets on their roll. Or bathroom jokes for Christmas."

"And what are the bathroom jokes of the accounting world?"

"Guarantees. Audit insurance. Your accountant will stand not just by you but in front of you all the way to San Quentin."

I glanced at Pereira. She hesitated, then, realizing that I wouldn't know about such assurances—with no income but salary, no property, no investments, I'd never had anything worthy of an accountant—she nodded. Her expression suggested she was beginning to lump me in the same pile with Moon.

"What kind of guarantees?" I persisted.

"Well, the audit insurance and—" Moon hesitated. "Well, okay, here's the latest. There's a rumor that Rick Lamott—he's the new hotshot in Berkeley—will be doing a money-back guarantee, guaranteeing that certain of his accounts will not be audited."

"Money-back?" Pereira said, horrified. Clearly, money-back was a concept held in poor esteem in all financial circles.

For a guy who'd been in the business only a few years, Rick Lamott had certainly commanded attention. He was, in his way, not unlike Mason Moon. I could picture Lamott whipping around a corner in that red Lotus sports car of his and thumbing his nose at the IRS office. Just as he'd parked in the red zone in front of the police station.

Pereira gave a snort. "When the IRS finds out about that, it'll be his business in ruins."

Moon grinned the same evil look he had when he started to make demands of me by Drem's body. "Yeah, it's a quick ticket to the problem-preparer's list."

"Yeah, Moon, you'd better hope Lamott has no talent for sculpting. 'Cause he'll have plenty of free time to learn." Pereira laughed.

"Hey, wait up here," I said. "What's the problem-preparer's list?"

Moon leaned back in his chair. It was an old wooden armless swivel, the type of chair that would have been at home in Herman Ott's office. The spring for the backrest was loose, and Moon had to catch his feet under the desk to keep from flailing backward. Regaining equilibrium, he pushed off and rolled to the rear wall where he could face both Pereira and me. "After a trip to this rugged nation, Vita Sackville-West—or her husband, Harold Nicolson—pronounced: 'All Americans are more or less vulgar.' To the minions of the Internal Revenue Service, ladies, all taxpayers are more or less thieves. It galls the minions that they can't catch every one and make them pay. If they find that you went to a police meeting in San Francisco and deducted your travel expenses and then went to the symphony that night, it doesn't just irk them—it gnaws all the way to their marrow. If they had the manpower to comb through every return, they'd disallow the whole trip because you had symphony tickets and would have gone to the City anyway. They hate stuff like that."

I could have told him the department would have paid the rapid-transit fees, but I decided not to distract him. Moon leaned forward and made an inward circle with his arms, as if sweeping us into his confidence. "They hate taxpayers who cheat. More than that, they hate people who don't report income at all. But the people they hate the most are the tax preparers who show you how to get away with overdeducting or not reporting. There are crooked accountants, of course, and, alas, incompetents. Incompetents cause them a lot of work. But the ones they're after are the guys who find loopholes they *know* shouldn't be in the law but are. The clever guys. The guys who beat the Service at its own game. It galls them."

Moon reached up by his forehead, then let his hand drop. He'd intended to tip the floppy hat to accentuate his performance, but he was bareheaded. Undaunted, he went on. "So what they've got for the whole lot of these guys is something called the problem-preparers list. Of course, they'd never admit it exists. It's like a blacklist of accountants. They watch these guys. They can audit their clients year after year. You don't have any way of knowing if your accountant is on it, not until the third year your taxes are audited for no apparent reason."

I eyed Pereira. She nodded. "Rumor is, they've run guys out of business. You can imagine, Smith, that when the word gets around that all of Lamott's clients are being audited, he's not likely to pick up new business. Or keep the old."

"And that's legal?"

Pereira and Moon nodded in unison. It was he who said, "It's all legal for them. You can't sue an IRS agent for harassment."

"And in a case like this, if Lamott took it to court," said Pereira, "the agency would say they'd found a pattern of abuse in his records and were checking it. He'd have a helluva time proving otherwise."

"It's not known as the Internal Kafka Service for nothing." Moon was hitting his stride.

Behind him, the pounding stopped. A woman's voice yelled something. A hammer hit, and again, mocking her, or so it sounded. Lyn Takai stalked out through the door, her short brown hair and gray sweatshirt covered in dust, her olivey skin flushed orange. Spotting our entourage at the desk, her scowl deepened.

It was a wonder this hotel had guests at all. I said, "What's going on back there?"

"As little as humanly possible," she grumbled, thrusting a foot onto the edge of the counter and leaning forward over her sleekly muscled leg. She clasped her hands around the foot, pulled her chest forward over the leg in what I assumed to be some yoga position, and said to Moon, "Ethan must have advertised in the uncoordinated-and-unwilling column. Those guys back there are working at capacity figuring out which end of the hammer to hold. And considering the skill they show hitting nails, the wrong choice probably wouldn't make any difference."

Taking advantage of Takai and Moon's presence and their parallel bad moods, I said, "Lyn, Philip Drem was auditing you. Had he pulled the returns for the hotel too?" I didn't move my head, but it was Moon I was watching now. He stiffened.

Takai released her foot and lowered her leg. "No. He asked me about the hotel, but he had his nose in my classes. He didn't have time to worry about this place."

"Not yet," Pereira said with just the hint of a smile. She'd upped the ante before in situations like this. Nervously, Moon eyed the mess on the desk.

I considered asking what it was Drem would have been seeking here the night he died but decided against it. That was a question that needed to be asked the owners individually. Instead I said, "You don't mind if I look around, do you?" That casual request worked about half the time. Some of the innocents were interested in getting things over with quickly, the guilty in looking innocent. But in Berkeley plenty of citizens would demand a warrant on principle. When neither Moon nor Takai answered, I focused on Takai, to whom I was a small nuisance compared to the more pressing problem of the workmen. I started for the stairs to the second floor, *away* from her problem. "Okay?"

"Yeah, sure. But you won't bother the guests, will you? If the rooms are empty, the doors are open. If the doors are closed, chances are there's someone in there. Some of our guests keep odd hours. Scookie's finished cleaning, isn't she?" she asked Moon.

He glanced at his watch. "Should be."

I made my way up the wide oak stairs. The second floor still had the marks of deferred maintenance, but with work the dirt-darkened oak wainscoting could be beautiful. Put an antique table at the head of the stairs, add four-poster beds, quilts, vases of flowers, and the Inspiration could be a great rendez-vous spot.

It reminded me of my grandmother's house, except that there was never a question of renovation there. I didn't want to think about that. I'd have to, I realized—both buildings were too much like Howard's house. But I didn't have to think about it now.

I looked through the empty rooms, but the only extra accoutrements in the drab cells were metal hangers, and not many of them. Nothing to titillate Agent Drem. And nothing to indicate he'd been here. But of course even if Drem had decided to come Friday night, he hadn't arrived. Had he been looking for the person who stood him up at the Film Archives? Or was he headed here for something connected with the hotel books? Of course, if Lyn Takai was being straight when she said Drem hadn't audited the hotel books, it didn't really matter what they said. What mattered was what Drem *thought* might be in them.

I headed downstairs. When I passed the desk, Pereira was scouring the registration records and looked in her element. Moon, on the other hand, was fingering his stuffed clouds. I walked on past them to the back of the hotel where I'd been last night.

Down here, dust covered the hallway. The pounding, more regular now, came from room 3 with the easy-access entrance window and pile of boards.

I was halfway through the door when I spotted Ron, the blond linebacker type, Saturday night's host at the window. He stood there now, hammer in hand. In the corner behind him was a tiny corner bathroom sink with a big forked crack in it. It took me a moment to recognize it as the one I'd seen outside Lyn Takai's.

Ron stopped, wiped his plaid sleeve across his forehead, and turned around. "You back?"

I smiled. "You still here?"

"Hey, lady, I live here."

"Looks more like slaving than living," I said, slipping into Ron's view of life.

"The only reason I haven't got two hammers is Simonov's too cheap."

"And the reason you don't care about that lumpy cot is you're too exhausted?"

He sighed. There was a yellow-Labrador-retriever quality about him. He'd look right at home flopped on the lawn. But you wouldn't want to throw the ball too often and expect him to bring it back.

"You doing Lyn Takai's plumbing in your spare time?" I asked, letting a note of irony come through. Extra work in spare time was surely a concept that hadn't darkened Ron's brow.

"Not plumbing. I don't do pipes. I just swapped the sink for her."

"Looks like that was a wise decision on her part," I said, recalling the sink with the blue-tulip design, now in her bathroom.

"Yeah, but it's going to be a pain in the ass for whoever takes care of this place. Guys they're renting to now aren't going to complain, but when they get ready for real money guests, they're going to have to yank this baby out again."

"And the sink she got is better, right?"

"It'd have to be. For one thing, it's twenty years newer. And it doesn't have a big crack." Ron leaned back against the wall. Had he been a yellow Lab, he would have started scratching behind his ear with his hind leg. Clearly, he was prepared to make the most of this diversion. "Old is only good if you're talking good condition."

"Right." I gave a wave and headed back toward the lobby. I was almost to the front desk before I heard a tentative tap of the hammer. Pereira was still at the registration book. Moon was seated in the swivel, arms crossed. Lyn Takai was headed to the front door.

"Lyn," I called. "One more thing."

Irritably, she stopped. I said, "Can you show me the financial records for exchanging the sink in your studio for the one in back?"

"Records? They're just two old sinks." She was glaring at me, but it was the unsteady stare of someone who's on shaky ground.

Pereira looked up, eyes widening. "You exchanged your personal property for hotel property?"

"Yeah, so? Look, I oversee half the work here. I have to make decisions all the time. We're not talking about brand-new items with prices on them. Things like these sinks are from the salvage."

"But they still have value." Pereira put up her hand to forestall comment. "It doesn't matter if you think it's a waste of time. The IRS won't. They take a real dim view of using rental property for your own house and not having sales figures both ways."

"Philip Drem found out about that, didn't he?" I insisted.

She shook her head angrily, then stopped. "Hell, I don't know. He asked to use the bathroom last week at my house. So he saw the old one there and the new one in the yard. He asked me where I got it. That took me by surprise. But by then, I didn't assume anything was a friendly question. I told him it came from a friend. He didn't say anything else. I hoped he'd forgotten it."

"Did he seem like he might have recognized the sink from here?"

"How could he? He's never been here."

"You're sure?"

"Believe it," Moon said. "Scookie's carried on about the guy so much that we'd sooner rent a room to the devil."

"We were renovating the room. We had the sink out anyway," she said—poor explanation.

"So you rented out the room up till last week?"

"Yeah," said Lyn, just as Moon said, "No."

Pereira flipped back a page in the registration book. "Room three?"

"Right." Lyn moved closer, eyeing the book with the same intensity Pereira had. "Hey, there's just a line through it. Go back another week." Pereira flipped another page. "Line there too. Mason, what's going on here?"

If Moon could have rolled his chair out the front door, he would have. As it was, he slipped to the farthest corner from Takai. "It was a comp. Ron had a room upstairs last week, and he's been in number three since Saturday. Before that, it was the girl who cleaned the rooms."

"The blond?" Lyn demanded. That didn't sound like a recommendation for housekeeping standards.

"Right. Maria."

"Maria Zalles?" I asked.

He nodded.

Maria Zalles had had room 3 Friday night when Philip Drem was killed. By Saturday, she was gone from the hotel. She'd left *before* I talked to her. She hadn't left Berkeley then, or even deviated from her routine of going to the Film Archives. "How did she come to work here, Moon?"

"She needed the work. She was, you know, between things. We didn't want to throw her out. We needed a maid. She was here."

"Whose decision was that?" Lyn demanded.

Moon shrugged. "You know how things are."

"So, Mason," I said, "your agreement with her was what? Straight trade, room for work?"

"Yeah."

"What did she do for food?" She wasn't hungry and destitute when I'd run into her at the Film Archives.

He shrugged again. "She must have had something else. But
whatever it was, it didn't keep her from cleaning here. She did a
good job."

Now it was clear why Maria Zalles had given me a false
address—to keep from telling me she lived here. Philip Drem
left the Film Archives where he'd been with Maria, felt woozy,
aimed his bike down here. The question was, was he coming
here for help or because he felt the prick of the needle and
figured Maria had done it?

"Where is Maria?" I asked.

"Gone," Mason said. "You can search her room, but I've
been in there, and there's not a thing of hers left."

"Why did she leave Saturday?"

He shrugged again. "She just said she was quitting and going
to stay with a friend. I figured she'd gotten a better job."

"Who's the friend?"

"Got me."

I asked about forwarding address, other friends, phone calls,
letters. But from what Moon and Takai admitted knowing of
Maria Zalles, she could have been a hermit instead of a woman
with a friend who happens to offer her a room.

Maria Zalles had seemed shocked when I told her of Drem's
death. If she hadn't known about Drem's death earlier, why
would she have left the hotel? Coincidence? Or it was not Maria but the friend who wanted her out of the hotel? A friend
who was nervous about the murder and Maria's connection to
Philip Drem?

I spent half an hour searching room 3, hoping for some lead
to the mysterious friend. But for all the connection to Maria
Zalles it held, it might always have been Ron the workman's
room.

When I was finished going over it, Pereira was waiting. She followed me back to the station, into my office and settled herself on Howard's desk. Automatically she glanced around the office, checking for food or drink.

I gave her the background on Maria Zalles. "And so, Connie, it would take a naive trust to believe Maria Zalles's story that she just happened to run into Drem at the Archives."

"The hell with that, Smith. Let's look at this from a tax agent's point of view. Maria mentions that sink that they took out of her room, moans about how nice the tulip design was, and complains about the rotten cracked one they're replacing it with. Drem may remember the cracked one from Lyn Takai's yard. But even if not, he sees the tulip sink in Lyn Takai's bathroom. For a bulldog, that's steak tartare. He'd have moved on from Takai's returns to the hotel's in a flash."

"And Lyn Takai would have been in a lot of trouble?"

"Depends. The sink switch is illegal, but it's not a big financial swindle. It depends on what Drem chose to do. And, of course, what else he might uncover about Takai."

"And what he might uncover about the hotel?"

Pereira nodded. "Right. And believe me, Smith, with the state of those books, even if Drem couldn't get thousands of dollars from Moon and company, he'd have had Mason Moon chained to those books for weeks."

CHAPTER

18

It wasn't till I got home and was standing on the stoop over-looking Howard's newly replanted azalea that I realized I hadn't had dinner. And there was not likely to be any food in the fridge here.

But suddenly the exhaustion from the day hit. Even the prospect of Chocolate Chocolate Shower ice cream couldn't tempt me back into the car. I trudged past the resettled azalea and opened the door.

Heaven.

Or more accurately, pizza. Or utterly accurately, the smell thereof.

In the living room was the second surprise. Howard.

"You still working on your taxes?" I asked, looking from him to the pizza—pepperoni, anchovy, black olive, and green onion. It looked wonderful. Howard, on the other hand, looked like the pizza might two days from now: dry, lifeless, and curled in at the edges. His arms were crossed, his head down, his brow wrinkled. In front of him, the pizza lay untouched.

"I can't do any more till tomorrow. I've got a meeting with the bookkeeper for Fancy Food Restaurant Service. That's where the Nob Hill Club gets its ingredients."

"Then how come you're not out taking advantage of your

freedom? You've been in the house all weekend. Aren't you going stir-crazy?" I certainly would have.

"Can't leave here."

The light was beginning to dawn. If I'd felt bad before . . . I waited.

"Sunday night. I've spent the whole damned weekend watching for the plant thief. I'm not going to leave now. I know the criminal mind. Sunday, when no one suspects . . ."

I sank onto the sofa beside him. We'd always handled issues circumspectly, lightly, jokingly—trusting that the other would get the point and appreciate the lack of leaden touch. We'd laughed at Quality Time and Serious Talk. But now I wondered if fifteen minutes of serious talk three days ago would have saved the lunacy I'd made of the weekend. I'd turned him into a hostage and myself into my grandmother. I could almost feel the clammy air-conditioned air of that East Coast house and hear the whir of the sawmill outside.

Howard motioned to the pizza. Suddenly I wasn't hungry. Or almost not. But it wouldn't do to refuse food—too out of character for me. I picked up a slice and bit into it an instant before Howard said, "Watch out—it's hot!"

As I swished his beer over the burned roof of my mouth, I steeled myself to keep from racing out, throwing myself into the car, and heading for the freeway to anywhere. I looked over at him. His face was drawn, and the skin on his cheeks hung inward as if it were too tired to stand up. His eyes were half closed, not tired by weighing, pondering, ready to be amused. The fun guy, the guy willing to take a chance—that was how most everyone saw Howard. I'd seen beneath that to the man who took lots of chances on things that didn't really matter but few on those that counted.

One of those chances had been on me, on showing me that nugget of what he really was. I just hoped I hadn't yanked it out and trampled it. I pulled back from the thought. It was too painful to think I'd never again see that nugget but only the public Howard.

Howard had fallen in so beautifully with the theme of my sting. I'd almost have thought he was a co-conspirator. Maybe he'd spent too much time in sting mode. He leaned back, his left hand holding the pizza, the right on my thigh. The stereo was playing "City of New Orleans," traveling music. I wanted to . . .

But I'd spent my childhood and teenage years watching out, being careful, walking nervously at night when I was alone. I'd heard the tales of girls whose clothes were too tight, short, skimpy, sexy; girls who "got what they deserved." I'd heard them, I realized, from my grandmother in that prison of a house as we sat on the horsehair sofa by the front window looking out at the normal teenage girls I was terrified I'd never be like. I had blocked that memory all these years. I hadn't felt really free till I'd joined the force. And even now, I had to admit, the message of those myths was ingrained in my cells. Now I fought against it, purposely didn't take safe routes, made myself face dangers I could have avoided. But no matter how hard I fought, that ingrained message—"watch out; be careful; don't get yourself raped"—would never disappear.

I took another bite of pizza, chewed, swallowed, and forced myself to return to the question of the azalea. Surely Howard of all people would agree it would be a pity to waste such a good educational setup as this one. And at the bottom of it all was the fact that the need not to be caged by society, by *him*, was too integral to me to ignore.

I shrugged. In for a flower, in for a bush. "So you figure the plant thief will be back. It's always more dangerous at night. You don't think of this as a bad neighborhood. It's not a place where you're afraid to walk alone. But"—I let myself sigh—"in times like these there's no place an azalea is really safe." It wasn't quite "A woman always has to be careful to avoid certain areas of town." But unless the plant grew feet, it was as close as I was going to come. Hoping I wasn't laying it on too thick, I said, "You could bring them all indoors."

"They'd die."

My God! Had he thought of that? He was in a lot deeper than I'd realized. But in one sense it was good. When the sting stung, he'd have little trouble getting the point. God, my grandmother would have been proud. "And you wouldn't want to put them in front of the windows." (I wished I could say scantily dressed.) "It could just be too much of a temptation for the thief."

Howard snatched the beer. The can was empty. He hurled it to the floor and crushed it with his heel. "Just let him try, dammit."

"If he's obsessed, you'd be creating such a temptation. I can see his lawyer saying, 'Detective Howard, you should have known the kind of drives my client has. He's not a well man. He couldn't help himself.' "

"What!" Howard stared at me. "What kind of bullshit . . ."

"Come on, Howard. He'd be saying it's nearly entrapment. And then, if the lawyer questioned you about your past, if he found out how many stings you'd planned . . . The promiscuity of it." I couldn't keep from laughing.

Howard was not amused. With a snort, he leapt up and strode to the fridge for more beer—with a detour past the front window. Looking at Howard's short angry steps, his tense jaw, the laugh lines pulled into a scowl, I wondered if I'd delved into a level of him that I didn't want to know.

But it was too late now. I said, "It really must be frustrating for you to be stuck in here because of someone else's inability to control their urges."

" 'Inability'! Jeez, Jill, you sound like a social worker. Inability nothing. No one *has* to steal plants. This guy's stealing because he figures he can get away with it. The guy's a thief!"

"The rape of the leaf."

"Huh?"

I picked up another piece of pizza and waited. But the Popeian penny didn't drop then. Howard paced to the window and back, snatched a slice of pizza, sat down, sprang up, checked the window. His tension, and mine, filled the room more thickly than that air-conditioned air ever had. I finished my beer and announced I was going to take advantage of the empty house to have a long bath. "Care to join me?"

Howard grinned. For the first time tonight he looked like *Howard*: eyes sparkling, secret grin with just a soupçon of come-hither leer. Then the grin faded. "It'd be too noisy. He could dig up half the yard, and I wouldn't hear."

I stood up and kissed the top of his head. "I'll miss you."

His hand wandered down my back. "Maybe if we left the door open and . . ." He let his hand drop. "No. We'd have to be so careful, it'd be ridiculous."

I gave his hand a squeeze and headed upstairs.

I had barely slid into the water when Howard stuck his head in the room, stood listening, muttered, "Nah," and left.

"He's got till midnight," I said to myself.

Half an hour later, I got out of the tub, pulled on a T-shirt, and headed for bed. Howard was sitting atop the comforter in jeans and the L. L. Bean snap-front sweatshirt I'd gotten him for Arbor Day. The french blue matched his eyes; the cut outlined the angles of his sleekly muscled shoulders. I pulled the top snap free. "Coming to bed?"

"I'll just be overdressed," he said, weaving his fingers between mine.

"Jeans and sweats? That *will* limit things. How about mittens?"

"It'll only be for tonight," he muttered.

Clearly it wasn't just clothes that would inhibit us. I slid under the covers. "And if the thief doesn't come tonight?"

"Well, then tomorrow. We'll have the morning, Jill. He won't come in daylight." He ran his hand under the covers down the side of my breast. "I thought you liked mornings."

"What if he doesn't come tomorrow either? Yours aren't the only azaleas in town. He could be digging up northside tonight and saving yours till the weekend."

"I'll worry about that then." He was massaging my breast as he spoke.

"And even if you catch him," I forced myself to say, "once there's a market for stolen plants, there'll be other thieves. Are you going to sleep in your clothes for the rest of your life, or the azalea's?"

"Jill—"

"No—"

He stared down at me, his hand still now. "You want me to just let the guy steal my plants—"

"No, I want you to think, really think, how it'd be watching over them all night, every night, night after night, forever, never being able to go out and leave them unguarded, or having to get a guard for them, never being able to leave them out because they might entice some man who'd want to dig them up"—Howard's eyes widened—"never being too provocative" —his mouth dropped open—"never exciting the lust of—"

"You?" He yanked his hand free. His body was quivering as if he were afraid to move, for fear of what he'd do. I don't think I'd ever seen him so angry. It was as if time had stopped and then inched forward, and his face flashed between disbelief, hurt, and fury. "The plants are okay? No one is . . ."

". . . going to rape your plants. No."

His face was dead white, his voice very soft, as he said, "How could you do this to me?"

I swallowed hard and pushed myself up. The air was icy on my back. "I wanted you to feel what it's like to be confined—"

"Well, you certainly succeeded." He jumped up and stood leaning over the bed, squeezing the comforter in the middle of his fists. "Maybe you'd like me to feel what it's like to have a leg amputated. Or an eye out. Or maybe you'd just like to go straight to being God."

"Howard, this is how women feel every day of our lives."

He yanked the comforter off the bed. "You lied to me."

"I'm sorry about that," I said. God, I *was* sorry. "But society lies to women all the time: We love you; we'll protect you *until* you go where you're not allowed, *until* you complain about harassment, *until* you pretend you're equal, or free!"

He stared, but his expression didn't soften. "How could you?"

I gritted my teeth to keep from yelling. "Do you really want to know?"

Still holding the corner of the quilt, he crossed his arms over his chest. He wasn't tapping his foot as he waited, but he might as well.

I chose my words carefully. "It is asking a great deal of anyone to know what someone else is going through. But it's asking even more of someone who is sure he will never have to go through that himself."

"Well, I'm sorry I'm such a lout. It was magnanimous of you to put up with me all this time."

"Howard, if you can't make the effort to understand what it's like to always be kept in second place, then much as you think you love me, you'll always be looking down at me."

Howard walked slowly toward the door. Halfway there he realized he was dragging the quilt and dropped it. "I'll never be able to trust you again." He opened the door and walked out.

I got up, grabbed the quilt, and ran to the window to throw it down on him. I couldn't get the sash up! I stood shaking with anger, and desolation. Howard and I had never had an argument like this. Wrapping the quilt around me, I stood at the window and watched his Land-Rover back out of the driveway; turn, tires squealing; and roar away. Then I recalled the other thing my grandmother had said, not of me but of my father. "Failure," she'd muttered every time. "The man'll never amount to anything." And each time, her dry fingers had tightened on my shoulder. I was too young then to know if my anger and my fear were for him or for me.

Then I would have run after the car all the way to Allentown, Pennsylvania, or Bayside, Queens. Now it was all I could do to restrain myself from grabbing my belongings and slamming out of the house.

But I couldn't leave. I had to stay here, for Howard and for me.

I pulled the quilt tighter and stared into the dark. I don't know how long it was before I'd calmed down enough to admit that with the azalea sting I'd chosen the worst vehicle to make my point. I'd been asking Howard to put himself in the one-down position he'd spent his life avoiding, and to be the butt of a sting while he did it. I should apologize. . . .

But women spend their lives apologizing, thinking of others, making nice. I couldn't do that, not if Howard didn't speak first. A lifetime of suppressed anger would clench my throat closed.

Howard of all people might excuse the sting. Would he, the Master of Stings, be willing to swear off for life? No way. If he swore off, he'd mourn every situation that cried "sting." Being the Master of Sting was part of his aura. I couldn't imagine him giving up that little grin and swagger that went with it. I pulled the blankets tighter around me, but neither it nor all my analysis of this warmed me.

■ ■ ■

Monday morning, I rose before the alarm. Howard hadn't come to bed. I was halfway to the bathroom before I realized that it had been Howard's steps in the hall outside that had woken me. And once in the bathroom, I could hear him walking across the bedroom to his closet.

We didn't argue well. But we did silence great. From my grandmother I'd learned that the person who holds her breath longest wins. I'd won with a few lovers that way—waited them out while they screamed, looked at them like they were jerks. The game works well when you play with a screamer, but when two strong silents go at it, it's hell. I picked up my swimbag and headed for the pool.

I'd already done a lap when Howard arrived. I do flip turns, head down, no time to look around at the end of a lap. So I had only a vague sense of Howard standing in the next lane talking to Betty Davis, one of the regulars, talking a long time.

Monday is always rushed with the weekend's in-custodys. Detectives' Morning Meeting is always crowded with the weekend's crimes. Howard didn't come back to the office afterward. Sometimes he didn't. Any other time I wouldn't have noted it. My IN box was full. I had notes from Sunday's interviews that still needed to be dictated. I had to round up Pereira's reports and Leonard's and Heling's, and I couldn't do that till I'd dictated my own. No way to avoid an hour in the dictating cubicle.

When I was through, I veered past Pereira's desk. Howard pushed himself up and headed for the door. I let a moment pass, giving Pereira a chance to fill me in. She stared down at the hot-car report from Evening Watch, even though it would have been read at the Day Watch meeting. What had Howard said to her?

"So, Connie, how're you coming with the Inspiration books?"

She laughed a little too enthusiastically. "With them, you're talking an hour or a lifetime. Anything could be hidden in there, but you couldn't pay me enough to find it. No way to tell whether half the rooms were empty or every inch was filled with carpenters, roofers, and maids."

I started to ask Pereira if it would have been worth Drem's while to plow through. But I knew the answer. It would have depended on how badly he'd wanted to get Mason Moon. And only Tori Iversen could tell me that.

CHAPTER

19

The fog was beginning to clear by the time I got to Tori Iversen's flat. Tori peered out the window. Recognizing me, she said, "Go on to Phil's place."

On the other side of the building two days' mail was poking out of Philip Drem's box like a welcome flag for thieves. I pulled it out and carried it inside, stepping over his bicycle in the middle of the living-room floor. As I was dropping the mail on his desk beneath the *Ban Styrofoam* and *Clean Up Toxic Waste* posters, the curtain to the window to Tori's living room pulled back.

Tori's living room was unchanged—bare wood, white cotton sofa, the wooden-slat chair nearly touching the window to Drem's flat. That chair must have been there since yesterday afternoon when I told her her husband was dead, with its back to the room, facing a curtain no one would open again.

"How are you holding up?" I asked.

"Okay. I've had to make some arrangements. It's taken time, but I've got plenty of time."

In fact, Tori looked okay. Her skin seemed less dry and wan than it had before. Her light hair looked less dry too. Maybe that was because she had the overhead light on in the dimness of the foggy morning. But when I looked more closely, I realized she hadn't washed her hair. Because, I suspected, she assumed no one would be coming home to see it. Again the awful aloneness of her caged life struck me—days that faded into nights that became days, with no change but the amount of light. Like being dead. Entombed. I swallowed hard, pushed the thought away. And I wondered how often Philip Drem had been taken unawares by thoughts like this and shoved them away.

Tori was standing behind her chair. Her hands tightened on the top slat of the back, and her voice was shaky as she said, "Have you found Phil's killer?"

I'd seen that mixed reaction from other survivors. They were anxious to know who the villain was. But the investigation was the last extension of their husband's, wife's, lover's life, and just as desperately, they did not want that to end. "No, Tori. I've come to clarify a few questions."

She nodded slowly, then walked around the wooden chair and sat.

I took the place in Phil's chair facing her, so that our knees almost met at the window glass. "Are you sure Phil didn't blame Mason Moon for the accident?"

"I told him often enough. Mason was a victim too."

I leaned forward. "Tori, suppose Phil did get the chance to harass Mason Moon?"

"Phil wouldn't do that."

That didn't convince me. I was sure it wouldn't have reassured Moon. I wondered just how far Moon would go to keep Agent Drem from his hotel books.

"Tori, let's try a different tack. Have you heard the names Lyn Takai, Ethan Simonov, or Scookie Hogan?"

"No," she said slowly.

"How about Maria Zalles?"

There was no hesitation there. "Never heard of her. Who are these people?"

"The first three are taxpayers Philip either was or might have been auditing."

"Phil never talked about his work," she said quickly.

"Never?" I asked, amazed.

"I told you Phil hated his job. He sold them his forty hours, no more."

"So what did you talk about?"

She leaned back against the hard slats. "Phil told me about bicycling, the races, the courses, his training. He was proud of his times. He really was a good racer. And then there was the news—what was going on in the legislature, how antismoking bills were progressing, what congressmen needed to be lobbied about genetic research. Phil was always on top of who we had to write or who I should call the next day."

For the first time today I picked up a thin whine in her voice. "Who *you* should call?"

"Well, he couldn't be calling Sacramento from work, could he? But I was here all day with nothing to do." The whine was clearer.

I said, "Did you talk about your illness too?"

"Oh, yeah. It was always the first thing Phil asked when he got home: How was I today? Any reaction to the newsprint? Or to the dyes in the tissues or the chemicals they use to decaffeinate coffee?"

"You drink coffee?" The question came out before I could censor it.

Her eyes narrowed. "You're just like Phil! I'm not a porcelain statue, for chrissake. If Phil had had his way, he would have found a mechanism for me to stop eating and breathing altogether. He would have wrapped me in cellophane and taped the package safely shut." She laughed bitterly. "Except that I react to petroleum products."

"He wanted you to be safe," I put in.

"Mummified!" She sank back farther in the chair, shaking

her head. "You're right, of course. He just wanted me to be safe."

I began to see their relationship more clearly now, all too clearly. "You've already had to give up so much, it must be wrenching to forgo anything else, particularly coffee," I said with feeling, "especially if it's not doing you any harm."

She leaned forward, "But see, we can't be sure it's not. If I get an attack a day later, how do we know the coffee, the residue of caffeine, or the uric acid didn't combine with something else and set things off?"

"But you could say that about anything."

She held up a finger. "Now you're beginning to see. Once your immune system goes, everything out there is potentially lethal. It's like this: You're wearing a tweed suit. One kind of thread in it makes you itch. You don't know which one. You narrow the choices and pull the blue thread. But maybe by that time the irritants have rubbed off on the yellow threads next to the blues, and now the yellows seem like bad guys, so you pull them. But you don't get any better. You start over pulling tan and azure and mauve, thread after thread. But you don't feel better. In fact, you're worse because now you've been stressed out from the allergy and worrying about it, and trying to find the lethal thread. But you can't stop. You've got to find the thread. And so the whole process keeps going on and on until you're naked and freezing."

I shivered. I wished I could reach out to her, but of course the glass separated us. Glass, and the murder, and my gut-level fear of a life like hers. I said, "It's really hard when you don't know what you're looking for. Or what you've done. Like you're playing a game without having been told all the rules."

She nodded, as people do when you've seen the tip of the iceberg. I waited for her to fill me in on the ice beneath the water, but she didn't. Again I was impressed with how controlled she was. I thought about her and Drem and the coffee.

And about Howard and me. Howard and I had handled our frustrations by stomping out. Tori couldn't do that. She couldn't even pull her curtain and be assured Drem wouldn't yank it back open. She could never do much more than she was doing right now—purse her lips and block him, or me, out.

It took me a moment to formulate my question. I understood her situation so well, it made it all too easy for me to poke into the open sore. I glanced quickly at Tori's tense, controlled posture, her tight lips. In a flat, emotionless voice I said, "Philip changed his whole life because of your illness. How could you continue to drink coffee if it would aggravate your allergies and make you more of a burden to him?"

Her hands flew up from the armrests. "Why didn't I just fucking kill myself, right? And let poor Phil out from under!" She smacked her fist against the glass. I jolted back.

"Do you know what it's like living with a martyr?" she demanded. "He brought my food, he opened my packages, he showered three times, then waited till I went into the bathroom and came over and vacuumed. He never wanted thanks, never accepted it. There was nothing I could ever do to repay him. Every day I got further in debt!" She stood up, stalked around to the back of her chair, and plopped her arm atop it. "What could I give him?"

"Love?"

"If you mean sex, it was too dangerous. I had an attack two years ago, right afterwards." She shook her head. "No, nothing so simple for Philip. You want to know? Look around you."

I turned and stared at the officelike room with its posters.

"Phil was always an obsessive. I just didn't realize it before I got sick. Before that, he was caught up in travel, in our plans to go around the world, to make the trip last as long as possible. That's a socially acceptable obsession. But then the explosion burned out my immune system, and no more travel. So Phil got into bicycle racing and environmental illness. If he's not out on a timed course, he's protesting perfume sales, or chemicals in new carpeting, or fumes from copy machines. Or car exhaust, or motorcycles. It became his goddamn life!"

I said softly, "Mentally, he was as imprisoned by your illness as you are?"

"He chose to be." She held out a hand. "That sounds crass, doesn't it? He devotes his life to me, and I shrug it off. But look, the thing is, it wasn't me he was devoted to. He was a disciple of my illness. After a while it was like I was merely the host body for these allergies. Look at those posters: smoke, fumes, Styrofoam. They're not my causes. They were his." She sank back against the slats of her chair. "I was a stained-glass artist. I loved creating beautiful windows—the planning, the buying glass, sketching the patterns on oil paper, cutting the paper, scoring the glass, tapping the line till it broke. I loved the soldering. The whole process. I'll never even be able to have a window like that in my house, much less make one again. Gone, forever. Okay, I've accepted that. I've given up going out. Being able to touch other people. Feeling any material but cotton. I know I'll never again taste Coca-Cola, chocolate, alcohol, bread, cheese, meat—anything that makes eating more than a chore."

"And then Phil starts on the coffee."

"Yeah, the coffee. And if I'd given that up, he'd have moved on to some other poison."

Her hands were shaking, but still she kept them on the chair arms. By now, I would have killed for a cup of Peet's coffee. Drem had audited her life and disallowed her everything but her illness. Or was his constantly recharged anger about environmental assaults his way of avoiding the bottom of the iceberg—because he couldn't bear to see her life through her eyes?

Slowly I said, "You'd given up everything and had nothing but your illness, and he co-opted that."

Her look told me I hadn't seen the bottom of the ice either.

"There was a point when I realized Phil had gotten so caught up in environmental illness that he'd forgotten me altogether. He was like sediment that hardened around a bird's egg millennia ago. The fossil is still there, but the egg's decayed and disappeared, nothing more than a hole in the fossil." Tears ran down her face. It was the first time I'd seen her cry, and I knew it wasn't for Drem but herself. I swallowed hard, wishing I could reach out to her, knowing no one could, ever. Finally she dragged her hand across her face, wiping away the tears, a rough movement she would never have allowed herself in front of Drem. "I haven't cried for years," she said softly. "I don't know whether I was more caged by the illness or his protectiveness of it."

Caged! I sat forward, shocked out of my emotions. Like a bird in a cage. A canary in a cage. "You're Canary's Keen, aren't you. You're the death-game master."

Probably another time she would not have admitted it. Even now she hesitated, balancing the Homicide detective against the confidante. She searched me with her eyes.

I watched her as she laughed, and her whole body relaxed as if the varnish of tension had dissolved. She'd given up so much. What more could I do to her? Imprisoned behind her glass, she was free.

Finally she said, "It's one of the few hobbies I can do like a normal person." She laughed sardonically. "Or maybe I just like celebrating that others are worse off than I."

I restrained a sigh. I'd tried hard to feel what she felt—police-manual writers would call it getting overinvolved. I was relieved it had paid off. As game master, she'd have copies of every death-game player's list. I said, "Phil was on a few lists. Whose?"

She shook her head. "I can't betray my players. It's just a game. The rules clearly state that you don't get points for a death you're involved in. No San Quentin branch."

Normally I would have reminded her that it was her husband's murder we were dealing with. But I knew that wouldn't work here. Asking her to betray the game meant taking that too away from her. Drem taking it away. I didn't think she was ready to be that free. I said, "I could get a warrant and force you to show me those lists."

She nodded.

"Scookie Hogan, Mason Moon, Ethan Simonov, Lyn Takai. Who among them were players?"

She sat tapping her teeth, deciding. "You won't ask me any more names, just these?"

"Deal."

"Okay, among them, just Scookie."

"She got a lot of points for Phil's death. Was he her bonus choice?"

"Yeah. But to be fair to her, Phil was another person's bonus choice. It was a real shock to find how well known a minor bureaucrat could be."

"A tax agent," I reminded her.

"I was wrong about not having cried for years. I cried the day those forms came in." She walked stiffly around the chair and leaned over the back. "Phil was a wonderful guy once. He wanted to go everywhere, see new things, let them stretch his mind. Instead, my illness chained him here to a job he loathed and shrank him down to a despot." Tears rolled from her eyes, but she seemed not to notice them.

Was it worse, I wondered, to have the man you loved die or to find he'd changed so much that only memory reminds you you once loved him? I pulled my jacket tighter around my shoulders. "I have to ask you this. Are you sure he never got involved with other women?"

She shrugged. "As much as I can be."

"Did he have no other outlet? Nothing to look forward to? No long bike trips, for instance?"

"No. Racers don't ride for scenery. Phil rode to win. It was like everything else he did, a contest. His reward was when he got a restaurant to go all nonsmoking, or a company to install windows that opened."

I nodded. Nothing in Drem's flat suggested otherwise. "But still, your immune system could regenerate. You might get better."

"Maybe. We both gave up thinking about that a couple of years ago. Phil even started looking around for a place we could live that would be free of irritants."

"Like where?"

"Good question. People used to go to Arizona for their health, but now with the copper smelting they *get* allergies there. In Alaska I'd be indoors all the time, surrounded by housing synthetics. There's nowhere on the continent that would be safe. Phil started thinking about islands in the middle of the ocean." She laughed, a scratchy sound. "Of course, he got obsessed. He has a ton of vacation days. So he was going to check out an island off Samoa."

"When?"

"Some time this week—he didn't know which day it'd be. He picked up the ticket on his lunch hour Friday."

"Which airline?"

"I don't know. It never came up."

I asked for the name of his travel agent. No travel agent. He'd taken BART to the airport for it. But if Drem had gotten his ticket Friday, it would have been in his briefcase when he died. Where was that briefcase? And despite Tori Iversen's certainty, I couldn't help wondering if Philip Drem wouldn't have found a week or so in Samoa more pleasant with a companion, particularly one who was the next thing to Tori. And the last person known to have seen that briefcase.

But a ticket to Samoa wouldn't be cheap. And if the islands worked out for Tori—something I doubted—surely a chemical-free paradise would be a tourist mecca and become chemical-full within a year. But if the plan did work, how would Drem have supported the couple once they moved there? I asked.

"Phil made decent money. And there's not much we spend it on."

That answer showed her financial innocence more than anything else. But Drem wouldn't have thought that way. I tried another tack. "Tori, when did Phil start looking for places to move?"

She lifted her foot and rested it on the edge of the chair. "I had a bad attack a couple of months ago. Phil panicked. He said anything was worth a try rather than watching me die here."

"A couple of months ago. Winter. Is that a normal time for an allergy attack?"

"I don't have 'normal' times. And that attack might not have been so bad, but Phil was away that week, and I let it go on longer than he would."

"He was in Fresno, IRS meeting, substituting for his group manager?"

"Right."

"Did he talk about the TCMP when he got back?"

"Only that they set the local standards for a couple of things, like business meals. Nothing interesting. Phil hated the meetings even more than he hated the job normally."

But he had come home from that meeting and begun to think about expensive travel.

20

"Drem didn't use a travel agent," I said to Pereira, Acosta, and Leonard. "He picked up his ticket from the airport. If he wrote a check, he didn't record it."

"An IRS agent?" Pereira asked, amazed.

"If he paid with a credit card, he could be in Samoa in less time than it would take us to track that down. So where is that ticket?"

Pereira was sitting on Howard's desk. Leonard was propped against the wall between desk and door with a stance so out of kilter that he could have slid into the Avenue scene without a ripple. Acosta stood on the other side of the door in the narrow space between the ends of the desks and the walls. Nothing on his person touched desk or wall; there was just the suggestion of a flare to his chiseled nostrils.

"Drem picked up the ticket Friday at noon. It's not in his desk at work."

"Smith," Acosta said, "obsessives don't leave their papers around. Trust me on this."

I glanced at Acosta. There was the slimmest suggestion of a smile on his angular face. He went on. "Ten to one, Drem had his ticket in his briefcase, and whoever lifted that has it. It'll just be a matter of going to the airport and seeing who comes as Philip Drem."

"Or Philippa Drem," Leonard offered.

I said, "The last person who saw Drem with his briefcase was Maria Zalles. Zalles is missing. Chances are, she'll be Philippa Drem. What airline would put up a fight against the argument that their agent had misheard Ms. Drem's name?"

"Let's hope she's not flying out of San Francisco. If there is one place you could lose a suspect flying out, that's it," Pereira said. "A flight to Hawaii, in a foggy April, with passengers who've chilled their butts all winter . . . It'll be jammed. More flights than from Oakland, thus more flyers, more friends, relatives, kids running through crowds, toddlers wandering around the waiting areas—just try setting up a chase there. Luggage carts, cabs coming and going, hotel vans, buses, and cars. And rush-hour traffic on the freeway—"

"Enough!" I said. "I take your point. If I can get the whole department over there, maybe I have a chance. I need to find Zalles before she leaves town."

"If she hasn't already," Acosta said. "The woman had a free room at the Inspiration Hotel. She's been gone from there for days."

Leonard leaned forward. He looked as if he would have liked to clamber up on Howard's desk, but Pereira already occupied most of that. "Zalles could have taken the connector van to the airport Saturday right after you left her and gotten a room at one of the hotels."

"With an alias. She is not a stupid woman, so by now"—Acosta glanced down at his watch—"she has checked out and gone to the airport."

Leonard moved in closer, virtually arm-to-arm with Pereira. "She could be at the gate for any flight on any airline, in any concourse. Just another passenger. When one flight boards, she moves to another, and another, see?" Leonard grabbed Pereira's arm, shaking it with enthusiasm. "If she didn't need to sleep, she could live out there at SFO the rest of her life."

Pereira extricated her arm, but Leonard didn't notice. "In O'Hare she could probably do it, sleep and all."

I sighed. "I can't tell you what a comfort this is to me. If Zalles is still in Berkeley, we've got a chance to catch her here on our own turf and avoid the airport horrors you've all been kind enough to describe. Acosta, you call the airlines and have them check reservations."

"For how long?"

"All week. We only know Drem was leaving this week. Then start on the airport van companies, have them check the last two days for Zalles or Drem. Give them her description too. Chances are, she'd have left from the Durant Hotel pickup. Leonard, try the airport hotels—your reward for the suggestion. We need to have another go at anyone who might know her whereabouts. Connie, you take the Inspiration Hotel crew —Simonov, Moon, and Takai."

Leonard nodded his shaggy head, turned, and started out, his gun slapping against his tan pantleg. "Leonard," I said as he reached for the door, "what's the word on the street person who said he saw a patrol officer at the Drem scene?"

Leonard shrugged. "Vanished. Probably boosted a better bike and pedaled off into the sunset."

"No one on the Avenue has an idea where he went?"

"Not that twenty bucks would buy. Unless I'm wrong, fifty wouldn't do it either. I'd say Sierra just decided Berkeley was too hot, and split." He waited a moment, then walked out.

Leonard was so at home on the Avenue, he'd know whom to trust, whom to get rid of. He'd been at the scene. He . . . I pushed back the suspicion. Leonard had been a veteran when I was a rookie. You don't toss away your career for a trip to the South Pacific.

"What about you, Jill?" Pereira said. "Who're you checking out?"

"Scookie Hogan." I paused. "And if that doesn't pan out, Herman Ott."

"How is your favorite PI involved in this one?" Acosta looked down the length of his perfectly straight nose, wrinkling it just a bit at the thought of Ott. It amazed me that immaculate Acosta had chosen this messy profession. There is a saying my Zen friend told me: "Exist in muddy waters with the purity of the lotus flower." I couldn't help imagining Acosta rinsing Berkeley off his stems each night. I wondered if his very compulsiveness made his partner Leonard so laid back.

I grabbed a donut on the way out of the station. It was maplenut, the brussels sprouts of the donut world, but there was no other choice.

By the time I got to Telegraph, the sky was gray again. Strong winds off the Pacific push the summer fog inland every afternoon and let it ease back over the ocean around ten in the morning. But winter fogs are land fogs, scummy gray layers that dim the sky and mute life beneath them. April this year clung to winter.

I left the car in a red zone off Telegraph and ran around the corner to the Med. The Med is too much an old Lefty place to have bourgeois patio seating. It does have a wall of windows that make life on the Avenue an extension of the room. But today there was nothing to see outside except people pulling their sweaters tighter and hurrying up the Avenue. Inside, the place smelled of smoke, coffee, and wet wool.

Scookie Hogan was at the same table she'd been at two days ago. *Her* table? But in contrast to the drab sixties cottons she'd been wearing then, today she sported a soft violet sweater and one of those scarves that cost more than sweaters.

I got a cappuccino and sat down at her table. "Celebrating the bonus you got for Philip Drem's death?"

"How did you know?" she asked, amazed.

"I'm a cop, Scookie. I've got connections all over town." Before the implications of that statement could fade, I said, "Where is Maria Zalles?"

"I don't know."

"Maria was the hotel maid. When she disappeared, you took over. You'd done that job before, right?"

"Well, yes. Someone has to."

"You trained Maria, right?"

"It's not a difficult job. I—"

"You were close to her. Of all the people at the hotel, you were the closest, weren't you?" Pereira would be using this same line with Moon or Takai about now.

"I suppose."

"When she came looking for the job, you arranged for her to have a room at the hotel, right?"

Scookie hesitated, then nodded a bit too quickly. She looked relieved. There was a step, a slant, something, I'd missed here. What? But I couldn't afford to slow down to worry about that. The quick pressure was forcing her answers. "What did she say when she left?"

"She didn't. She just didn't show up for work."

"You don't not show up for work when you work where you live." Maria hadn't been in room 3 Saturday. The workman had had it. "Did she sleep in another room at the hotel Saturday night?"

"No." Again the answer was too quick.

I leaned closer. "Scookie, you are the one person we know of who profited by Phil Drem's murder. In more ways than one. You got your bonus points." I shushed her with my hand. "I know you don't kill just for that, but you liked the idea of Drem dead so much that you singled him out as the person you most wanted to die. Juries are swayed by odd things, and I can promise you, Scookie, a bonus choice in the death game will be a killer with any jury."

Her face paled.

I went on. "I'll give you another chance to be straight with me. Where is Maria Zalles?"

She drew her shoulders in protectively. The fringe of her violet sweater shook. I let her think, let her contemplate the ominous possibilities. Finally she said, "She was scared. She came back Friday night and said she was going to get out of town. Go back home."

"Where's home?"

"Jersey. Someplace in Jersey."

I nodded. Then I let her create a story of how Maria Zalles had planned her departure and trip. I grew up in Jersey. I may not be able to spot every ex-Jerseyan, but I can sure as hell tell a woman who has never lived in or near the state. Maria Zalles had a bit of an accent. It wasn't from Jersey.

I gave Scookie the normal warning about not leaving town. Then I left my cup at the counter, stepped into the bathroom, and peered out through the crack in the door. Scookie Hogan was hiding something. I was betting what she was hiding was Maria Zalles. Chances were she'd take advantage of my absence and rush out to find Maria. If not, I'd have to wait outside until she decided it was safe to leave.

But the door had barely closed when Scookie headed for the street.

CHAPTER

21

Telegraph Avenue is never an easy place on which to tail. On sunny days street artists' tables and display cases line the curbs. Browsers meander beside them, half-looking at mushroom-shaped candles or braided bracelets, half-averting crashes with other distracted browsers. Pressing in against the tables, potential customers finger piles of Peruvian sweaters, displays of feather earrings lavish enough to have turned parrots into fryers, or stars-and-stripes long johns. Shopping is serious business here. And we on the force can make a month's worth of enemies barging between stained-glass panels and potential buyers.

But today, in the fog, the Avenue was as barren as the day after a closeout sale. Nearer to campus there'd be a sprinkling of the hardier or hungrier street artists and their wares, but here only a few students hurried to coffeehouses or bookstores. I might as well have had a blinking red light on my head and a sign: *Police Tail*. My only camouflages were my gray jacket and Scookie Hogan's obliviousness. I wouldn't even have tried with anyone less glazed than she.

I stood in front of the Med and watched as she meandered bareheaded across the street as if experiencing the first spring day after a Minnesota winter. The mist-laden fog coated her long gray-streaked hair; it matted into her violet sweater. She strolled on, oblivious. At the corner she turned and looked around. I stepped back into the Med's doorway, brushing against a guy with a cup of espresso who was watching the scene.

"Hey, you want in or out?" he demanded.

"Sorry," I muttered irritably, wiping a drop of his coffee off my sleeve. I couldn't afford to get involved in a territorial dispute here. I looked back at Scookie. She was crossing Haste Street and heading toward campus. When she stepped up on the sidewalk kitty-corner from me, she took another look, and then, satisfied she wasn't being followed, moved on at a faster clip.

I darted through traffic to the other side of Haste Street and hurried along the empty Telegraph sidewalk. There are no convenient doorways there. I had to count on the meager camouflage of my jacket. Single-man tailing is a sucker's job. On the force we always use at least two officers. I'd had no chance to call in help, but that didn't make me feel any better.

Scookie was halfway up the block. She slowed. She was going to check around. There was no doorway to hide in. I squatted against the wall, head on knees and pulled my collar up over my neck. There were no street people sitting out in the cold fog, but had there been, no one would have been surprised. And peering out through my eyelashes, I could see that Scookie didn't find my slumped gray mass odd either. She picked up speed again and hurried to the corner.

I poised on the balls of my feet, ready to run if she turned the corner. Already my thigh muscles screamed. Traffic poured across Channing. Clearly, every Berkeleyan who would ordinarily have been on the sidewalk was in a car. Scookie jumped back as a truck shot in front of her. Again she glanced behind her. But by now she wasn't even looking at my side of the street. For her, the game of tailing had very narrow rules.

The light changed. I stood up as she started across Channing.

Now I was beginning to see where she was headed. I could have loped up the empty sidewalk and between the slow-moving cars across Telegraph and into Herman Ott's building before her, but I waited till she'd entered the door.

She was at the top of the first flight of stairs when I rounded the old elevator cage. I hurried after her, pausing as I came to the landing to let her clamber up the second flight. Then I raced up the stairs and turned north instead of south to Ott's office. The hallway makes a square. Ott's rooms are in the southeast corner. I reached the northeast corner just as Scookie was knocking on his door. He didn't open it on the first knock, of course. Ott opens instantly for no one. She'd have to go through the two-rap, identify-self ritual that was the Ottian equivalent of a welcome mat. I had plenty of time to brace for takeoff before Scookie would start inside.

I waited till the door was full open to make my move. Doubtless, Ott intended to shut it after her, but I was inside before he got the chance.

"Where is she?" I demanded. "Maria Zalles."

"What the hell are you doing barging into my office?" Ott never misses a chance to be outraged.

Scookie took a step toward the door. "Don't even think about leaving," I said. "You're in enough trouble already. How long has Maria been here?" I stepped in front of her, blocking Ott from her view.

"I don't know." Her voice was quavering.

I spun to face Ott. He was so close behind me, I nearly ended up nose-to-forehead with him. "So, Ott, this is the way you deal fairly. I'll remember that. Has Maria Zalles been here ever since I saw her at the Swallow? There is such a thing as interfering with a police investigation."

"Smith, you never asked where she was, and I never told you." The corners of his narrow mouth twitched in triumph.

It hadn't occurred to me she might have been here, hiding

under one of his repulsive piles of blankets, sheets, and yellow garb. Or maybe she'd been behind the bedroom door, squeezed in between the radiator and the hot plate. I glared down at Ott. If Scookie hadn't been there, I'd have shaken him. I took a step back and waited till my breathing was calmer. "Ott, Maria Zalles was the last person who saw Drem alive. She lied to me. She made me look like a fool. Do I have to explain what that means?"

Ott looked over my shoulder. I should have let Scookie go right away. With her here, I'd put Ott in the position of losing face. But I'd been too mad, *was* too mad. Let him lose face. Let him lose his whole goddamn head! "Ott, if I have to put out an all-points on Maria Zalles, I will. I'll call in every favor from every patrol officer in the department, and from everyone I know on the street. We will press people. And, Ott, every time any officer does that, he'll mention your name, because, Ott, you"—I turned around to face Scookie—"and *you* are responsible for this. Now, if you want to save yourselves the hassle, save the people who might have seen Maria Zalles, and keep her from being in a lot worse trouble than she already is, you'll tell me where to find her. Now!"

Behind me, Ott drew in his breath, ready to retort.

"Where?" I yelled at Scookie as I took a step back into Ott. It pushed him off-balance and against his table.

"Gone," she said with smug defiance. "Gone where you won't find her."

"To the airport?"

Scookie gasped.

"To Samoa?"

Scookie's eyes widened.

"When does the flight leave?"

She stared. She could have been Mrs. Lot, dripping grains of salt.

"Abetting a felon is a very serious offense, Scookie." I turned and glared at Ott. "Tell her what it's like in jail, Ott."

Ott didn't respond, but he didn't protest either. Looking back at Scookie, I could see that she'd gotten the point. As icing on the point, I added, "You'd make a tasty meal for one of the tough girls. Fresh meat's always a treat."

"Four forty-four," she muttered. "On United."

"Four forty-four *today*?" I demanded. It was already 3:00 P.M.

"Yes."

"That had better be the truth." But she was too scared to lie. "Be at the station in an hour. You've both got statements—factual statements this time—to make."

I ran to the patrol car. Ott wasn't going anywhere, and I didn't expect Scookie Hogan was either. But Maria Zalles certainly was. Her flight would be boarding in an hour and a quarter. SFO was a forty-five-minute drive in the middle of the night. Now, with rush hour beginning, it could take a lot longer. And I had to go back to the station and change cars first. Maria Zalles could be on the beach at Waikiki before I pulled up at passenger drop-off.

At the station I found Pereira. Leonard and Acosta followed in a second car. I called Airport Security, gave them a brief background and a description of Zalles, and hoped they weren't distracted by suspicious items at the luggage check, or disturbances, or one of those runway "mishaps" that are frighteningly common all over the country. If anything else came up, Maria Zalles would plummet to the bottom of their list.

Pereira drove, code 3, lights and siren, down University, weaving lane to lane, cutting in front of a van at Sacramento, causing three cars to screech to a stop at San Pablo. The siren screamed as we mounted the overpass; cars squeezed left. The fog was getting thicker nearer the bay. It was clammy inside the car, and I cracked the window. The cold wind only made the contrast greater.

I looked down at the freeway. "It's packed. Take the frontage road."

But Pereira was already moving into the left lane. Behind us, brakes squealed, horns honked. Pereira cut left onto the frontage road. It's one lane there. In front of us, drivers jolted, most swinging onto the edge of the waterfront marsh, but a few froze like deer in headlights. Pereira had to weave around them into the oncoming lane. Sweat coated her face. She drove braced forward, her back an inch from the seat.

I called the dispatcher to alert Highway Patrol of our route and to get United and find out the Hawaii gate number. He'd tell them to hold the flight.

The frontage road stops half a mile before the turnoff to the bridge. Once we got on the freeway, the siren didn't help. Here drivers might have been willing to move out of our way, but there was no place for them to go. "Use the shoulder." But even as I said it, I could see a car stopped a hundred yards ahead.

As we came up behind it, Pereira put on the siren again and cut into traffic, Leonard and Acosta right behind us. The fog was thicker here next to the bay. Pereira had the wipers on, but they cleared the windshield only momentarily, and it was opaque gray by the time they made the next pass.

I grabbed the mike again and called CHP. "Berkeley five two seven," I said, giving my badge number. "We're passing the toll plaza." My voice was strained.

"Take lane five, Berkeley. It's not fast, but it's moving. Check back with me at Yerba Buena."

"Thanks." We moved up to the far right lane.

"*Moving's* a euphemism," Pereira muttered.

"Four o'clock. Forty-four minutes, it'll be off the ground."

The dispatcher called. The Hawaii flight would be leaving from gate 12B.

I could see Yerba Buena Island ahead. The Oakland span of the Bay Bridge ends there, and a short tunnel leads through the rock to the San Francisco span. I called CHP before we hit the tunnel.

"Lane four after the tunnel, then ease over into one. You can siren into two before one cuts off at Fifth Street."

I'd driven to San Francisco enough to plan on that maneuver. "How's it after that, on one-oh-one?"

"How d'ya think?"

"Like a sit-down dinner."

"You got it, Berkeley."

"Okay, how about we get off at Fifth and back on at Seventh?"

"Yeah, sure." The radio crackled. "I didn't think you'd know that one."

Despite the tension, I laughed. "Hey, Chip, I'm always up on the shortcuts. I learned to drive in Jersey."

I called the dispatcher again to do a courtesy notify to SFPD of our bounce off the freeway into the City, and to San Mateo south of the City. Pereira was already on the off ramp at Fifth Street. She hit the siren again. Cars moved aside grudgingly.

"Four-nineteen, Connie. We can't count on Airport Security. With the best of intentions—"

"I know, I know. If we could do more than ten miles per hour . . ." She was nearly on the bumper of a beige Chrysler. "What do these people think when there are sirens blasting in both ears and they see red lights flashing in their rearview mirror?" She rolled down the window and stuck her head out, just as the Chrysler eased around the corner at Seventh Street. Then she wove her way through the slow-clearing intersection, muttering at each driver. It wasn't till we were back on 101 that she turned off the siren, and using just the pulser, moved into the fast lane.

I called Airport Security again. They had no sighting of Zalles. I checked in with the San Mateo Sheriff's Department.

Traffic on 101 south was packed. Rush hour proper. Ten miles per hour tops. I held the mike, button off, smacking my fingernail against it. Sweat pasted my shirt to my back. Cars pulled to the right for the 280 turnoff. Pereira reached for the siren.

"No!" I barked. "Too crowded. One of these guys panics, and we've got a pancake."

We passed the exit. Connie stepped on the gas—30 mph, 40 mph. By the time we hit Candlestick Park, we were almost up to speed limit.

"Four thirty-five. Give it the trumpets."

She hit the button, and the siren ripped the air. Cars veered out of our lane. I loved it. I flicked a glance at Pereira—she loved it too. She moved left and stepped on the gas, waiting till the last moment before veering right, across all four lanes onto the airport ramp.

It was 4:42 P.M. when we pulled up in front of the United counter. The passengers would be on board by now. In two minutes the plane would leave the gate.

"Which way to twelve-B?" I yelled at the baggage handler. He pointed to the right.

If Security hadn't held the flight it would be gone. I ran through the doors, sidestepping a couple with a luggage carrier. Pereira shot around the other side. Businessmen hurried toward the gates; toddlers wandered unheeded. I pushed in front of a gray-haired man with a briefcase, ran around a mother with two small children, squeezed between a couple, and slowed at the luggage X ray to flash my badge. Before they could decide, I ran on.

Boarding Area B forks halfway down. I nearly ran over a couple in front of me as I tried to read the overhead directions.

"Left," I called back to Pereira. I could hear her panting behind me. I was panting too. Every time I do this kind of thing, I think I should run in the mornings instead of swim. Why is it one sport does nothing to prepare you for another? Pereira did aerobics. I didn't know what Acosta did to keep his long, lovely body in shape, but I was surprised he hadn't passed me already. I hated to think how far back Leonard might be.

The line at 12B was still moving toward the gate. Thank God for airport delays. I pushed through to the front, pulling out my shield as I ran. I extended it toward the stewardess at the gate. "How many passengers have boarded?"

"Just first class. We started boarding a few minutes late."

No way would Philip Drem have been flying first class.

"Have you gotten word from Security on this flight?"

Her eyes widened. "No. Nothing."

Behind me, passengers shoved closer. "Hold it up till we check the line."

I could see Pereira at the far end, Acosta blocking the escape into the terminal. And no Maria Zalles on line.

"Okay," I said to the stewardess. "Go ahead letting them on."

Leonard staggered into view. To Acosta I said, "Check the manifest. Get the seat number."

I moved to the side and watched the line dissolve into the gate's maw. The past dies quickly at airports. By the time the last few passengers showed their boarding passes, they'd forgotten me. I looked around the boarding area. The only people there now were the ground crew, two families standing by the windows looking toward the lighted portholes of the plane. Had Maria Zalles changed her mind? Or was she in the same hideout I'd used myself? Motioning Pereira to take my spot by the gate, Acosta and Leonard to either side of the aisle, I walked into the ladies' room.

Maria Zalles was standing right inside.

CHAPTER

22

Frequently I interview suspects in the station's glass-windowed booths off the meeting room. I like to seat them so they can look past me at the full force of the department—officers rushing to the communications center, sergeants giving orders. I let them see witnesses being interviewed in the comparative freedom of the tables in the middle of the room, freedom they don't have in the tiny closed booths, with me between them and the door.

But an even better psychological setting for an interview is the back of the squad car—the cage.

In the airport I read Maria Zalles her rights and led her through the terminal to the patrol car like a stunned but obedient child. She looked gray and shaky in a white cotton dress, suitable for Hawaii or American Samoa or wherever she planned to deplane, but much too thin for San Francisco Airport in April. Huddling in the far corner of the backseat, her arms pressed to her sides, useless protection against cold, despair, and fear, she looked more like Tori Iversen than ever.

I signaled Leonard to drive. After they'd dealt with Zalles's luggage, Pereira would go back with Acosta, an arrangement I suspected would appeal to both. However, that was not my focus. What I wanted from this was the back of Leonard's head right beyond the mesh of the cage, his thick gray hair, his muscular neck, an image that said "no give."

I climbed in beside Zalles. She looked terrified. I didn't blame her. At the best of times, being in the back of the patrol car is degrading. Cigarette smoke settled into the upholstery years ago; every surface is coated with grime that the occasional departmental cleaning only smears; windows are stained on the inside and streaked on the out. And even in spring you feel that bottom-of-the-well cold that makes you sure you'll never be warm again.

Leonard's hair was dark in the back; it hung a bit over his regulation collar. I couldn't ask for anything more official, more "cop." I thought of Sierra, the street person—the street person Leonard couldn't find—and shivered.

Blotchy bumps stood out on Maria's arms. Later I would give her my jacket or put the heat on. Now the cold suited my purpose. I pushed aside any sympathy for the shivering girl and focused on the woman who had run, the murder suspect. "You thought this was a game, Maria. Philip Drem was murdered. You were the last person to see him alive—"

Her blue eyes widened. "But I wasn't. He was waiting for someone else."

I motioned Leonard to start the car. "So *you* say. You lied to me Saturday night. You didn't show up when you agreed to Sunday morning. Now you're trying to leave the country. Why should I think your word is worth anything?"

"But he *was* waiting for someone. Honest. Look, I know I wasn't straight with you. But I was so shocked. I never expected Phil to be killed. Half the time I was talking to you that night I was trying to figure out if you were part of a joke."

"A joke?" I let my scorn come through. "Who would play a joke like that?"

"I don't know. I was just hoping you were an actress, maybe a friend of Ethan's. Maybe he'd swapped you a room for your performance or a voucher for something someone else in the swap club did. I just couldn't believe Phil was dead."

An interesting take on our conversation indeed. Leonard pulled sharply right onto the freeway *on* ramp. Gusts off the Pacific rattled the car windows and made the chill in here colder. Maria was clutching her arms; there were white spots on the skin around her fingertips.

I said, "Tell me about your meeting Phil. You were an actress, right? Playing the part of a potential"—I chose my term carefully—"admirer."

She looked up, a hint of a proud smile flickering on her pale lips. "No. I'm no actress. I mean, not a professional." She hesitated. "I'm an investigator."

I laughed. "An investigator? Licensed?" In California a licensed private investigator needs five thousand hours of experience. Pigs may fly, as Pereira had said, but they'd have a greater likelihood of getting a pilot's license than Maria Zalles a PI's.

"Well, no."

"If you're not licensed, you're not an investigator. You're just dishonest."

"No. Look, I was going to start working for an investigator. He'll tell you. I checked with him about Phil. For background, you know."

Only a triumph of will kept me from laughing. Scruffy, grumpy Herman Ott with a young, pretty blond assistant was a concept that would tickle half of Berkeley. No wonder Ott had reacted so defensively when I told him about Maria. Later I would find out from Ott exactly what their "professional relationship" was or if it existed only in Maria Zalles's mind.

"I've already talked to Herman Ott," I said, letting her jump to the conclusion that he'd already enlightened me. "You were about to tell me how you met Philip Drem."

"I never meant for him to die. Honest."

"Start from the beginning." I let my voice slide into a friendlier tone. I wanted to give her my coat—she was pressing her teeth together to keep them from chattering—but it was still too soon. We were almost to Candlestick Park, where the 49ers and the Giants play. The flags above it were snapping in the wind. Looking past it, I suspected Maria could see her future snapping about in reaction to forces she could no longer control—if she was ever in charge of them.

"I've only been in Berkeley since New Year's," she said. "Christmas was a bummer in Portland, and I decided to split and see how things went here. I had a little money, not much, but you can always find something to do, right? I got a temp job right away." She relaxed a bit, recalling things she had controlled. "I can transcribe. But that office wasn't a place to make friends. I mean, when you're a temp, you're invisible. None of the regulars even notice you, much less treat you like a person. But I've moved around enough to know that. If you want to meet people, you've got to go out, take classes, go to places like the Film Archives, or lectures, or work on some environmental project or something. I mean, I'm sorry I never had a drinking problem; AA's supposed to be one of the hot social spots."

"Drem?" I prompted.

"I'm getting to that," she said with almost normal irritability. "I just wanted you to see where I was coming from. I couldn't just be sitting home. So I took a yoga class."

"Lyn Takai's?"

"Right. She's real good."

"And did Lyn mention Philip Drem?"

"No."

"No?"

"Not Lyn. It was another student. I was surprised. I mean, I was looking for friends, but I've been around enough to know that yoga classes aren't great spots for friend-making. I mean, you'd think they would be—all that doing poses together, working in partners, and stuff. But people are too into what's going on in their own bodies, whether they've stretched their left leg as much as their right, if their headstands are straight. Teachers don't like you to talk, you know. And then at the end they have the *savasana*, the relaxation. You're lying on the floor, sort of letting relaxation wash through you. It almost puts you to sleep. By the time you leave, it's too much of an effort to talk to anyone."

"But this other student did talk to you."

"Yeah. I noticed her in the middle of the class looking at me. I mean, she wasn't just glancing over like you do if someone's got on an interesting T-shirt. She was staring, not even trying to hide it. I mean, for a while I wondered if she was hot for me. So I wasn't surprised when she came up to me at the end of the class. When she invited me for coffee, I figured I was probably right. But what did I have to lose, see?"

A black sports car squealed, braking frantically beside us. Maria paused but didn't turn, as if she were afraid looking away would mean abandoning what little safety she had in the story that bound us. The driver paralleled us, taking time to read the logo on the side of the patrol car, and then, clearly infuriated he'd broken stride for a car that was not Highway Patrol, hit the gas.

"So we went to the Med," she said quickly, "and got a table along the far wall, and she made small talk—she hadn't seen me around before, how long had I been here, what kind of work did I do? It took me a while to realize that she wasn't just trying to get to know me; she was sizing me up. And when she discovered I was new and had a temp job and was open to other things, she made her offer. She said I was almost a dead ringer for another woman, the wife of the man who had ruined her life. She'd already told me about the cookie business and how that was the only thing she'd ever done herself and how Phil had destroyed it."

Maria reached up for a clump of hair and began running her finger and thumb back and forth across the blond strands. "It sounds dumb to get that upset because you can't operate a cookie stand, but I could feel for Scookie. I mean, she grew up in times when women couldn't even get credit in their own names. She'd been a housewife for years and no one, not even she, thought she was competent enough to do anything more. And then she goes out and creates this business. And suddenly she's being written up in the newspapers. She's going to expand and open a shop. She's legitimate, a success. And then Drem comes along and basically says to her, 'What you're good at doesn't matter. The only thing that counts is columns of figures and lots of receipts.' She's an artist, an artist with her stove, right brain all the way. You can't expect her to suddenly be left brain and catalog every receipt. But Drem did, and he screwed her."

It was unconscious, but she was so wrapped up in Scookie's story that she saw Phil as "Drem," and she spit out the hated syllable just the way Scookie Hogan did.

"What did she offer you?"

"A room at the hotel. I figured it had to be better than where I was staying. And free."

"In return for?"

"Cozying up to Drem. Finding out what was as important to him as Scookie's business was to her. Investigating," she said proudly.

"And?"

"Nothing. That's it."

"Maria, if that was it, it wouldn't have mattered what you looked like."

For the first time she smiled. "Not true. Anybody else would have had to approach him. Phil wasn't much in the friendly department. I think maybe Scookie tried with someone else, and it didn't work out. But I looked so much like his wife that all I had to do was be someplace he was. I didn't have to compromise my role. Phil came up to me."

I was sure I knew the answer, but I asked, "And what did you decide was indeed the most important thing to Drem?"

"His wife."

Was Maria right, or had she merely found the superficial answer and not yet uncovered the truth as Tori saw it—not "his wife" but "his wife's illness." But for Scookie Hogan's purpose it didn't make much difference. If Drem lost Tori to anything other than death, he lost his claim as the avenger of her illness too. If she divorced him, he'd become just another spouse who couldn't handle illness—and I was willing to bet that was a group of people Philip Drem had despised. For him to think people might assume he was one of them would have been the ultimate humiliation. I wondered if Scookie could have come to that conclusion.

"So then what, Maria?"

"Nothing."

"The truth! The most important thing to Drem was his wife. You look like her. He was attracted to you, right?"

"Oh, yeah. In his way."

"Don't ask me to believe Scookie could pass up that combination. What did she ask you to do?"

Maria hesitated.

"Go on a trip with him, like this one to Samoa?"

She twisted the blond hairs around her finger—an effective ingenue move. "Well, yeah. I mean, I had some qualms. I mean, Phil was nice to me. He was a little stiff, but you know, he really did care about his wife, and he cared a whole lot about getting the air pure again. And when he started talking about going away someplace and living simply and stuff, I could kind of see what he must have been like before her illness."

The skin around her eyes tightened. I believed Maria really had had some concern for Drem. I could picture her sitting opposite him in the Swallow drinking cappuccino, with that look of sympathy drawing him out. "I've done enough temp work to know what it's like to hate your job. He didn't talk about his job, and I didn't ask, because I wasn't supposed to know. But he said enough for me to realize that he gave it the least emotional energy possible."

She paused, waiting for me to acknowledge her Berkeleyan observation. "But you know, that type of thing gets you. It backfired on him. It was like he walled himself off from the people he audited, but once he got the wall up, he couldn't get it back down when he wanted. You know what I mean?" she asked, more secure in the scene she'd created—two colleagues comparing notes about Drem.

I nodded. I hadn't asked her whether the ticket she was using was one Drem had given her money for or his, altered to Philippa. There was a big difference, legally for Maria, emotionally for Tori, and for me—knowing how deep Drem's loyalty was would affect my strategies. But I held off, saving the question for the right moment. I didn't need that big a gun to shoot down Maria's security now. "Tell me about Friday night."

She let go of the hair she'd been twisting and pressed her arms close around her. "I did tell you! That was completely true. I mean, when I found out Phil got killed right after he left the Archives, I was too scared to lie."

I couldn't help but believe her. Which left me with the same nagging question I'd had for days. "Who was Phil waiting for at the Film Archives?"

"I don't know."

"I'm sure you do want to help us," I said, pausing to let the implicit offer prod her. "You watched him for the better part of an hour. What kind of person was he looking for? Was he watching the street for a car? Was he looking at men or women? Blacks, whites, Asians?"

She glanced at the metal mesh of the cage, then back at me,

her face pale. "He wasn't out on the street looking. He was waiting in the courtyard. The only thing I know is that he was planning to sell something, and that's what was going to make this trip possible."

I tensed. "What was he going to sell?"

"I don't know."

"Did he have it with him? Think."

"I don't know."

"Don't give up." I could hear the tightness in my voice. "Did this meeting he was planning seem like it would be the final one, the culmination of the sale?"

"Well, it had to be. He already had the airline ticket. It cost a lot. He had to get money."

"Okay, so whatever he was selling he had with him. He was carrying his briefcase. Was his briefcase bulkier than normal?"

"No. It was more like a manila folder with a zipper. He couldn't have had anything more than papers in there."

He'd have had Lyn Takai's tax return, his airline ticket he'd picked up that day, and probably just one more piece of paper. Drem had one particularly valuable bit of information to sell, the thing he'd gotten by a fluke the same weekend Tori had had her last attack. "Maria, I'm going to ask you again. Who was he waiting for? Was he looking for a car? Did you see any cars slowing down like they were looking for him?"

She made an odd squeak. It took me a moment to realize it was a laugh escaping from a tense mouth and throat, reminding me that in that area of town drivers are always moving slowly, on the lookout for friends, girls, boys, or even more rare and desirable, an on-street parking spot. "A car," I persisted, "that slowed just in front of the museum? Or double-parked across the street?"

She closed her eyes as if she were thinking. Her eyes didn't move under the lids. She was faking.

"Maria, you were apprehended attempting flight to impede a

murder investigation. That's a felony. Think of what it's like to be locked in a cell, with someone watching you all the time. To never even pee in private."

She stiffened. She looked almost too scared to tell me what she was hiding.

I had to up the ante. Taking a chance, I said, "And you were using a stolen airline ticket. That's grand theft. This is not a game. We're talking years in jail. Look out the window, at the cars. People driving south to San Diego, north to Oregon, or east through Nevada, Nebraska, to New York." I shook my head. "You won't be able to walk eight feet without checking with a guard. In jail, Maria, nothing is yours, not your pencils and papers, not your time, not your body." I waited. I could almost hear her heart thumping. "Now, tell me what you saw outside the museum. And give me Philip Drem's ticket."

She fumbled in her purse for the ticket. She had to swallow twice before she could say, "No one was hanging around. It was cold out; misty. It was all I could do to go back there and stay myself. People were rushing up the street. There was a red car that came around three times and stopped across the street. Double-parked. Once, the driver almost got out. The door opened. But he must have changed his mind."

"He never got out?"

"No."

"What time was this?"

"Late." She shrugged. "He might have been there earlier when I was gone. I didn't come back till about ten. It was a little after that."

"Describe the car."

"What?" She stared at me. "This isn't the fifties. Cars are cars, just transportation. If I weren't a detective, I wouldn't remember it was red."

California, car capital of the nation, and I had to find the one person who couldn't tell a Mercedes from a Morris Minor. So much for Herman Ott's detective tutorage. But Maria was a young single woman; she might not differentiate between cars, but she would between men. "The guy driving the car—what did he look like? Young, old, big, small . . . ?"

She shrugged. "He was too short."

My shoulders tightened in anticipation. "Then you must have gotten a good view of his hair? Dark? Blond? Straight?"

"Brown and slicked back, like he was walking into a gust of wind."

The muscles across my shoulders clenched tight. Rick Lamott. No wonder he was so anxious to keep in touch with me, or more accurately to keep up on the progress of the investigation. Bastard!

We were coming onto the lower level of the San Francisco–Oakland Bay Bridge now. Twice in the last couple of years drivers had gotten out of their stalled cars on the top level and been knocked over the railing to their deaths. I glanced uncomfortably out the window at the icy Bay water two hundred feet below. Turning back to Maria, I put out my hand for the ticket. She hesitated, then sighed and turned it over. I didn't have to look at it to know it would be for Philippa Drem. "How did you get this?"

"I didn't kill him, honest. I shouldn't have taken it. I know that. But I couldn't not go to Samoa, could I? I mean just because I was afraid?" She had been nervous before, but clearly this was what she'd been worried about. Now her words poured out frantically. "I mean, I am a detective."

"Stealing—"

"I didn't steal it. It was on my bed."

"Whoa. How did it get there? And when? And why?"

"The night you and I talked at the Swallow. I was really upset. You saw that. I didn't know Phil had been killed."

Was it possible that Maria Zalles, would-be detective, was one of the few people on the Avenue not to know about Drem?

I had to admit it was. "So you were unnerved. What did you do?"

"I went home. To the hotel. I guess I was babbling. I told everyone there Phil was dead."

"Everyone? Who?"

"A couple of guys who were going to do some work, and all the owners—they were in the lobby fussing about how long the repairs were taking."

"And you told them Phil had been murdered? How did they react?"

"I don't know. *I* was upset. They didn't know Phil like I did. They could see how upset I was. Somebody got me a drink. I was crying. I just remember having my head in my hands and then stumbling down the hall to the bathroom to wash my face."

"Down the hall?"

"They'd taken out the sink in my room," she said. In spite of all that had happened since, she was clearly still put out about that. "After that, I went to my room. The ticket was on the bed."

I stared at her, forcing her to stop and see my disbelief. "The ticket just turned up on your bed?"

"Well, somebody must have put it there while I was washing up."

I swallowed sarcastic comments. Sarcasm's an easy route to losing a witness. "Who?"

"I don't know."

"Didn't you ask?"

"No. I figured if someone wanted me to know—"

"And you call yourself a detective!" I said, exasperated.

"I'd had enough of detecting, with Phil dead and all. I just wanted to get away. I took the ticket, and I left."

I asked who she thought might have given it to her. I re-phrased the question three times, but the only thing I learned was that Maria Zalles had thought about only one person that night—herself.

I left her at the station with Leonard. But I couldn't overcome a queasy spot of fear about it. I still didn't know who had stolen the briefcase, still couldn't swear it hadn't been the cop that Sierra fingered, Sierra, whom Leonard couldn't find. It was ludicrous to consider Leonard. Unreasonable. And he was the one who'd heard the whole Zalles interview. He'd go over her statement once more, then get it in writing. He'd make sure the process took long enough to keep her there in case I needed another go at her. She'd be safe with him, surely. . . .

I considered rounding up Scookie Hogan, Ethan Simonov, Mason Moon, and Lyn Takai, but there was no reason for any of them to admit having Drem's ticket. And they were all savvy enough to realize that. If I didn't come up with something solid, they could stonewall me into the twenty-first century.

But stonewalling was one thing Rick Lamott was not going to do.

CHAPTER

23

I could have called around for Pereira. But to get answers to the questions I was going to ask, I didn't need esoteric tax knowledge.

I didn't turn on the pulsers, but I might as well have, as fast as I was driving. They would have suited my frame of mind. By the time I pulled into Rick Lamott's driveway behind his red Lotus Elan SE, I was steaming.

No wonder the man had made a point of coming to the station, asking me out for a drink, calling me. God, I hate to be a patsy. I had a lot to make clear to him, and I wasn't about to have Pereira witness that. Much less provide commentary on it for weeks afterward.

I walked around the Lotus in the driveway. I was surprised Lamott didn't keep it in the garage. But of course that would mean it would be out of sight. And what's the point of having a red sports car if no one sees it?

Lamott's house was just what I would have expected—a glassy modern job hanging down off the hillside. Nothing special in itself, downright precarious in earthquake country, but with a view of the bay, the San Francisco skyline, and the Golden Gate Bridge. It seemed fitting for Lamott that the appeal of his house would be external.

As I walked past the Lotus, I couldn't resist a glance down at the black leather interior and all the red gauges on the dashboard. And the driver's seat on the right. Like most Berkeleyans, I found the car bourgeois and superficial, but still, well, there was something so Scott Fitzgerald about it all.

Jazz poured through the door, and I had to ring the bell three times before Rick Lamott opened it. He was wearing a forest-green sweatshirt with a collar and acid-washed jeans—one of those processes that contribute to killing the rain forests. His light-brown hair was a bit ruffled, and his narrow face and sharp features seemed less sleek than they had in the Lotus. Even his eyes now looked closer to hazel than cat-yellow. But he was still idling faster than normal.

He grinned, giving those hazel-yellow eyes a slitty quality. "So, Jill, you found me. I'm flattered. Should I credit this to the lure of my charm or to your detective training, or both?"

Now that half-egotistical banter that had amused me before irritated me. "Tell me about the TCMP and DIF again."

He shrugged, a movement closer to a bounce of the collar-bones than an expressive lift and *c'est-la-vie* drop. A nervous gesture, even for Lamott. He ushered me into the living room, which indeed was essentially an anteroom to the view of the lights of Oakland and the San Francisco skyline. It smelled of particularly sweet incense. Sitting on a beige leather chair, I refused the offer of wine and repeated my question about the TCMP and DIF.

In the middle of the glass coffee table was a clay sculpture of the Lotus sports car. Rick Lamott moved to the other side of the table and poised on the edge of the sofa. To be farther from me, he'd have to have been out the window. Any question whether the TCMP and DIF were the issue Lamott's suddenly wary behavior answered.

He was already tapping a foot when he said, "I'm sure you remember, but I'll tell you again, Jill. The TCMP is the Tax-payer Compliance Measurement Program. Key info IRS's got on TPs, taxpayers. Dragged a bunch of people through audit, made them verify every cent of every deduction. Took the average. Put it together with their discriminant-function methodology, and voilà! You claim too far above the local average, you get points against you. The more points, the more likely you are to be audited." He grinned and held his feet still. "Unless, of course, you're my client."

"Tell me about the local adjustments to the TCMP."

Both feet started, alternating. "They'd waste a bunch of time if they held Angelenos to car-expense standards they have for Boston. A Bean Town guy drives forty miles round trip, he's putting in a lot of miles. In LA, a hundred's good. IRS doesn't want to haul in half of Los Angeles and find those folks can prove every mile. Makes 'em look bad. Also wastes a lot of time, and time's money."

The clay sculpture looked as if it had half-melted. Like a deflated tire. A sculpture that said "I can laugh about my status symbol." Or maybe "I can give the appearance of laughing about my status symbol." We'd see how good a laugher Rick Lamott was. The concept of melted appealed to me. I said, "Give me Philip Drem's TCMP figures."

"Hey, wha—"

"I've got a witness who saw you and your car at PFA Friday night, when Drem was killed. Three times you stopped across the street. I'm not going to waste time here. You've got them. I can get a search warrant."

"I don't have them."

Ignoring that, I went on. "And if I have to go to the hassle of getting a warrant, I'll assume the paper is hidden somewhere in the Lotus. And, Rick, we'll take that car apart."

He gulped.

"Now get it."

"I don't have any figures."

"We'll start with the interior, pull out the seats, all those gauges, and the gearshift. And then—"

"Goddammit, I don't have anything from Philip Drem!" His sleek face was flushed. He looked as if he'd skidded into a tree.

I let a beat pass, then said softly, "Convince me."

He leaned forward and made a show of fiddling with something under the table, playing for time.

I couldn't keep the sarcasm out of my voice as I said, "If you're going to pretend you're fooling with something on the floor, you'd be better off not having a glass table." He jerked up, smacking his forearm against the table edge.

"Okay, Rick, tell me the whole story from the top."

There was just a tiny twitch of head movement to indicate he was deciding between answers. "Yeah, well, see, Drem called me. He offered me the figure. I kept my options open."

I waited. Lamott was not a man to be comfortable with silence.

"It made sense he'd call me. I'm known for getting the best deal for doctors." His foot began tapping again.

"Drem was offering you a chance to bribe a government official to give you the local TCMP/DIF figures so you could keep your clients' deductions within the local average. So, barring a fluke, your clients would not be audited."

"Offers don't matter. You can offer the lease on the Brooklyn Bridge. Point is, I didn't buy."

"So you say. Go on."

"Okay, I was real tempted. A lot of accountants think you can get the gist of those figures from trade publications. But to have the actual figures . . ." Lamott inhaled slowly, covetously. He must have had just that look when he first saw the Lotus. With a small quick shake of the head, he said, "I stopped across the street from the Film Archives. I saw Drem. He didn't know my car. I sat there as long as I could. Then . . ." He swallowed and said in a small voice, "Then I wimped out. The thing is, I've never done anything illegal, and, well, I was afraid. It was a big chance. And I was doing okay without the actual figures. So I drove on."

"And came back."

"Well, yeah."

"Three times, all together."

He looked more humiliated than frightened now.

"And when he finally left, you followed him."

"I was going to forget the whole thing, but by the time he rode his bicycle across Durant, he looked funny. He wasn't pedaling anymore. The bike was swaying. Then he turned down Dwight. I couldn't follow in my car because it's one-way east. Cars kept coming. I couldn't even make a left. Finally I got across and turned down the next street. I almost passed Regent. I would have if I hadn't seen Drem stumble into the street and fall." He swallowed again, then made himself look directly at me. "If I hadn't called nine-one-one, he could still be lying there."

I laughed. "So you called nine-one-one. Then you ripped off his briefcase and left."

"Hey, that's a lousy suggestion. I never touched his briefcase. His bicycle was halfway down the street."

"The TCMP figures were a couple of hundred feet away, and you didn't even go down and look?"

To a game player like Lamott that idea had to sound preposterous. "Okay, I looked. It was after ten at night—dark. By the time I got to Drem, then stopped to call for help and walked down the street to the bicycle, the basket was empty." He looked directly at me, indignation etched in his face. "The goddamned briefcase was gone."

"Are you saying someone else stole it?" I asked, amazed.

"It was gone."

"Who took it?"

"Don't you think if I knew I'd tell you?"

I had to admit I did. Nothing would have been more to Lamott's advantage. Except having the TCMP figures himself. Still I asked, "Who else was around?"

"No one but a cop. I—"

"Which patrol officer? Describe him!" My throat was so tight, my voice squeaked, but Drem was too caught up in his own worries to notice. Please, I muttered silently to the powers that be, don't say "shambling, gray-haired, middle-aged guy with wrinkled clothes." Leonard. "Describe him!" I repeated.

Lamott shook his head. "Average cop. But look, it was dark; he was in the shadows. I spotted the uniform and the gun belt. That's it."

"Thin? Fat? Short? Tall? You sure it was a man?"

Lamott threw up his hands. "Look, it was just a glance. I didn't care about him. I just wanted him out of the way and me out of his sight, see?"

I repeated my question.

"Average, okay?" he yelled. "Probably a guy, but some of you broads are pretty tough. That's it!"

"Where was he?"

"Down the street near the bicycle."

I stared at Lamott, amazed. "And you didn't wonder why with a body in the street the only cop was half a block away?"

Lamott gave a big shrug. Shrug with attitude.

"And so you didn't even call him back to Drem's body. You just walked away, leaving Drem lying in the middle of the street?"

"Hey, come on. What was I going to do? I'm not a doctor. He was damned lucky I stopped at all."

I shook my head. How had I ever found this man intriguing? It was so embarrassing. "Leaving the scene of an accident is a crime." When he didn't react, I stuck it to him. "When IRS hears about this, they'll wonder what else you've been up to. If my guess is correct, they'll feel the need to audit some of your clients' returns for the last couple of years. Maybe all their returns. Certainly all of them for this year, wouldn't you say?"

It was the first time I'd seen Rick Lamott speechless. I sat a moment, savoring my small triumph. It was petty and really only managed to cover a problem caused by my own lack of perception. Later, I'd be disgusted. But for the moment I felt like a lion with its paw on a gazelle and a roar deafening the countryside. We don't get these situations much in Homicide-Felony Assault. But I could remember them from a stint in Traffic, ticketing Mercedeses. And I could imagine the controlled delight of the IRS agent, the former accounting major who drove a used beige sedan and dated girls with pimples, as he gave the coup de grace to the adult BMOC with the red sports car.

It was a moment before he said, "There's no need for you to inform IRS." It wasn't begging, but it was close.

"The truth?"

"Okay. But look—I didn't approach Drem. Who would have imagined Drem, the straight arrow, would think of selling figures?"

"Why did he?"

"He didn't say."

"You were suspicious of him. You wouldn't have taken his offer with no explanation. The truth!"

"Okay. He was planning to leave the country, and he needed the money. He wanted a lot of money, fast."

"So he offered you more than just the TCMP figures?"

"Yeah."

"What?"

"This is off the record, isn't it?"

"I'll only use what I need. I'm not after your hide."

Lamott had no choice but to take that offer. "Okay, he offered to throw an audit. My biggest client. Audit had been going on for weeks. Me, him, and the client. Me and the client yelling at him, Drem just sitting there like a sphinx, waiting to throw a levy on my client's assets and seize his property. Client was scared shitless, calling me in the middle of the night, worrying about jail. Good chance, too."

"But if you could pull it out, you'd have looked like God to that client, right? And to everyone he told."

Lamott nodded.

"For how much?"

"Hundred thousand."

I restrained the urge to whistle at that amount. Instead I waited Lamott out.

"When word got around, I'd have been representing half the money in Berkeley." He hung his head.

I was sure his grief was not from guilt but for lost opportunity. "You were the last person to see Philip Drem alive. You followed him."

Suddenly the reality of my charges struck him. "But I didn't kill him! Why would I kill him? If I'd killed him, I wouldn't have done it in a half-assed way like that, where I had to follow him and get the briefcase. Look, he was desperate for the money. I could have arranged to meet him anywhere. He and I are accountants, not mafiosi. Accountants don't think of murder; they worry about double entries. If I had planned to kill him, he wouldn't have suspected. He would have come to some secluded place. I could have killed him and taken the briefcase. I wouldn't have had to trail him all over town. I'm not a fool, Jill."

I probably felt worse than he did. I believed him. The best I could do was call Patrol, haul him down to the station in the cage, and make him go through the whole statement again. He was embarrassed and afraid. But I was left with a dead end.

24

Getting the final statement from Rick Lamott took nearly two hours. He tried to make deals. He jockeyed for position. His open-throttle face was flushed with the thrill of the game, the same expression he'd had driving his Lotus. By the end of the first half hour, I could picture Lamott at an audit with that same look, eyeing the competition, making moves, tossing out deals, trying to slip in five thousand dollars of questionable travel and entertainment for deleting three thousand of office supplies (which he could then claim under publicity). But this investigation was not a game or a race, and in any case Lamott was running on empty. By the time he signed his statement, he was as deflated as the driver of the last car in the Indianapolis 500.

Energy doesn't disappear; it merely moves on. In the normal run of things it should have moved on to me. But it hadn't. I felt as if I'd been driving in a circle too. Maria Zalles had turned out to be no more than a pit stop. With Rick Lamott I'd seen the checkered flag. But that had been a mirage.

It was eleven o'clock. I couldn't remember when I'd last eaten. No, I could: the stale donut I'd grabbed as we raced to the airport. It was still poking its crystallized sugar corners into the edges of my stomach. I trudged out of the station. The fog had rolled in and was now so thick, I had to use the windshield wipers. It seemed appropriate.

I sat in my Volkswagen waiting while the engine warmed and realized that despite my exhaustion, the thing I wanted most was to hash over the case, to stretch it like pie dough, sticking a finger in one option, maybe Lyn Takai, and pulling that as far as it would go before the dough split and I had to discard her as a suspect. Howard was great at that. He'd been known to stretch the pizza dough of a case so far that it ended up as a breadstick. But Howard, if he was home, was going to be in no mood to talk.

I shifted into first. Till now, I hadn't realized just how much I'd missed the old Howard—the guy who threw everything into the chase, the lighthearted plotter who could sniff out foibles at two hundred paces and weave them into a museum-quality net, who basked in being the ultimate sting artist—Howard whom I'd loved and maybe lost to his prison of a house and the prison of society's rules for women. It made me cringe to think that he of all men couldn't see the bars all the safety precautions made.

Again I had to fight the urge to get on the freeway, turn the radio up, and just keep driving.

Howard was asleep when I got home. His tax forms were still spread ominously and haphazardly over the door cum table.

I took a shower and climbed into bed. It's a big bed. He wasn't near me. But I heard the rustle of the sheet against his skin, and felt the tension of his body. His breathing was tight, angry. He was awake. I waited, but his breathing didn't ease, and he didn't say anything. And I was damned if I was going to. I'd put up with the taxes, the renovations, and the paint fumes that suddenly clogged my nostrils with that milk-of-magnesia smell. I could feel my neck tensing. My eyes refused to close. Dammit, I couldn't afford to be so pissed off it kept me awake. Not while *he* lay there playing possum. I—

"Your case," he murmured. "What happened?"

It wasn't a giant step into admission of error. It was a toe inching forward, testing the waters of truce, a toe pushing out the first of those prison bars. Shoptalk—it was the way we always handled situations we couldn't handle. But it was only a toe, not the whole foot or leg. But once I grabbed that toe, the foot would come. Tomorrow, when we weren't exhausted, we'd talk about the prisons and the jogger and the house. We'd talk on a level we hadn't before. I wasn't looking forward to it at all. For now, the toe was plenty. My eyes welled with tears of relief. "The case has dead-ended," I said, my voice tight.

He started to roll over toward me but stopped. Clearly, he knew what he'd committed himself to tomorrow and that a truce is no more than a truce. "Nothing has to be a dead end. What have you got?" His voice cracked.

I threaded my fingers through his. I hadn't realized he was so upset, that I'd hurt him that much. I could feel the nearness of his body, the heat almost warming me as I lay icily still. "Philip Drem wanted to get his wife away from the toxins in the air here. He needed money, so he offered to sell the TCMP figures to Rick Lamott. They arranged a meeting at PFA. Lamott drove around the block three times but chickened out. He couldn't quite bring himself to do something so dangerous."

"Kind of ruins him as a murder candidate."

"I know. I really had hopes for Lamott."

Howard sat up, awkwardly pulling the cover over his chest with his right hand, keeping his left clasped with mine. I had to sit too, or smother. Clumsily, I stuffed the ends of the covers around my shoulder. Howard didn't offer to help. I'm sure he didn't dare. I could hardly ask. And I couldn't do more than catch one fold of blanket behind my shoulder. The cold air poured down my side. Freedom isn't free.

"So," I said in a soft voice, "Drem's in the theater where he goes every Friday night, and while he's in there, the killer comes and sticks a tiny hypodermic between the double seats of his bicycle. He uses a plaster-of-paris-type substance that he could have gotten anywhere." I pressed my arm against my side. I was freezing.

"Okay, Jill, so the needle is planted. Drem sits on it. Then what?"

"He rides the bicycle up to College Avenue and turns right."

"That tips the killer that he's not going home."

"Right. Home would have meant a left turn. With the poison beginning to work, Drem couldn't have been moving fast. It would have been easy for the killer to follow him."

"And by the time Drem rode a block or two, he would have been shaky, right?" Not waiting for an answer, Howard went on. "Drem pedals along to Dwight. He's either got to turn uphill or down. Well, down's a safe guess, even if it's against the traffic."

"Figuring that, the killer can run downhill on Dwight, probably faster than Drem's pedaling. He can keep an eye on Drem, who's too out of it to be looking right or left. Drem comes to the corner and makes his final turn—"

"He watches Drem stagger off the bike and into the street. Then, while Drem's collapsing half a block away, he sidles up to the bike and steals the briefcase. Ta-da!" he said, with the wave of a hand.

The covers fell forward. I laughed and grabbed. Howard yanked them back up and tucked them back in place, but he didn't let go of my hand.

I snuggled back into the pillow, wishing I were certain of his conclusion about the killer. "That's fine, Howard, except that Lamott said the only person around was a cop. And one of the street guys swore the cop took the briefcase."

"Course, both of those guys were there, and they didn't see each other."

"They wouldn't have to have. Regent's a long block there.

Lamott was occupied with Drem and calling for help. The street person could have been at the other end by the bicycle then. He was planning to boost it. So when he realized he wasn't alone, of course he split."

"But they both said there was a cop at the scene. And we know there wasn't, right?"

"We sure hope that's right. If you accept Lamott's description of his cop, at least it wasn't Leonard."

"What about Acosta?"

"Description doesn't rule him out. But, Howard, I just can't imagine—"

"No, not Mercurio." Howard's fingers tightened on my hand. I hadn't ridden down this cop thing. I'd put it off as a road of last resort. Nothing wrecks a department like the idea that one of its members, one of our *friends*, has been light-fingered. And lying to the rest of us. We can't trust many people. When we can't trust each other, it's like driving on ice with bald tires. Neither of us even mentioned Pereira. We couldn't face that thought.

Howard sat up straighter. "But there could have been someone who looked like a cop. Or sort of like a cop."

I pictured Pereira with her blond hair hanging just over the edge of her tan jacket collar, strolling forward, her revolver swaying, the bullets and cuffs and the rest of the gear on the belt riding awkwardly on her hips. It reminded me how glad I'd been to get out of uniform.

Howard turned away, grappling on the floor beside the bed. The light was still off—we weren't ready to face each other—and I could hear a paper bag rustling. He sat back up and held the bag in front of me. Another time we would have sparred about the dangers of my sticking my hand in. But we weren't ready to face that either.

I reached in. "Ah, chocolate old-fashioneds. You knew I'd be starved."

"Safe guess."

At times like this, there's something to be said for subliminating one appetite by sating another.

"Let's move on to motive, Jill. Takai's being audited. Drem knows she's switched her bathroom sink for the better one at the hotel. Probably he's wondering what else she's taken."

"Likely," I said between bites of chocolate.

"Scookie Hogan already hates him."

I stuffed the rest of the donut in my mouth. I had really been starved. "Scookie's bitterness is old stuff. You don't kill for the past. You kill for the future. She wouldn't kill him because she lost her business last year but because he knew something that would make her lose her home this year, or go to jail."

"Hmmm." Howard was tapping his fingers on my arm.

"Hmmm, indeed." I thought about Howard and giving up his image, about the "cop" and the briefcase—and prison. "I've thought a lot about being imprisoned. It breaks your spirit, suffocates you emotionally, spiritually. But on a strict physical level, jail is a real nasty place. I'd do almost anything to avoid it. And if that thing was killing someone despicable . . ." I shrugged. "Stay out of jail and don't lose the things that matter to you. It'd be real tempting. Too tempting for Drem's killer."

I reached over and turned on the light. Smiling, I said, "Howard, I believe I can tell you who that killer is. But you know what I need for proof?"

He grinned. It wasn't quite the old Howard, but I'd deal with that later. He said, "You need a sting."

25

It didn't take much to get Lamott to cooperate in the sting. He'd been anxious to deal before. And the idea of wearing a wire appealed to him almost as much as not being reported to the IRS. The problem I was going to have with Rick Lamott was not forcing him to confront the owners of the Inspiration Hotel but reining him in.

Lamott set up the meeting for 8:00 P.M. Wednesday, April 15. Mason Moon squawked about the time—he hadn't finished his taxes—but he was overruled.

I cleared the operation with Inspector Doyle. He wasn't wild about it, but he admitted there was no other option, and since it didn't take much manpower . . .

The rest of my day was devoted to rechecking backgrounds, vainly trying to goose the lab, and being informed that the residents of petri dishes can't step up the tempo. And listening to Eggs bemoan his automotive misfortune. Finally the Mazda dealer had gotten his RX-7 in. Eggs had shifted the down-payment money to his checking account. He'd taken half a day of personal leave for the test drive. He'd gone to the dealership, opened the car door, climbed in, and found that his head scraped the roof. "Tilt the seat back," the salesman said. Eggs tilted. Now his head was fine. He fitted into the sporty car of his dreams, the car he'd waited years to own. He fastened the seat belt, rested his hand on the gearstick, and looked through the windshield.

Or more accurately, didn't look through the windshield. At this point in the telling Eggs glared at me. "I couldn't sit at that angle and see through my bifocals!"

With Herculean restraint, I had neither laughed nor commented on midlife crisis. I went back to my own office with the sting ready to go and the hope that nothing happened during the day to screw it up.

By 8:00 P.M. Howard, Pereira, and I were down the street in a van. Howard was fingering a manila envelope addressed to the IRS. I'd promised Howard we'd swing the van by the main post office so he could get his return in the mail before midnight. I couldn't imagine how he'd created order out of the heap of papers that had covered his door-desk last night. He hadn't mentioned the outcome of his calls to the restaurant suppliers. I didn't want to ask.

Rick Lamott strolled into the Inspiration Hotel lobby. "Pretty empty lobby. No tax-night party?" Lamott asked. Soft crackles of static flickered on the line, but the sarcastic tone of his voice came through loud and clear.

"Damn," I muttered to Howard. "I knew Lamott was too much of a grandstander. He's going to blow it."

"Too late to change," Howard said. "Just keep yourself in a three-point stance."

"Very funny," a woman answered Lamott. I realized how much Lyn Takai's sharp voice reflected her appearance: small, spare, sharp-boned. I found myself picturing her in a leotard and jeans.

"We can pull up chairs behind the desk. No one's going to be coming in here at this hour on a Wednesday," Mason Moon said petulantly.

"Parts of what I say may be private." Lamott.

"Somebody's got to stay by the phone." Scookie Hogan.

"Guess it's Scookie's night to work the desk," Howard whispered, laughing at her put-out tone.

"You said you had a proposition. Go on." Ethan Simonov.

Feet shuffled. The static was louder. I pictured the five of them moving behind the mahogany counter. Moon would prop himself against the back wall, cape hanging loose from his shoulders, his bushy Flemish-painter hair puffing out from his head just as the cotton double moon billowed on his T-shirt. Scookie would be in the desk clerk's chair, her mouth drooping victimlike; she'd be dressed in swirls of blue and purple. Lyn Takai I envisioned nearest the exit, shifting from foot to foot. And Ethan Simonov would have planted himself directly across from Lamott, the other dealer here. Simonov, his dark ponytail hanging over his collar, would be tapping his fist with a hammer he'd pulled from his tool belt, like a judge calling for order.

Lamott said, "One of you has been audited. The trail has led to the hotel books, right?"

"Nobody's asked for my books." Moon, defensive.

"It's just a matter of time. You all know that." I could imagine Lamott in his expensive suit, waving an expensive arm in front of the sputtering Moon. "And, Mason, you were shit as an accountant. What you call books here is Swiss cheese."

A babble of voices protested, but Lamott must have quieted them. "I can fix them." Silence. "Look, I've seen books like you wouldn't believe. I've had doctors arrive in my office without a single receipt and expect me to deduct thousands of dollars in entertainment. No verif whatsoever. But I handled it. Your problems are small potatoes. A little double-booking? We delete another guest. You ordered a chandelier for the lobby here, and it's hanging in one of your dining rooms? We create a receipt for your payment to the hotel. No problem to create documentation—if you're smart enough."

"Cook the books, you mean," Moon snorted.

"Semantics. Can it, Mason." Takai.

"Are you saying you can do our books so that no matter who takes over Drem's cases, they won't find anything wrong?" Scookie sounded disbelieving.

"They'll find an error here, a judgment call there. Flawless returns make them suspicious. But they won't have red flags—nothing to make them search further."

"Hey, wait!" Moon. "There won't be any more audit anyway. When an investigator buys it, IRS has to start all over. The chain of evidence is broken, scattered in a million pieces."

The line crackled. Otherwise, there was silence. Had I misjudged Lamott? But then he said, "You're right, Moon. That's what happens—normally. Not cost-effective for a new man to go over the same tracks. That's if things are normal, Moon. If Drem had kicked the bucket from the big C, they'd have buried his cases with him. But IRS gets suspicious when one of their own is murdered. Could be they'll figure it's worth the time to have another look. Of course, the choice is yours. If you're all willing to take your chances, okay." It was a moment before he said, "I'll leave you alone to discuss it."

Howard groaned. I nodded, seconding that groan. Scenario A ended with the killer admitting his guilt now. I had hoped for that, but I really hadn't expected it in front of a stranger like Lamott, much less the rest of the Inspiration crew.

The hotel door closed. Lamott was on the stoop. A car passed. I heard it first live, then over the wire—delayed stereo. The wind rattled the sides of the van, strong wind off the Bay like the ones we normally get in late summer afternoons. It smacks the smog back against the Berkeley hills. Now it rattled the palm fronds and plane-tree leaves and tossed discarded newspapers against our fenders.

Howard shoved his tax papers back into a manila envelope. I wished we could see outside. We could have doused the lights and crept into the cab for a peek. Odds of being spotted were slim, but any chance was too great a risk.

After what seemed an hour but couldn't have been more than ten minutes, Lamott walked back into the hotel. "So?" he asked, the soft thump of his footsteps forming a sort of background music. He was still walking, so the owners must still have been behind the desk.

"We may deal." It was Simonov. The swap king was the logical spokesman in this type of situation. "You do our books, in return for . . . ?"

"The TCMP figures from Drem's briefcase."

A couple of them gasped. But it was Simonov who said, "TC —what figures?"

"One of you knows what I'm talking about."

"How would we have anything of Drem's? He didn't give Maria anything." Scookie sounded defensive.

"Drem's briefcase." Takai. "You're saying one of us got these figures out of his briefcase."

There was a slurring sound on the wire, as if cloth had swished or Lamott had shrugged.

"Hey, man, you saying one of us killed him?" Moon.

"I don't care about killing. I'm just interested in the figures."

"Killing, figures—they're inseparable," Takai insisted.

There was a pause. I could picture Lamott looking down his sleek nose with that same smug expression he'd had when he told me he'd parked in the red zone outside the station. It didn't fill me with confidence.

"Lamott, any of us who admits to having Drem's briefcase is giving you a hold over him that could be a lot worse than an IRS audit," Takai insisted.

"Maybe. Unless you're going to jail. Tax avoidance is your right. Tax evasion is illegal. And jail is a dangerous place for innocents like you. Right, Simonov? You've been in the can."

"Years ago. And that was only a few months in a 'country club jail.' "

It was so quiet, I could hear their breathing. Then Scookie Hogan said what they all must have been thinking. "People go to jail for murder, too. Admitting you have Drem's briefcase would be like calling the cops."

There was a murmur of agreement, then silence—no shuffling of feet, not even the soft hiss of their breath. By his presence Lamott was forcing them to sit together in silence, so that each of them had to see his separateness and face the fact that the group couldn't or wouldn't support him. Or maybe he was just drawing a blank.

After a minute or so he said, "No one has to make a statement here now. You've all agreed you need my services. The one who has the briefcase needs them most. I don't care which of you that is. I just want the figures in the briefcase. Let's choose a drop point for them. I don't need to know who has them. He or she just leaves them off. I pick them up, then I clean up your books. Simple as that."

"Lamott," Takai said acerbically, "don't you think it's a bit damning for one of us to announce we'll make the drop?"

So much for scenario B—the killer reveals himself before Lamott leaves. That left C, the last and none too reliable resort.

"Okay, we'll protect your anonymity," Lamott said, easing into C. "I'll ask each of you for a suggestion about the drop point, each suggestion built on the previous one. That way, no one will be giving him- or herself away. Agreed?"

There was a general murmuring that I took for agreement if not enthusiasm.

"Scookie, you start."

"Me? Why me?"

"A little nervous?" Howard observed.

"Someone has to be first." Lamott's tone was halfway between laughter and exasperation.

"Well, okay. What exactly do I have to deliver—just a slip of paper with the figures on it or the whole briefcase?"

"The briefcase."

"What do you want that for?" Lyn Takai demanded.

I held my breath. The chances of getting the IRS to verify any numbers as local TCMP figures was slim. Without that verification, figures typed on a fresh sheet could refer to anything and be valueless as evidence.

Lamott laughed. "I want Drem's briefcase to wipe my feet on."

There was a shrill sound I took to be Scookie's laugh. "Okay, if I were choosing a drop point, I'd need someplace nearby."

"Ethan?" Lamott asked.

"Only a fool would chance his freedom on a game like this. Twenty questions chooses the spot? Or is it four suggestions?"

"We'll narrow down till you're all comfortable. As long as it takes."

I could hear more grumbles. Then Simonov suggested someplace with a number of entries and exits. Lyn Takai wanted a spot where she could be at least as comfortable as Lamott. The narrowing went on another two rounds, and it was Mason Moon who finally came up with People's Park. He named a spot at the near end behind the Med. Under the low wooden stage.

I slammed my fist into my thigh. "Damn!"

Howard whistled. "What you've got here is one of the worst spots in town, Jill. Maybe the worst."

"With the connections this crew has," Pereira said, "they could know a clerk or janitor or dishwasher in any of the businesses, or half the tenants in the motel that faces the park. They could come in from either side of the park, or from the far end. Or around the end of the motel. You're talking major surveillance."

I nodded. Ideally, uniforms in the closed shops, undercovers at either side of the park, by the far end, in the shadows of the shrubs, behind the apartment building, and on every street that led off. I could use up the department's overtime budget for the season. To get half that many officers, I'd have to get Inspector Doyle to pressure Chief Larkin, maybe to make a deal with the head of one of the other details who owed him. Then it'd still be a question of how many bodies we could pull in on over-time. I didn't know if we could do all that by tomorrow night.

"Okay," said Lamott, "the spot's set. You wanted the drop to be at night. So let's say three A.M. tomorrow night."

"No." Lyn Takai laughed. "No, you don't get to choose the time. Three in the morning's too late. About ten thirty is right. And not tomorrow. We'll do it tonight."

Ten thirty tonight. Two hours from now.

CHAPTER

26

A civilian might have asked why the Inspiration group chose 10:30 P.M. for the drop instead of 3:00 A.M. The answer is they were smart. At 3:00 A.M. the streets are deserted. The campus cops have swept and reswept People's Park. It's empty but for a street person who's willing to take the chance of being rousted out within the hour. At 3:00 A.M. People's Park belongs to us.

But at 10:30 P.M. the Avenue is crowded with students, neighborhood people coming out of cafés, other Berkeleyans who've been listening to jazz at Larry Blake's or strolling around after a reading at Cody's or a meeting on campus. At that hour it'd be easy for Scookie, Simonov, Takai, or even Mason Moon to make the drop, then fade into the crowd on Telegraph or take cover in a café, such a part of the scenery that everyone there would swear—and believe—he'd been sitting sipping a *latte* all evening.

Behind the row of stores on the Avenue, People's Park was dark. The wind that had rattled the van two hours ago was stronger now. It shook the acacia leaves at the far end, blew sheets of newsprint across the empty grass in the middle of the park, ruffled the shirts and jackets in the free box, and rustled the leaves of the shrubs in the protected area behind the stores where I hunkered down.

There was no good place to hide here. I wasn't surprised.
The drop site had been chosen by people who knew the area
and how to take advantage of it, people who had built a business from flour, raisins, and sweet tooths, a reputation from
stealing out under cover of night to plop a corpse bench on
public land. The drop site was under a wooden platform, a
small stage of sorts, that stood midway between sides of the
park and about fifteen feet from the back of the stores. The
killer could come from any direction and leave the briefcase
beneath any of the four sides of the stage. To make matters
worse, two Dumpsters lined the south side, blocking part of my
view no matter where I hid.

On a scale of 1 to 10 of ways I would have liked to set up the
catch, this was down close to a 1; 10 would have been half the
force entrenched all over the park. But even a 4 would have
included backup I could communicate with; 3 would have been
backup in places I'd decided on. With 2, I'd have at least been
sure there was backup. But 1 left me sure that no patrol officer
was the mysterious cop Sierra reported. But not certain enough
to have any of them on backup, which left me with only Howard and Pereira, and the whole of People's Park to cover.

As soon as we'd made the plan in the surveillance van, I left
the van and headed for the park. I had to make sure I was there
before any of the Inspiration crew arrived. I figured I'd need
every spare minute to check out the bushes to find a spot near
the stage that would give me cover.

I was right and wrong. Right I'd need the time. Wrong it
would be spent eyeing bushes. There were barely any. It amazes
me how different you discover a place is when you need it for a
specific purpose. Ask ten middle-class Berkeleyans to describe
People's Park, and they'd all call it a central lawn bordered by
trees at one end and thick bushes near the stage at the other.
Every one of them would be wrong.

What foliage there was near the stage was tall, willowy pampas grass or squat shrubs, none likely to conceal a 115-pound woman. Then there were the Dumpsters, big enough to hide all of Homicide-Felony Assault Detail. I held my breath. Surely I wouldn't have to . . . But no, the Dumpsters wouldn't work. As I traipsed over the rotten food and filthy papers, looking for signs of the approaching murderer, I'd be virtually a sideshow.

Which left only one other choice, only slightly better—the free box. The free box, a receptacle for donated clothes, had been a landmark of the park for as long as I could remember. The boxes themselves had changed, but the spirit of the free box continued from incarnation to incarnation. This particular one looked like a summer house for a St. Bernard, a four-foot-square platform raised a couple of feet off the ground with a roof to keep off the rain and open sides to facilitate pawing through the offerings. My joining the heap of clothes in it had a number of drawbacks. The box was next to the sidewalk at the north side of the park, twenty yards from the stage. I'd have to cover myself with clothes and lie unmoving on the platform for an hour or more. The clothes may or may not have been clean, and after taking them, some recipients had donated their own well-worn, not-well-washed raiment. With the inviting odor of sweat and dirt and the crumbs of muffins and enchiladas mixed in, the platform was on its way to being a biologist's dream.

But the free box was my only choice. Crouched near the stage, I checked the sidewalks, then the shadows under the trees at the far end. It was ten minutes before the area looked empty enough for me to move. I stood, stretched—likely to be my last stretch for over an hour—sauntered over, and sat on the edge of the free box. Glancing around, I took a deep breath, knelt on shins and elbows, and yanked piles of parkas and scratchy sweaters over me. My shoulder holster jabbed into my ribs, and the weight of the revolver dragged the harness into my back. It must have been a hundred degrees under the pile. My knees and ankles screamed. I stuffed jackets and shirts underneath, but it didn't help much, and the stench of old sweat was almost overwhelming. It was like a sauna that hadn't been cleaned since Leif Eriksson left Norway.

And people call Homicide the glamour job of the department!

The wind whipped the ends of a shawl near my head. Behind me a radio blared and died as a car passed. The park was a black rectangle, made blacker by the streetlights around it.

Something bit my ankle. A flea! I steeled myself to keep from slapping at it.

Footsteps. On the far side of the Dumpster. I held my breath. Feet crunching gravel. Slow, cautious, the walker was invisible in the dark. If the killer moved around the Dumpsters and slid the briefcase under the far side of the stage, I would miss the whole thing. If the footsteps stopped there, I'd have to choose blind and give chase or stay here and wonder if I'd blown the whole case.

The steps slowed. They were softer. Behind the Dumpsters. They stopped. I leaned forward, stretching my neck, straining to see, to hear leather being shoved along the gritty ground under the Dumpster. Car engines roared on the side streets. Radios cut the night. I forced myself to listen solely for the sound of the briefcase. Something scraped. If only I could see. The sound stopped. Had it gone on long enough for a shove? It seemed eternal. But . . . no time.

The footsteps began again, going back toward the far street, shielded by the Dumpsters. "Damn!" I muttered to myself. I'd never see the figure. The footsteps moved slowly. Too slow for an amateur making a drop. Amateurs drop and bolt.

I looked at my watch: 10:03; 10:05; 10:10. The park seemed too empty, too black. My skin quivered as it does when I wake up at four in the morning and can't get back to sleep. Something was wrong. I ran through the plan. No, things were okay. There was time. Things were okay.

I lay in the box sweating, the wood digging into my knees and elbows. Listening for the rustle of grass or cloth, I shifted position, trying to ease the pressure on my elbows and still prop up my head.

At 10:21 a car sped down Haste Street behind me, windows open, radio blaring, pounding of the bass shaking the box floor. I could feel my shoulders tense and in my chest an ashen cold I hadn't had since I'd stopped smoking years ago. I wanted to cough. I pressed my lips together hard, and for a moment I was seventeen again in my stalled car on a dark two-lane road with all my mother's warnings about what can happen to girls alone running through my mind. The heavy wool blankets blocked out the free night wind, leaving only dank airless air like my grandmother's closed-up house.

The wind ruffled the coats and sweaters on top of me. It was after 10:30. The killer should be here. Berkeleyans were chronically late, but surely not . . . I listened for footsteps. The only noises were the reedy whine of the pampas grass and the rumble of voices on the Avenue two hundred yards and a different reality away.

It was 10:37. A noise coming from the far side of the park. A voice. No, two voices. Could the killer have brought a friend or lover? Quickly I paired the Inspiration owners. Simonov and Scookie Hogan? Takai and Mason Moon? But no two of them would have spent an evening alone together, much less a whole night. And certainly there was not enough love between them for one of the innocents to endanger his freedom for the guilty one.

The voices grew louder, the words longer, melting together. Slurring together. Slurring period. Damn! Neither of these was the killer. What I had here was a pair of drunks. Now I could make out their figures, weaving slightly like cars avoiding the potholes on Henry Street. Tall, heavy. They veered toward the Dumpsters. One peered over the edge and said something incomprehensible to me but infuriating to his companion, who yanked the climber back. They fell on the stage. The old boards squealed at the impact. Together they looked like a dark furry ball. Arms flung out. Fists hit the boards. One of them groaned, then the other. The ball rolled again, this time slower.

I looked at my watch: 10:40. The killer certainly wasn't going to break up a fight to leave the briefcase. I just hoped they'd end their tussle quickly and be in decent enough shape to walk off. If one decided to sleep it off on the stage, the whole sting was shot.

The ball separated into halves. Slowly the two men stood. They veered toward each other and entwined arms, their squabble apparently forgotten. They staggered across the grass, two steps to the right toward the trees, two toward the free box, toward me. The dry cave of cold pressed out against my breastbone. The drunks weaved closer. Slowly they headed toward the free box, their voices low-pitched, almost growling now.

The wind stopped. I was sweating. The coats and shirts and blankets weighed down on me, imprisoning my legs and arms. My ribs shook from the gnawing cold inside while my skin cringed against the heat, and the hard edge of the shoulder holster dug into my side. Where were Pereira and Howard? Were they at the far end of the park? Was I alone here, with these two huge men, drunk . . .

I pressed my forearm against the holster and shoved it hard against my ribs. Why was I frightened? I was a police detective. I'd been trained in self-defense, in taking out suspects. I was in a lot better shape than these two men, I was sober, and I had a gun. I turned my toes under, soles down to the box, ready to push off.

The two veered closer, grumbling now. I poised, ready to jump up. Probably the shock of seeing me would do these guys in. I knew that, but the icy hollow in my chest didn't shrink.

Howard and Pereira were on the street. There was no reason to be afraid. But I couldn't shake the fear; it was too deeply embedded in my body. *Be careful, little girl! Watch out for strange men! Don't go there alone!*

Dammit, it had been over twenty years since I was a little girl. How could I, a police detective, still be captive after all these years? Would those fears I thought I'd banished run me forever? *Be careful! Find someone to protect you!*

Suddenly I was shaking, but now with fury. I'd damn well protect myself. I could jump up, grab the drunks, and slam them to the ground.

But I couldn't, not without blowing the sting.

In that flashback of panic, I'd almost forgotten about the sting. The two were ten feet away, clinging to each other, stumbling toward me. Trying to block them out, I looked toward the stage. It still seemed dark.

They veered to the right, beside the box. Maybe they'd amble on to the sidewalk. I held my breath. They stopped.

"Hey, Gray, looka this." Cloth swished. I could feel a sleeve being pulled up through the pile. "Whadaya think?"

"Dunno."

"This?" He lifted another garment.

"Dunno." How long before they got down to me? I kept my eyes on the stage. Nothing moved there.

"Whadaya mean, ya don' know? This iss great."

"Dunno."

Dust from the clothes got in my eyes. I blinked, desperately trying to focus between blinks. Failing, I forced myself to keep my eyes open. My eyes stung. That was when I spotted the figure shoving something under the stage.

I kicked the clothes off and started for the stage.

"Hey, who-do-you . . ." One of the drunks grabbed my ankle.

By the stage, the killer was shoving the briefcase underneath.

He jerked toward the commotion, then reached back under and grabbed the briefcase.

I kicked the drunk. He screamed and let go. But now the killer was running full out, nearly to the sidewalk. The street-lights showed the figure clearly now. Tan pants, tan jacket. Above the collar, dark hair. A cop? No. But close enough to pass for one.

I ran after, shouting, "Stop! Stop or you'll lose more than Drem's briefcase!"

The tan legs moved faster, racing into the street, cutting in front of a Jeep.

My gun clanked against my ribs. It might as well have been a hammer for all the use it was going to be in a crowded area like this. I ran faster, but I wasn't gaining. I raced into the street. A sedan screeched to a halt, but the pickup in the next lane didn't. It came within an inch of mowing me down.

Ahead, Regent Street, where Drem had died, was dark. One of the streetlights was out. I slowed down. The street was empty. No cars moving. No pedestrians. No one looking out his window.

Footsteps came up behind me. I spun around. Pereira.

"Vanished," I said. "Take the other side of the street. Between the cars. There we've got a chance. Between houses . . ." I shrugged and moved onto the sidewalk.

Cars filled every inch of free curb. I moved quickly, checking the cars near me with half my attention and with the other watching for movement in the shadows farther up.

Howard ran toward me. "Sorry. I got caught with a snitch. I—"

"Call for backup. Take the far end of the street. Check the backyards." But Howard was already gone.

I kept moving down the street, knowing with each step the likelihood of collaring the killer lessened. Tires squealed. The backup must have been patrolling the Avenue. They raced for the far end of the street. Other than ours there was still no movement. The killer was gone, I was sure of it.

I passed the pole Drem's bicycle had been attached to. The house next to it looked as if it were on stilts. Foundation work. Earthquake damage. "Pereira!" I called, and motioned her around the far side as I headed toward the foundation. I bent down, peering under, but it was too dark to see.

Pereira swept her flashlight from front to back. Boards, boxes, nothing big enough to hide behind and no one hiding. "Damn," she said. "Not here."

"No, wait." I pictured the "cop," dressed in his tans, his workbelt hanging like our equipment belts. I moved around to the back and motioned Pereira to the garage. She shone her light in. No car. No one.

Then I spotted it. The accoutrement of a big building job. The only other place to hide. Pereira saw it too—the idea must have come to us at the same moment. We moved almost silently to the Porta Potty. I could picture, inside, tan-clad legs braced against the edge, arms holding the door shut.

Pereira and I moved around back, caught the corners, and tipped it forward on its door.

27

I pulled open the door of the Porta Potty. Ethan Simonov was slumped against one side. He was clutching a knife, about to drag it across his throat.

I stared at him in that tiny dank room, precursor to other closed cells for years to come. I froze, desperately wanting to leave him his way out. So much less painful—one slice of the carotid—than bleeding out your life drop by drop, day by day, hour by endless hour, in jail. Then I braced my foot and yanked the knife out of his hands.

Pereira was already calling the dispatcher for an ambulance.

We lifted Simonov out onto the lawn and sat him against an upright of the foundation. The pipe behind it was a good place to attach the handcuffs. Simonov's cut was bleeding but not spurting. He'd live. I read him his rights.

He glared up at me, his dark ponytail now pulled free from his tan collar. "I've done time. I know what it's like inside. I'm not going back to jail."

"You killed Drem to keep from going back to jail?" I asked.

"I've got a record. Tax bastards got me once for not reporting. Drem would have made a sideshow of me this time: 'Swap king does it again!' There's nothing those bastards hate more than taxpayers not reporting income at all. *I* didn't get any income from the swaps, but the bastards would get me for taxes on the cost of services received, services I received, and conspiracy to keep everybody else's from being taxed."

You knew all that, and still you couldn't give up being the swap king, I thought. Just like Howard, who would quit the force before he'd stop masterminding stings. And Mason Moon couldn't give up the notoriety of the plop artist (or for that matter even his tacky T-shirt). Losing the business that was her whole identity undid Scookie Hogan.

And me—I wondered what it was that I couldn't part with. Maybe open doors, long straight highways, my options always open. Knowing what had filled me with the need to escape hadn't eradicated the urge to get on the freeway, turn up the stereo till it hurt my ears, and keep driving. But when I had to take an off ramp, I couldn't imagine it leading anywhere but Berkeley, bringing me home to the other 120,000 people who were drinking *latte*s, looking nervously over their shoulders, and fighting for their open doors.

The wind flapped Simonov's tan jacket. It rattled the plastic sheets over the lumber. "Give me back the knife," he pleaded.

"Why didn't you just pay the taxes, Ethan?"

His eyes scrunched, and he looked at me in disbelief. I remembered him the first time I saw him, standing behind the counter like a bazaar trader. For him, giving up the contest would be giving up entirely. "IRS'd never have bothered with me. I was too small potatoes. The swap club was all informal, nothing written. No way for them to find out. They'd never have looked at me at all if it hadn't been for Lyn's audit. And even then—if it had been anyone but Drem." He shook his head. "There were no records. Nothing. I made sure of that. And then Drem found that damned sink, and the workman, and . . . He was a bulldog. He'd have hung on till he got me. Then it wouldn't be county time; it'd be federal prison. I know what that's like. I can't be locked up!"

I thought of Tori Iversen, locked in twice as tight now. But what I said was "You killed a man."

"He deserved to die. Guy was a bastard. Institutionalized reneger. Damn IRS gives you rules, then they don't follow them themselves. Tell you one thing on the phone—if they're wrong, they don't stand behind it. Renegers. Can't trust 'em on a deal. You do your part, you're honest, they screw you. Drem, he was all of that. Then he even reneged on them, the IRS!"

I could hear sirens in the distance—not for Simonov, too soon. I felt numb, as I always do when a perp gives his rationalization for ending another person's life. But for the swap king nothing was worse than reneging. And yet when he looked up again and pleaded, "Give me back the knife," I was as tempted as I'd ever been.

I was still thinking about imprisonment—Simonov's, Tori's, the prison of a life Drem had made for himself, and Howard's house—hours later, after Simonov had been taken to the hospital, after he'd called his lawyer and stopped talking.

When I got home, the living room was dark but for a fire—a big bustling, crackling red-and-yellow fire—in the hearth that had never hosted more than embers. The room smelled not of wood shavings but burning pine. And on the stereo Kris Kristofferson was singing "Me and Bobby McGee." As my eyes adjusted to the dark, I could make out Howard sprawled on the couch, his legs flung over the back like an afghan. In the shadowy light his face looked gaunt, and his red curls were gray. As if the curtains of the future had parted.

I'd never really considered whether he'd be there twenty years from now. I'd never thought that far at all.

He swung his legs down and sat up. "So, Jill, is everything set with Simonov?"

I nodded, glancing under the coffee table till I found an open beer can. I took a long drink. It was still cold.

"Plenty more in the fridge." Howard grinned. "It's nice to have them all gone." The tenants, he meant.

Settling down next to him, I said, "This is great. It's like a different place. Smells like Yosemite." But still I felt a tug of panic as I spoke. Windows may open, but you can't always get out.

"The house has always had potential."

"I never saw it."

Howard laughed. "Well, Jill, it's very, very difficult to truly understand something that you think you'll never experience."

"Touché." I smiled.

Before I could speak, he said, "You know how pissed I was that you'd gotten me with the azalea. A whole lot more pissed than I'd been about Damon Hentry slipping through my fingers. I guess that was no secret, huh?" His voice was rough, unsure, as if he were speaking from a level he wasn't used to treading. "I couldn't believe you'd done that. I felt so, well, betrayed." He was staring at the fire, away from me. He laughed uncomfortably. "I asked Connie, made it real awkward for her. I could tell she'd have done my taxes, meal deductions and all, for the rest of my life before she'd get in the middle of this."

I felt my shoulders tighten. I felt a bit betrayed myself. *I* hadn't talked to Pereira about any of this. But then, this relationship stuff was more virgin territory for a guy like Howard. And I owed him one. I put a hand on his arm. "I wondered what you and Connie were so edgy about. I thought she was going to kill you over your taxes."

"No. That's all worked out."

The road forked here: Easy Unemotional Tax Discussion or Quicksand of Emotion. I leapt at the former. "You got all the restaurant food figures already?"

"No."

"You gave up?"

"No." He sounded at once sheepish and smug. "I filed for an extension. Then I cut a deal with Pereira. I never mention our problems again, and she'll do my tax return."

I laughed. "God, you must have really been a pain."

He took my hand in both of his, but he didn't look at me, and he didn't laugh. "I operate in a world of stings, counter-stings, drug dealers, lies, double crosses. You know how it is in Vice. Or maybe you don't, quite. Maybe, like me, you don't really know what life's like for someone else. Nothing's real. Other than the guys in Detail, there's nothing you can count on, no one to trust, no firm ground at all." He squeezed my hand hard.

I pressed my teeth together against the pain.

He didn't look at me, but the intensity of that avoidance was greater than any gaze. "I count on the reality of what we have. And on my house." His voice was trembling.

Mine was too, as I said, "I don't want to be without you. But I need my doors open. When your arms are around me, I need to know they're there for love, not protection, not squeezing me in."

He did the last thing I expected. He laughed. "Okay, okay. Just promise me you'll never tell anyone in Berkeley you even thought I was"—he swallowed and forced out the word—"conservative."

I leaned against his chest and felt the warmth of his body. I hadn't had vision of how this issue would resolve. But if I'd thought of it, I would have hoped that Howard would understand about freedom and still we'd return to the comfortable status quo. It hadn't occurred to me that it would kick us to a different level, one that would leave us more exposed. We'd had that easy relationship so long. It had seemed it was attuned to Howard's temperament.

Maybe. Or maybe it had been more in line with my own than I'd realized.

Now I felt disoriented, like when you're hurrying downstairs and you miscount steps and there's one more than you expected. You step off, and for an instant you're in nothingness, and you don't know how you'll land, or even if you'll be able to keep your balance.